Didja' Ever Make Butter?

and Other Hilarious Childhood Survival Tales

by

gary michael corbett

Copyright © 1995 by Gary Michael Corbett

All rights reserved. No part, or all, of this book may be reproduced or transmitted in any form or by any means, electronic or mechanical, including photocopy, recording or any information storage and retrieval system, without permission in writing from the publisher. Any resemblance of characters to real people is purely imaginary. For information address:
Polo Springs Publishing, 1658 Polo Club,
Tarpon Springs, Florida 34689.

Library of Congress Catalog Card Number: 94-93975
ISBN 1-886882-00-2

Published by
Polo Springs Publishing Co.
1658 Polo Club Drive
Tarpon Springs, Florida 34689

Printed and bound by Walsworth Publishing Co., Marceline, Missouri
Typography by Mary Jo Kaffai, Belleair Beach, Florida
Jacket Design by Tracy Hall, Palm Harbor, Florida

Printed in the United States of America
Publication Data: January 24, 1995

First Edition

Dedication

*For my grandparents and aunts —
they first exposed me to love.*

Acknowledgements

There is never one person to accept all the credit for a project, save perhaps Robinson Crusoe before Friday. The efforts of many are responsible for bringing this book to fruition. Therefore plaudits and my sincere appreciation is extended to the following:

My antecedents for adding me to their lineage and sharing their lives.

Thanks to Eugene Lamb, retired and deceased from Missouri Military Academy, for demanding that the Class of 1951 knew how to write.

Dr. Walter Dillard, my blind mentor, who challenged me to write in a style that enabled him to see.

The Fellowship Club Creative Writers for lending me your ears, patience and comments.

Barbara Hagen, my gentle drill sergeant for leading a novice through the rigors of turning a manuscript into a book and Mary Jo Kaffai for doing it.

Mike and Gena Lewis for providing the setting for *Solitude* and becoming the first outlet in Tennessee for the sale of this book. Lewis Family Crafts will host my first signing session. You ain't Regis and Kathy, but then I ain't Mark Twain, either.

Ann Bevard, my very dear friend who has encouraged and counseled me for a major portion of my life.

Contents

1. **Rommel's Raid** --------------------------------------- 1
   A Boy, Some Shade And Some Dust
      Irons Left To Rust
        Imagination

2. **Setting Hen** --- 4
   A coward in feathers, not she
      Protected her eggs
        From predator — me

3. **Kate & Pete** --- 7
   One was gray, the other brown
      Doubletree married
        To wagon and plow

4. **Spring Cycle** --------------------------------------- 11
   Muscles ached, sweat poured
      The sun created dry throats
        Seeds returned to earth

5. **Prince Of Wales** ------------------------------------ 13
   Christmas Shopping in the Snow
      Bored Boys Wearing Gloves
        Inevitable

6. **Till The Cows Come Home** ---------------------------- 17
   Sloshing homeward to the barn
      Leaves crunch underfoot
        Udders full to bursting

7. **Didja' Ever Make Butter?** --------------------------- 20
   Yellow thick cream, so heavy
      Churned by hand in ice
        Golden sweet butter

8. **Spot, Spot Where Have You Been?** -------------------- 25
   Straw, golden soft in a barn
      Secluded, hidden
        Squirming balls of fur

9. **Summer Storms** 31
    Heavy Air, Blackening Sky
      Gusts — Flash, Boom, Shudder
        Squishy Mud — New Life

10. **The Hunt** 37
    Leaves crunch; chattering squirrels
      White dust from Jack Frost
        Branches or antlers?

11. **Didja' Ever Make Blood Sausage?** 42
    Pigs squealing as if they knew
      Kettles on the fire
        Hams in the smokehouse

12. **Wash Day** 47
    Cistern water, warmed by sun
      Lye from the ashes
        Fatback from the pigs

13. **Harrowing Experience** 50
    Two furrow spiked toothed harrow
      A singletree hitch
        Giddyap, Kate! Haw!

14. **Seat In The Garden** 55
    Bare bleached wood, odor so rare
      Flies hum, wasps can sting
        The wealthy sat two

15. **Pickin' Berries** 58
    Purple fingers, itchy hands
      Backs tired, buckets full
        Crisp crust cobbler, ummm

16. **Thrashin' Day** 62
    Golden cascade of fresh straw
      Incessant chug chug
        Creaking wagon wheels

17. **Hoein' Rows** 68
    Jungles hid the enemy
      Machete chopped path
        Imagination

18. **Canning** 71
    Aromatic scents
      Wooden spoons and wax
        Bounty preserved in green jars

19. **Tractors** 77
    Bang, clang, rumble, lurch
        Antithesis to nature
            Godsend to old mules

20. **Model A** 83
    Stubborn as a mule it stood
        Dressed in lustrous black
            Would it go to town?

21. **The Crusade** 87
    Four cylinders roar
        Black steed carries bold, brave knight
            Infidels await

22. **Is There Life After The Crusade?** 92
    Crashing chunks of crystal ice
        Candy in a jar
            Shopping Spree in Town

23. **Player Piano** 97
    Hypnotizing Holes
        Bellows Produced Sound
            Voilá! Concert Pianist

24. **Maggots** 101
    Quivering red and white mess
        Nature's own horror
            Maggots in a wound

25. **The Calving** 104
    Huge brown eyes drown you with love
        Spindly legs barely stand
            Milk coats soft muzzle

26. **Betsy** 107
    Calico dress, eyes of blue
        Skin like ripe peaches
            Plump, cherry ripe lips

27. **World's Funnest Playground** 111
    Wide gray boards; rusty tin roof
        Wide open doorways
            Lofts full of hay bales

28. **Herbie** 117
    Blotchy freckles on pale skin
        Hanging head alert
            Penetrating eyes

29. **The Queen Mary** 121
    Screws, glue, ancient wood
        Paddles cut to size
            Look out catfish, here we come!

30. **Watermelon Time** 124
    Verdant, rotund balls
        Bursting with juicy delights
            Painted sticky pink

31. **The Flood** 129
    Roaring wild water
        Layer of new life
            Rain's thundering symphony

32. **Learning To Frog** 134
    Beady eyes Alert
        Heart pounding like a tom tom
            Escape, or capture

33. **Grape Coffeecake** 140
    Purple clusters on the vine
        Yeast making bubbles
            Come home from the fields

34. **Rodeo!** 143
    Cowboys for an afternoon
        Wash line in ruins
            Angry grandfather

35. **Catfishin'** 150
    Complacent waters
        Curved rod, taut stretched line
            Moby Dick on six pound test

36. **Summer Fun** 156
    Dark, damp, constant cool
        Candles flicker, then expire
            Claustrophobia

37. **Floating** 165
    Surprise everyone!
        Unexpected visitor
            How about a swim?

38. **Fencing Is Fun** 170
    Strands of wire, posts of cedar
        Horseshoe shaped staples
            Be careful it bites

39. Stove Wood And Bunnies 176
    Carrot in a box — Beware!
      Best to dig 'em up
        Oops! You're in a stew

40. Iron Crazy Horse 183
    Kids in disfavor
      Aromatic Incident
        Iron Crazy Horse

41. Growing Pains 188
    From cocoon, the butterfly
      Long limbs, rounded flesh
        Emerge young woman

42. Helmet Potato Salad 196
    Rich, dark earth; forest green vines
      Rounded mounded rows
        Kartoffel below

43. Fraidy Cat 199
    Tranquility reigns
      Broached by dis-harmonic cats
        Let sleeping dogs lie

44. Watchin' And Walkin' 202
    Panorama of color
      Yellow, red, green, brown
        Joseph's autumn coat

45. Solitude 208
    Quiet solitude
      Tree filtered sunlight
        Nature's Holy Communion

46. Eternal Rest 212
    Mourn the crying sky
      Tears flow from man and nature
        Embrace them warm earth

47. Epilogue 216
    Sad separation behind
      Put to rest the past
        New dawns, new friends, begin again

Introduction

Fantasy is the stuff of dreams. Entertainment is the object. Imagination was entertainment on a dirt rich farm. An eight-year-old boy grows to pubescence sharing love, chores, friends and animals with his aging grandparents. You will enjoy his experiences as painted by a palette of vivid imaginations. Each of the forty-six stories are steeped in Americana. Most of the anecdotes are based on personal history, but written to entertain, some fanciful, some surprising and most with humor.

Names of real people, important to my life, are included. Some, like Herbie, my real childhood friend, won't recognize a single farm incident, as he never set a foot on the farm to the best of my knowledge. However, he would agree that the adventures could have happened, if he had. The reference to the frying pan brouhaha is true, but that had a different setting. I include my wife's name, Betsy to honor my love and appreciation for her.

This is a work of fiction. *Didja' Ever Make Butter?* is not the maudlin autobiographical discourse of an aging man. It is rather, a work of love. I try to capture in generic fashion the adventures of a boy in a setting familiar to my peers and unfamiliar to those younger.

Most of the characters are real, Kate and Pete, Helga, Grandma, the farm itself and of course, Rommel, the rooster. Minotaur is pure fiction as is the character Betsy, named for my loving wife. Grandpa is a composite of several people. Spot is a generic pooch. She was Pal on our farm, but many of her adventures belong to Tramp and Rocky, my two most memorable dogs, both male.

Most of the settings are real. The spring on Wiedman Road, the old town of Manchester, everything on the farm except the cave. Many incidents described in the book really happened. Most have sugar and spice added, like any hand-me-down, oft told family story. The rest, well, they could have happened and maybe did, to you.

Gary Michael Corbett

"Which of us has looked into his father's heart?"

— Thomas Wolfe
Look Homeward Angel!

Rommel's Raid

A Boy, Some Shade And Some Dust
Irons Left To Rust
Imagination

Small puffs of dust wafted about. Somewhere in the distance, my imagination heard the rumble of diesel engines creeping forward, hidden by the clouds of milled dirt. My camouflaged, make believe tank was invisible to the attacking forces. Quiet orders were issued to my illusory army. Expected was an attack from the feared "Desert Fox."

It was 1943. The radio gave daily reports of the real war, a fierce desert war between opposing armored forces in North Africa. A raging, real war between good and evil, the Allies and the Nazis. This same war was being fought in a nine year old boy's imagination. I was that nine year old boy. Each day I reconstructed in the dirt that which had been reported the night before. Today's imaginary battle was about to rage on the 116 acre farm of my grandparents near Manchester, Missouri.

A patch of dust, clumps of grass, twigs and discarded stove top flat irons contributed to a summer day's make believe. Fired by the news from far away battles imaginary wars could be won in minutes. In these sanitized clashes, the Allies rarely lost a battle and never a war.

Didja' Ever Make Butter?

Under a gnarled tree of forgotten heritage were the supply depots and battlegrounds for the armies. A junk pile, hard dry dirt, sticks and a smattering of grass provided a miniature oasis, or two. The stunted tree aided the allies with a respite of shade during the hot summer day. It grew east of the wash house and provided a strategic view of the stable, the cistern, the barn and the chicken house. Although bent and ugly, the crooked woody growth was spared a fiery death in the wood stove. You see, one stout branch paralleled the ground six feet up. Two wires were twisted around its girth. Close examination revealed rabbit hairs crusted to the wires. Was it rust, or bloodstains? Ah, but that's another story.

The battle was imminent. My tank, in a previous life, had worked in concert with its clones on the hot stove. Unlike my hero, General George S. Patton, who claimed in a previous reincarnation to have witnessed Thermopylae and the Peloponnesian Wars, my imaginary tank and I had not. My tank, before its reincarnation, was parked on the always hot wood stove. A wooden handle lifted it from the stove to the table which was converted to an ironing board every other week. A quick pass over a cloth permeated with old candle stubs lubricated its gliding trip across a dress, or a shirt. When nicks, too deep to be filed away snagged Grandma's favorite dress one time too many, the iron was banished by Grandma to flat iron heaven. To my good fortune, I spotted the antique in the pile of rusty discards and it became truck, tank, or even a battleship for countless days of fun. A quark of creative energy could convert it from one to another. Today a tank, it manoeuvred at the will of my cleverly devised strategy. Reality was always the first casualty of the day, always wounded by a pre-battle surge of childish adrenalin.

"Steady there, boys. Hold your fire. Be brave." Rommel's forces were advancing. Intelligence had been excellent. The Desert Fox was headed straight into Patton's trap. Third Army units were well dispersed and dug in behind camouflaged positions. Swirls of dust appeared as angry portends from the advancing enemy forces. The dust covered our positions, as well, hiding us from their scouts.

Rommel's Raid

(I entertained no thought that Grandma would notice that in the process of battle this same dirt covered me from head to bare toes.) Rommel's columns advanced toward the jaws of the trap. The propitious moment had arrived.

"Now boys, fire! Hit them with everything you've got. Destroy the huns. Attack! Attack!" Heroic cries from my daydreams filled the air and startled the nearby chickens. Their unending search for food interrupted, they immediately took voice, squawking and flapping away in terror.

The enemy was reeling. The battle would be won. Rommel was about to slink away with his damaged forces. Defiantly observing the battlefield, I saw victory within reach. But wait, the enemy was regrouping. White flags had been pulled back inside the panzers. Far from surrendering, they were attacking, led by...

...Reality, having recovered from its wounds, destroyed the remnants of imagination, imposing its presence once again into the battle. The attacking menace was not imaginary at all. He had bayonet fixed and sabers bared. Fanaticism, unmistakably visible in this enemy's venomous eyes, reflected the spectre of death. This attacker clearly wanted nothing less than my life.

He was my arch enemy of the barnyard, the fright producing, ferocious, spur displaying cock of the walk. His fiery red comb swayed back and forth like a battle flag. His beak threatened like the eighty-eight cannon on a Tiger tank. It was aimed at my left eye. What a viscious rooster!

Petrified with fear at the sight of him, the battle was over. He knew my cowardice and used it against me, at will. I hoped once again that I was swift enough to reach the gate before he spurred me to death. In my worst nightmare, he served me on his dinner platter. Fear lent wings to my feet, spurring me toward the fenced yard just ahead of his deadly spurs and derisive crowing. It seemed as if an eternity of fear had frozen my heart before the sturdy gate finally slammed between us.

How quickly my bravery returned. I turned with a swagger, fully three feet inside the wire fence and taunted Erwin Rommel, the Nazi "chicken" from the safety of my fortress. The feud continued until...ah, but that's another story.

The Setting Hen

A coward in feathers, not she
Protected her eggs
From predator — me

The living symbol for cowardliness has long been the good old multi-purpose, tasty chicken. Seems like everyone except Colonel Harlan Sanders slaps insults on this egg laying fowl. Evidently, the inventor of this derogatory label had no experience with real live honest-to-goodness barnyard variety chickens. By contrast, the eagle — that national symbol we all praise as the epitome of courage — attacks silently, killing its victims from behind in sneak attacks, reminiscent of Pearl Harbor.

When I remember the setting hen, I suggest she is the prototype for primitive, heroic motherhood. Let me digress...

"Here's the basket, gather the eggs and check all around the barn," Grandma Rausch instructed. She handed the basket to me, patted my head fondly and sent me out the door. Sometimes our poorly trained hens didn't deposit their eggs in the wooden boxes provided for their convenience on the wall inside the hen house. The idea was to reach into each straw lined box and pluck any eggs from the man made nests.

The Setting Hen

The nests were built on the wall inside the door of the hen house about three and a half feet above the floor. (I never could figure out if the height was chosen for our convenience or for the inconvenience of the predators.) To the left, occupying most of the twelve foot square wooden structure was a rack that angled from low in the front to high on the back wall. Roosts trimmed from saplings made a rack that the chickens slept on at night.

The roosts and the floor were rich with nitrates gathered periodically for the garden. The odor of "Eau de poultry" never left the small house and gave evidence why chicken farming is frowned upon in urban areas. The tin roof leaked some and drafts sifted through the raw wood walls. It mainly was a good thing, the wind that is, 'cause I don't know how the chickens could have slept in there without some ventilation.

"Those fool chickens will drop an egg anywhere," Grandpa used to grumble. He showed me all their favorite spots - dust bowls by the barn, bran boxes in the milk shed, front seat of the ancient truck on blocks, the manure pile and occasionally the nesting boxes in the chicken coop.

"We could fence them in," he continued, "but if they don't eat grass the yolks turn as colorless as a bleached muslin sheet."

To this day I yearn for the rich orange yolks found in those "country eggs." I spent a lot of time finding where to buy those eggs for years. Even the infrequent red spots catered by the most energetic rooster couldn't deter me. If you ever tasted one, it's as unforgettable as Nat "King" Cole.

Digress? My goodness, I've wandered miles. Straight for the coop I headed that memorable day. After carefully checking the whereabouts of Rommel, the Rooster, I went out the yard gate. I had to pass the rabbit skinning tree on the left and pass the cistern to the right. The hen house stood thirty yards ahead in ramshackle glory. It was like an appendage to the barn. The much larger barn loomed to the right of the coop. The coop leaned meekly to its left trying to maintain contact with the barn.

Didja' Ever Make Butter?

I climbed the high step into the chicken coop and saw four unoccupied boxes yawning in the shadows. The fifth box was filled with a swollen old hen. Chickens make themselves look twice as big when they fluff all their feathers. One box contained two real eggs along with a fake one. Grandpa always put in the nest some "seed", a fake china egg or two, to urge the hens into the spirit of competition. I checked the other boxes, emptied the edible contents and stared at the nesting hen. Surely, she would leave. I patiently stared at her for all of five seconds.

"Shoo chicken. Leave!" I ordered. She pulled her head back, turtle like and fluffed her feathers to new dimensions.

"That's all right, don't be scared," I reassured her. Grandpa Phillip always reached right in and took the eggs from under such nesters. I never could see around him when he did this. Consequently, I was unsure of how to get the egg, without offending the scared old lady.

"Well, after all, chickens are cowards and cowards are chickens," I thought, as I reached for the box. WHAM! Like a bolt of lightning a red-eyed, white head shot forward and nailed my hand three times before I knew that I was under attack. I hastily took inventory and counted five digits, assuring a full quota of fingers. Three bright red marks peeked up at me from my hand. All but my pride was intact.

The outlook was bleak. That cantankerous old hen continued to glare, puff and I'll swear to this day, growl. She knew I was going to take her hoped for babies. That was one Pro-Life hen. Retreat seemed to be the order of the day. "If Grandpa wants those eggs that badly, he can debate the matter with that old hen, himself."

Unlike the eagle that attacks silently and unseen, this bastion of primitive motherhood sat nose to nose with her enemy, unblinking, defiant and courageous in defense of her progeny. Go ahead, call me chicken, it's a hallmark of courage to me.

Kate So Gentle and Pete So Mean

One was gray, the other brown
Doubletree married
To wagon and plow

Kate was a beautiful Missouri mule. Her muzzle felt like silk, as she curled her upper lip to pull a piece of carrot to her moist tongue. My young hand could barely resist the strength she chose to exhibit. Inevitably, I came away dabbed slick with saliva from her sponge soft mouth. Kate was always lips and tongue, moist and warm. With Pete, the gray, it was teeth and hooves. Women and children stayed at arms length from his stall. Wearing a heavy leather glove, adults only gingerly handed him his dinner box.

They lived together in a two horse, excuse me, two mule stable attached to the corral. An eight foot high, extra wide door gave them plenty of room to get in and out wearing full harness. It made sense to currycomb and brush them inside the stable most of the time, especially in cold or wet weather. A tin roof kept the shed reasonably dry. Being inside during a hail storm was like listening to "Drum Boogie" while sitting inside the drum. A gentle shower, by contrast, was hypnotically relaxing.

Matching harness hung on two by four racks nailed to the studs. The daily rubbing the racks received from dragging the harness on

Didja' Ever Make Butter?

and off twice daily made the wood shiny smooth. A can of lard sat on a narrow shelf. It was used with a rubbing cloth hanging nearby for cleaning and oiling the strong leather, blackened from the daily cleaning. Copper rivets glowed like small lights as they held the many pieces of leather together.

I was fascinated how Grandpa could harness two mules, so quickly. Somehow, when the leather covered wooden collars (you've seen them hanging in antique shops with mirrors inside) were fastened around their necks, Kate and Pete took on an air of royalty. Their heads rose a little higher. Their feet lifted prancingly, kind of like the huge Clydesdales do when pulling the big red Budweiser wagon. Grandpa used to call it mule pride. The collars had two brass knobs up on top. The padded collar rested against their shoulders and chest as the mules powered a double bottom plow through the tough Missouri clay, or pulled one of the other many farm implements. We had plows, harrows, rakes, planters, mower, combine and several multi-purpose wagons, all mule powered.

An early chore each day was mucking out the barn and the stable. Muck was a nice word for manure. Mucking was shoveling the final by-product of milk production from the barn, you know, digging out the last remnants of digested fodder left by the hard working mules. Horses and mules are neater than cows. The round, brown two inch pellets from a mule made perfect missiles whenever two or more kids had a minute of devil's time. It sounds gross to the uninitiated, but it was kind of like having snowballs available year round. I remember a rare occasion when Grandpa winged one at me. I can't remember if he was having fun or angry with me, probably the latter. Now with cows, you never touched the stuff until it was well dried, unless by accident, but that's another story.

We were lucky and had plenty of wood to burn. Further west, on the almost treeless Great Plains, cow and buffalo chips provided fuel with which to cook and heat.

Manure from the barn was forked into an iron wheeled wheelbarrow which in turn was taken to the pile in the corral. The fork was a

Kate So Gentle and Pete So Mean

five prong pitch fork about twelve inches wide. Fresh straw was spread in each stall before the evening milking. That wasn't just kindness for the cow, either. The milker had to get right close to the milkee and six separate feet shared the same floor space, clean or dirty, wet or dry. (Foot scrapers made a lot more sense after a week of practical living on the farm.) The stable had a four by four door that allowed access to the manure pile in the corral. We forked the manure from the mules right onto the pile. It was very important to keep the mules hooves dry and cared for to prevent hoof disease. Grandpa would clean their hooves daily with a curious looking instrument called a frog knife. The knife had a round wooden handle with a blade about three inches long. The end of the blade had a curl to clean around the frog, from which it got its name. The frog was a protrusion in the center of each hoof. Grandpa dug around and cleaned the frog most carefully. Once in a while Grandpa would trim the hooves with a long handled snipper. If Pete didn't hold still, a huge rasp had to be used to smooth the edges of the rough cut. Usually, even Pete behaved once you got his foot off the ground. You'd have to see it to believe it. That is, what Grandpa looked like when he worked on the hooves. He faced the rear of the mule while standing at the side of the target leg. He then reached down and brought the leg up between his legs where he held it up with his legs. That freed both hands to work on the hoof. Naturally, he was in a semi-squat and all bent over. It looked real hard to me and awfully dangerous if he he was doing Pete.

That smelly pile of manure was really important to a farm. Commercial fertilizers were too expensive during the depression, therefore most places had a manure spreader that was hauled slowly across the fields before the fall plowing. It spewed natural plant food in the form of dried manure, thereby helping to complete nature's cycle. One even got used to the odor. When compared with the European version of the spreader, called a honey wagon, American manure was like fine perfume. The honey wagon is probably the best example of a misnomer known to mankind. In Europe, human and animal waste are used together in liquid form. It creates an unbelievably harsh,

Didja' Ever Make Butter?

lingering smell.

Grandpa used to tell about the time Pete, the dappled gray, male mule, caught him unawares. Pete, unlike Kate, was mean spirited and just plain ornery. Whereas, gentle, brown Kate was all lips and love, Pete, as I said earlier, was all hooves and teeth. On this particular day, he lashed out and kicked Grandpa in the stomach with his huge hind hoof. The scar remained the rest of Grandpa's life. Grandpa said he feared that his life span was only minutes right after Pete had connected. He used to say that the gray leg had flicked out quicker than a spear of lightning slashing acorns from an oak tree. The force of the kick folded him in half, lifted him right off his feet, and propelled him right out that four foot square window onto the manure pile. He laughed at his own exaggerations in the telling of it later, but did go to the hospital at the time. He wore a rupture belt from the Sears catalog the rest of his life.

Now Kate, in contrast was a regular nanny, especially to kids. Nobody was permitted to play in the stable. I did anyway. The day Grandpa caught me, I was laying next to Kate with my arms wrapped around her front leg. I even sat under her on the straw bedding between her four legs. If given a choice, I would have taken my nap right there. I would rub her legs, currycomb her belly, walk under and around her with seeming impunity. The Lord watches over fools and children. At what age did I pass from one to the other?

Since Kate and Pete are featured elsewhere, I thought it might be nice for you to meet them. They were part of the family and seemed to fit right in. I had an uncle that wasn't much better humored than Pete and I had several aunts that were almost as sweet as Kate.

How the wind would whistle through the seams of that rickety old stable. A person could commune with nature in a very elemental way in that small building. I did a lot of thinking in those friendly confines near my four legged confidant. Got kind of misty just remembering that kindly animal. I'm glad that I don't recall when she died. I must have been away at school by then. Funny, teenagers have other things on their minds besides grandparents and mules.

Spring Cycle

Muscles ached, sweat poured
The sun created dry throats
Seeds returned to earth

Battle lines were clearly delineated in the bright sunlight. No one should die on such a glorious day. Yet the enemy was visible, finishing the trenches across the narrow strip of no man's land. Planes circled above. The craft dueled for the skies, darting hither and yon. Their weapons almost sounded like birds chirping at this distance. My lips were dry and parched. I longed for a thirst slaking drink of cool water and a bit of shade to rest in. Muscles were cramped and sore. Sweat streaked muddy rivulets ran down my face. Surely, we could stop the incessant digging, digging, digging. The relentless sergeants forced us onward. Their duty was to prepare the defense for any attack Rommel might launch upon us. We obeyed without question, for the sergeants talked to the officers and the officers talked only to God.

    I carefully placed row after row of mines in the soft earth. I used finely crumbled soil to cover the sensitive implants. The first rain would make everything uniform and no enemy would be able to see the mines. Some of the mines were round and slender, others round and flat. Some were white and some were brown. Some were thick and some

Didja' Ever Make Butter?

were slender. The smallest were like grains of sands, the largest no bigger than my thumb nail.

"That's too much dirt on those." The sergeant approached chiding my careless work.

"Aw, Grandma you told me to put an inch of soil on the bean seeds."

"That's right, but those are lettuce seeds." Reality interrupted my imagination and tiny lettuce seeds dribbled onto the finely prepared soil. Grandma followed and covered them quickly with only a fine sprinkle of dirt. The circling birds watched our every move, just daring us to leave a single seed exposed for them to steal.

"Boy, fetch a bucket of water from the cistern when you finish that row," she urged. Visions of cool water returned once again. I released the seeds from my hand more quickly and soon the row was finished. In my mind's eye, refreshingly cool water was already splashing into the tin drinking cup. I could imagine its stinging chill on my teeth. I could envision the dust turning to mud and trailing down my arms and hands to drip as gullies of brown water from my finger tips. My feet suddenly caught up with my mind and I darted for the cistern.

Prince of Wales

Christmas Shopping in the Snow
Bored Boys Wearing Gloves
Inevitable

Grandpa told a few rich stories, some of which were true, I'm sure. Many of these stories evolved in carefully measured segments. As a result, when the final commas and periods were in place, I had memorized each detail. One such story involved his childhood shopping trip in London. Whether this was before or after his permanent exodus to the United States, he never made clear. A taciturn man for the most part, he left out much of what could have helped distinguish tale from experience. Since I am unable to attest to its probity, the following entertaining lore remains Grandpa's favorite story. Over the years, I developed an accuracy test. If his memories were unfolded in front of Grandma, the liklihood of verity increased greatly. This story was told often, many times in the presence of Grandma, but who knows? Well anyway, here goes.

"The snow had trickled silently over the Dickensonian landscape while we slept," Grandpa began for the umpteenth time. Over the telling, he carefully formulated his words into carefully crafted dramatic dialogue. Otherwise he never spoke like this.

Didja' Ever Make Butter?

"I threw open the window and saw a city coming to life. People appeared as mimes acting out their business of daily living. Movement was purposeful and lively as they hustled and bustled toward predetermined destinations. The covering of snow muted all but nearby sounds and that of the horse drawn carriages wending their way along the whitened cobblestones. Wisps of smoke from a hundred chimneys climbed heavenward from snow covered roofs." He sighed, remembering this cherished moment from his childhood.

"Close the window, Phillip!" Grandpa continued, imitating with careful precision, the shrill voice of his aunt.

"Yes ma'am. Can I go outside in the snow?"

"No Phillip, we are going Christmas shopping at Harrod's today."

"Aw, Aunt Tillie..." He would moan convincingly. Nevertheless, the narrative continued as Grandpa related the elaborate measures taken by Aunt Tillie to protect him from the elements. She directed him to don his long woolen underwear, a shirt buttoned to the collar and knee high stockings carefully tucked under herringbone knickers. Then she bundled him a too long, black cashmere scarf, woollen mittens and flapped cap. A coat heavy enough for a horse blanket waited in the vestibule. A manipulative whine avoided the coat, but the mittens and the cap were firmly skewered to the appropriate appendages before they exited the chilled hallway into the bright sunshine of the streets.

The crowds were increasing. Bundled women, overdressed for the weather, gaily smiled and exchanged seasonal greetings with neighbors and strangers alike. Emancipated children obviously exempt from shopping expeditions ran and laughed, exemplifying the spirit of the coming holiday. In spite of his captivity, young Phillip was soon caught up in the conviviality of the streets and happily enjoying the Victorian displays. Hardly a shop was passed by. Aunt Tillie's festive air grew. Once again she chose yet another dress shop to enter, casting a temporary pall on her eager to play-in-the-snow young charge. Inside the shop were two others about his age, obviously young men of station, by their manner of dress. Nevertheless, they soon joined in the banter

Prince of Wales

and mischievous pursuits of young males. If by design or high spirits, the three young men were a hindrance to the concentration required for purposeful shopping. The cooperating fates, at the same time, provided a group of cockney youths, who filled the streets, pummeling each other from lamp post to doorway with freshly packed snowballs. Every person under sixteen was obviously enjoying the gay sport. In almost simultaneous plea, the three captive young shoppers implored of their respective parents to be permitted to go outside and *watch* the activities.

"Yes, but behave yourselves like gentlemen." Came the universal admonishment from three separate parents. Voices rang with agreement from the charged spirits, as they tumbled out the door.

In an instant, bonding with the other urchins occurred, resulting in the fire power of white missiles increasing by three. Inevitably, a stray clump of white ice struck and shattered the very window through which the three newcomers had espied the activity. A passing Bobby doing his duty to God, Queen and the merchants immediately gathered up as many of the frightened youths as he could collar, Grandpa included, and escorted them to the nearby station house. As with most incidents, it happened so quickly as to leave the shoppers in the dress shop aware only of the broken window.

In the station house an officious officer, attempting to identify culprits, questioned each lad. Careful scrutiny also revealed that two of the lads wore clothing that contrasted markedly with the cockneys and grandpa. Grandpa had gotten himself disarrayed in the skirmish and appeared as shabby as any of the other urchins. The duty sergeant, the one with the brusque attitude, approached the older of the two gentlemenly youngsters. He asked demeaningly, "What might your name be, sir?"

The young man drew himself to his full height, to a position of military attention and answered loudly and clearly in a most respectful manner, "I am Edward, Prince of Wales."

Obvious disbelief crossed the face of the Bobby, who to his credit, reserved his judgement and continued on. Two Bobbies in the back-

Didja' Ever Make Butter?

ground made a sincere effort to hide their mirth at the impertinence of the youth. The inquisitor then repeated his question for the younger gentlemanly lad.

In almost imitation of the first lad, the second assumed a soldier like stance and with no sign of impudence said, "I am George, Duke of Windsor."

Now, even Grandpa knew these names. The now sardonically smiling Bobby proceeded to repeat his who are you question a third time to what happened to be an opportunistic cockney lad, the next in line.

"Guvner, I must remain loyal to me mates," the smirking urchin replied, "Me, I'm Thomas, the Arch Bishop of Canterbury." None of the Bobbies could refrain from hilarity at his pluck. Laughter filled the station just as two liveried gentlemen and Aunt Tillie entered the station with a happy merchant in tow. Payment for the window with a little extra for the season had the dress shop owner in a jovial mood.

As Aunt Tillie hauled Grandpa away, they heard one of two gentlemen say, "Your highness, the carriage awaits." Attempts to question Grandpa further about the incident were met with carefully crafted smiles and twinkling eyes.

Till The Cows Come Home

Sloshing homeward to the barn
Leaves crunch underfoot
Udders full to bursting

Dark clouds fought for dominance with the failing sun. It was a ten minute fast hike to the back pasture where the two cows and a heifer had grazed away another sultry summer day. In spite of the looming battle between light and darkness, the oppressive humidity sapped too much energy for haste. At six years of age I thought I could do everything. At eight years of age I feared everything. At ten years of age I would admit no fear.

"Hurry back, supper will be ready soon," Grandma Rausch called after me, "Remember to shut the gates!"

"She treats me like a kid," I grumbled to no one in particular, making sure to loop the wire tether from the gate to the gate post. The warm powder of the dusty path felt silken on my feet. Each step brought small tan puffs through my toes. Soon the rain would turn it a slippery dark brown. The feel would change from talcum powder dry to chocolate pudding slick.

Clumps of grass, bitten short by the daily migration of milk making cuds, fought with shallow roots from nearby trees for sustenance. In many places the foot wide path was several inches deep, clearly

Didja' Ever Make Butter?

marked as it wound along the hillside, overlooking the barely wet creek at the bottom.

Then I heard the enemy issue a warning. Naturally, they spoke in code. My imagination knew that an ambush was being prepared. Would it be the sharp cut back around the deep gully? No, more likely they would rush over the hill by the persimmon tree and drive me into the creek by the flat rocks. (Grandpa could always spot the squirrels. More then one had graced our table, but he was cultivating the corn field today.) I was alone and outnumbered. Those chatterboxes of the nut trees became imaginary invaders. Tankers from Rommel's panzers, samurai from Tojo, or Sioux braves from Sitting Bull. Each whim of the mind conjured a new cast for the make believe scenario of the day. (Mine was a pre-television imagination, limited, but original.)

Darting down the hill, I stopped briefly on the flat white limestone rocks. Small pools excited with crawdads invited my toes for a drink. After polite acceptance, my feet leaked their way silently past the persimmon tree and its awaiting ambush. This day I would attack "them" from the rear with my army of cows.

Opening the back gate, I saw my three allies at once. One seemed to smile as her jaw ground inexorably on a half digested cud. She unfolded her legs into an lurching mass, causing her cavernous udder to sway precariously before beginning the trek to the stable. The Jersey quickly followed. The heifer, enjoying its year of independence gave a few last tugs on the lush alfalfa before remembering her particular ghosts of loneliness. My army filed its way into the woods of battle.

My tension increased as I noticed that the shadows had disappeared. Trees now blended into the growing darkness. The heat felt like grandma's wood stove on a Saturday morning. The air was thick with humidity. The first crack of lightning flashed and two seconds later rumbled its onerous warning. Grandpa could tell how far away the rain was, by the time between the flash and the sound of the thunder. Even I sensed that it was gonna' rain real soon. I slapped the heifer with a small switch and urged haste. Her nose bumped the Jersey. One glance from the irritable walking cream pot and the heifer dropped back a step. Me, I was more afraid of the Jersey than the rain and settled into the easy fluid stride of the lead cow.

The pockets of darkness united, surrounding us with the paralyzing fear of the unseen. You could still see for a hundred yards, but not through ten year old eyes. At last we passed the persimmon tree standing guard on the big hill. Safe at last. Suddenly my hair stood on end. The flash and crash exploded simultaneously. Their artillery had caught us. My brave army bellowed charge, and fled toward the barn. Bullets splattered on the path making little dust puffs where they missed us. I ran then, dodging each new bullet. Once again the lightning popped nearby and the battle ended as the cold rain drenched us, driving dust and demons away.

In record time we made it to the stalls. The four of us were safe. Grandpa Phillip had even served the bran. In a few moments the fresh straw bedding, a box of bran and a fork full of hay had our cows defining contentment like no Borden cow ever could. I pinched a handful of bran on the way to the house, thinking, "It doesn't get any better than this."

Didja' Ever Make Butter?

Yellow thick cream, so heavy
Churned by hand in ice
Golden sweet butter

Rich, pale yellow it poured from the right separator spout into a two gallon crock. White and frothy, the milk gushed into a clean bucket from the left spout. So plentiful most of the year that it clabbered and was fed to the dogs, pigs and the chickens. Of course, we drank milk warm from the cow or cold from the spring fed well in any desired amount, usually gluttonous.

Rarely in her old age did Grandma make cottage cheese or koch käse (cook cheese). The messy, odoriferous process of hanging clabber in cotton bags behind the wood stove to drain off the whey, took time and energy, both in short supply with septuagenarians. At the propitious moment it had to be processed into cottage cheese or cooked slowly on the stove with rye seeds to form the creamy smooth koch käse.

Every morning and evening after milking the cows, the buckets were carried two by two to the cellar. The separator, guarding the far wall of the cellar, appeared huge as it towered over me at age eight. Like a bulbous headed space alien, it stood topped by a broad aluminum tub into which the raw milk was poured. Even Grandpa had to

Didja' Ever Make Butter?

reach high to pour the warm from the cow milk into its maw. After the evening milking we would crank up the separator and centrifuge the cream from the whole milk. The rich thick cream was treated like liquid gold. Every drop was caught in carefully cleaned stoneware crocks. You know, the ones that bring ferocious bidding at today's auctions. We had a variety of those crocks that held from one to ten gallons. The ten-gallon one was used to make sauerkraut. While Grandpa steadily cranked the handle of the separator, I would slip away to explore the rest of the cellar.

In a small room adjacent to the separator area stood a generator, an ancient gasoline powered engine similar to one that powered the washing machine. The generator produced direct current electricity to charge an array of wet cell storage batteries stacked by the outer wall. Grandpa had it for emergencies, like if the kerosene lanterns wouldn't light. It was never used. Grandma preferred kerosene lamps saying, "That engine is too noisy and it makes the house smell."

A storage cellar, dark and cool was three steps down and under the rear of the house. A smaller storage area for dry foods and empty jars was beneath the steps. The main storage area occupied nearly half of the basement. Large wooden bins on the floor and shelves above held the bounty from the soil. Potatoes, onions, turnips, apples and squash were kept for surprisingly long periods. Occasionally a potato leaked and loudly announced its death as it slapped your nose most grievously upon opening the cellar door.

A cavernous ten-gallon crock held homemade sauerkraut. Layer upon layer of shredded cabbage covered with coarse salt filled the huge container. A double bladed cabbage slicer prepared enough of the freshly washed green orbs to fill the crock in less than half a day. Usually Grandma had help when preparing this staple. To this day one of my favorite meals involves mashed potatoes and sauerkraut. A wooden top fit inside the rim of the crock and was weighted with two or three well scrubbed large rocks.

"The cabbage must be covered by the brine in order to cure. If it gets air, it will spoil," Grandma would say. I was puzzled, as she

Didja' Ever Make Butter?

never poured any water in the crock. Years later I found out the salt reacted with the cabbage to "draw" liquid (brine) from the leaves that usually provided enough liquid to allow the fermentation while preventing spoilage.

Shelves above the bins held jars and cans of tomatoes, preserves, snipple beans, beets, apple sauce, cherries and more. It was a cornucopia of the harvest, provisions for the long cold spell between spring's early radishes and fall's last dug turnip. Tomatoes picked just before the first frost lasted all the way till Thanksgiving and once in a while till Christmas.

In the separator room was a work table fastened to the wall, always meticulously clean. On it stood the black balance scale, the weights and the butter molds. A box of square butter wrappers was handy. On the floor from one Friday till the next sat the crocks of cream. As sour cream is needed to make butter, the cream from early in the week would sour by Friday. Friday's fresh cream was added after the last milking and the butter churned Friday night for Saturday morning delivery.

On Friday the crocks of soured cream were emptied into the wooden barrel churn. A block of ice was chunked with an ice pick and added to the cream. Some of the cream — it looked like french vanilla ice cream — was so thick it wouldn't pour, but was ladled into the churn with a spoon. It looked like butter even before it was churned. I ate some that hadn't soured yet — right from the crock — you think Cool Whip tastes good. To this day, the British serve this "clotted cream" on desserts instead of whipped cream.

The sealed churn was then steadily turned with its cast iron crank. A rhythmic "kerplush", "kerplush" sound ticked off the minutes. When "kerplush" evolved to "kerflump" the liquid gold inside the churn had been transformed into solid gold. The seal was broken and the lump of butter was lifted to the work bench. It was carefully squeezed to work out the trapped drops of buttermilk, then patted into one pound lumps. The cast iron balance with a one pound counter weight verified the size to the nearest pinch. Always the pound of butter was

Didja' Ever Make Butter?

weighed heavy to the customer's benefit. Chunk after one pound chunk was gouged out with uncanny accuracy, weighed, and wrapped in the butter papers. Each brick was carefully patted into aesthetically uniform bricks of golden butter.

Fresh country butter, eggs, seasonal fruits and fresh garden vegetables were the main cash source for the farm. Most of the crops were used to feed the stock. Saturdays Grandpa would go to the city. He had several regular deliveries, but most of the week's harvest would be sold at the farmer's market. He and grandma talked about what to buy in the city at the supper table. Fresh buttermilk, cold from the churn and flecked with bits of butter was sipped in accompaniment with homemade bread and sausage. Of course, the homemade bread always tasted better with real butter.

"Grandma, you forgot to put this cream in the churn." I pointed to a one-gallon crock with a few cups of heavy cream in the bottom.

"Grandma didn't forget, come with me," Grandpa said. On the back porch stood a wooden bucket with a crank attached. Grandpa got out a chunk of ice, some rock salt and began to chip ice into a pile. Grandma took another jar of creamy looking milk from the icebox and mixed it with the cream I spotted in the gallon crock. She poured that mixture into a metal cylinder. Right into the middle of the cylinder went a paddle contraption that went through the lid and attached to the crank. The whole works fit inside the wooden bucket. Grandpa then piled layers of ice and salt around the cylinder. He told me to turn the handle. I did. After the ice had settled a bit the turning was quite easy.

"Hey, easy does it. Slow down a bit, we're in no hurry," Grandpa guided me gently. He knew cranking too fast would make butter. I learned to slow down and turn steady. The odor of fresh vanilla was in the air. I began to suspect what we were doing. For the first time, I cranked home made ice cream.

It didn't take long before Grandpa took over the crank as the mixture began to thicken. Before he finished it, even he squeezed a bead or two of perspiration from his forehead. Do I have to tell you

Didja' Ever Make Butter?

the rest? Carefully rinsing the salt from the top, we opened the churn and removed the paddle into a waiting pie plate.

"Quick, outside and lick it clean," Grandma ordered, smiling. Heaven, ecstasy, sheer delight, I was hooked for life. It is my Achilles heel of gluttony to this day — my unlimited capacity for homemade ice cream. That day, without adequate refrigeration, I felt obligated to complete the consumption of the entire gallon of ice cream before bedtime. Grandma and Grandpa were both astounded by my enthusiasm and promised me a well earned bellyache. The bellyache did not materialize, only a belly. Only thing I never got sick of from over eating. Never have, never will.

Spot, Spot Where Have You Been?

Straw, golden soft in a barn
Secluded, hidden
Squirming balls of fur

Joy, expressed by a wild enthusiasm for living, described our farm dogs. Collars were always optional. Collars can snag in a brush pile while burrowing after a bunny. Fences were designed to contain cattle and horses, not man's best friend. For dogs, the farm was open range, a blissful license to roam as far as energy and inclination would carry. This was the perquisite for serving perpetual guard duty. Raccoons, coyotes, wood chucks and many other critters gave our chickens wide berth. A loud mouthed farm dog has few enemies in the wilds of Missouri, especially when fortified by the smell of her human master. No creature knows the contentment of a napping dog curled in a shade covered dust bowl. Surely, she dreams of supper while awaiting the excitement of the next unsuspecting visitor that dares to challenge her seeming indifferent vigil.

Intruding into such a quiet moment came the chug of an automobile. It signalled the imminent arrival of a visitor. Spot reserved her most courageous and energetic performances for these occasions. Cars contained only humans. Humans posed absolutely no danger whatsoever to her. What better opportunity to display raw bravery. A whis-

Didja' Ever Make Butter?

pered growl began deep in her throat. It was caressed lovingly forward until it escaped as a brief, sharply pitched bark. This was the first alert. The car had turn onto the farm road, a mile away from the house. The first alert antic might be repeated if a visitor had not arrived within recent memory.

A neighbor shared the farm road with us and most of the sporadic traffic passed by us. The second alert identified the destination of the intruder. This notification actually caused Spot to move. We knew then, that the car was crossing the ford in the creek. Spot's scruff rose like the quills on an irritated porcupine giving her the appearance of a punk rocker born years too soon.

Just before the unsuspecting automobile reached our turnoff, a small hillside would hide the approaching car from view. If the vehicle slowed as it disappeared behind the hill, Spot chose that instant to charge stiff-legged down the road, while emitting a sharp, loud, challenging bark. It was never clear if this bark was a final warning to "git", or a dare to trespass and continue the game.

Cars just going by to the neighbor's farms were soon forgotten. Spot would trot proudly back to her dust bowl, head held high as if to say, "That one had better sense than to come on my property."

But should the front bumper, perchance, round the corner and trespass on our farm, the action began. Muzzle skimming the grass while traveling at warp speed, Spot galloped straight toward the offending monster. When about ten feet away, she would leap at the driver's door. Her loudest, teeth baring snarl blasting forth from her mouth. She didn't even smile. By the time she landed and bounced once or twice, the intruder, of course would have driven past and be fast approaching the house. Some unknowing drivers added to the hilarity by increasing their speed, a certain sign of cowardice to Spot.

The chase was on. Naturally no car could out run a healthy farm dog on a rutted rocky country road. It was now a joust between the chugging machine and one gloriously brave, flesh and blood dog. The rapid fire staccato barking from the black and white bundle of viciousness personified, filled the air. Chickens ran for cover. Cats dis-

Spot, Spot Where Have You Been?

appeared. Docile, more sensible, animals blatantly ignored the charade, concentrating instead on the serious business of grinding their cud, or splashing on a flat rock.

Grandma would come to the door, invariably wiping her hands on her apron. I cannot remember one event that was not preceded by this habit. She would continue down the steps and walk to the fence. Almost eighty by then, I think she had to get that close in order to see who it was.

"Stop it, Spot," Grandma would say calmly, only a tad louder than normal. Grandma always acted embarrassed, I think for the sake of the visitor. Yet she surreptitiously managed to pet Spot and whisper, "Good girl."

For gentle Spot it was always a game. A game that ended as soon as the car door opened or Grandma said, "Stop." Of course, some visitors weren't precogniscent of the script and it took some convincing before they allowed a vulnerable foot to touch the ground. You could never be certain, but I think this is how Spot kept score. She knew if she won the bluff. Of course, if she recognized the car, the game ended much sooner. When we returned from town in the Model A, she would bound along side trying to lick, or nip playfully an extended hand.

These highlights of her life in the 1940's were separated by a lot of long naps. Gasoline rationing kept folks from making unnecessary trips. In order to stay in peak watchdog condition, Spot had to bully a chicken or chase a cat up the elm tree. Boredom and fatigue led to another siesta in her favorite dust bowl under the snowball bush.

Spot lived to accompany any of us about the farm. Daily, she tagged along to bring the cows from the back pasture. She escorted us when taking the mules out. While everyone else worked, she patrolled the woods and the brush, guarding us from German or Japanese invaders that might be preparing to attack. She did an excellent job, we had not one invasion during all of WWII on our farm.

It could be a squirrel, a rabbit, a covey of quail, a rare wood chuck or even a fellow dog. Any of these critters were acceptable

Didja' Ever Make Butter?

distractions for Spot. Being a responsible sentry, Spot I'm certain, rationalized these forays, as training maneuvers. It would have pleased the heart of General George S. Patton to see the vigorous enthusiasm she put into her training, even though some of these exercises were of the briefest duration.

For example, an exploding bobwhite was startling and exciting, but the chase was quite short, as even Spot couldn't fly very far. Squirrel and cat chases lasted until a tree interfered. Tag games with rabbits and other dogs lasted from a few minutes to a few days. A skunk chase lasted over a week one time, but that was because Spot was banished from human companionship for quite apparent, odoriferous reasons.

She had been gone for two days now. She had missed this many meals only once before. That time, she had limped home battered and exhausted. Her head had been held low in shame, either for losing the battle, or for having been gone so long. Spot slept all that night and the whole next day, before she wolfed a meal that distended her belly to comical proportions. The memory made us smile for a moment, but this well loved rapscallion had us concerned once again. She was long overdue.

"We'll wander around the place and look for some ready firewood while we look for her," Grandpa promised me, more as bribe to let me sleep easy, than in real hope of finding Spot. More than likely she would find us. "We'll go right after the milking."

In a blue funk, I climbed the stairs and crawled under the feather bed. "Now I lay me down to sleep...," I prayed, "and please, God, if it isn't too much trouble, find Spot for us. Amen." Faith at that age wasn't deep enough to shake the worry. Sleep sneaked up on me long after the moon went down that night.

"Breakfast!" Grandma called up the stairs. Then, to let me know how long I had slept, she continued, "Grandpa is already on the way to the barn!"

Spot, Spot Where Have You Been?

Clothes were thrown over a warm, but rapidly chilling body. With shoes untied and buttons haphazardly finding the nearest hole, I flew down the stairs, stuffed a piece of bacon in my mouth, grabbed a biscuit from the plate and in spite of Grandma's objections assaulting my ears, I urged my feet to do their best in order to catch up with Grandpa.

I took my bucket from him as I caught him at the barn door. Grandpa would milk the Jersey and the heifer. I milked my beloved cow, Hilda. His big hands could squeeze a lot more milk from each squirt than I could. Try as I may, I could never empty an udder the way he could. He always "stripped" Hilda after I finished. "If you don't get 'em empty, they'll be hurting by evening," he'd say.

Hilda, eagerly awaited the handful of bran I'd sneak her. Her cold, hard, black nose would press against my hand as soon as it moved toward her feed box. A scratch or two behind her ears, a quick cleansing of my hands on my pants and the milking began.

Grandpa held the bucket between his knees, but mine sat on the straw. He sat on a stool. I did too. His hands reached down and his face was almost in the cows flank. My hands reached up and I was looking straight at the magnificent four. There were advantages and disadvantages. The cow's tail kept the flies from his face, but when the tail lacked certain qualities of sanitation, he got high lighted with aromatic ecru colored streaks from the living paint brush.

Squirts from his powerful hands rang loudly, echoing off the empty bucket. My piddles were as resonant as my 10 year old voice. His bucket filled rapidly covered with creamy foam. A visiting cat, with hope in her heart, would mew gently and be rewarded with a jet of milk in her waiting, open mouth. I tried it several times — to hit the cat. Got a lot of milk on my bare feet. The rough tongued cat would tickle cleaning up my mistake.

Milk crept slowly up the sides of my bucket, keeping pace with the cramps, creeping slowly up my forearms. Resting a minute to let my fingers shake the tightness out, I heard a discordant sound. It sounded like a tiny squeal. "Probably one of the cats," I thought.

Didja' Ever Make Butter?

Again the sound was heard from the far side of Hilda, from between her byre and the barn wall. Surely it was a tiny squeal. "It's probably mice being chased by the cat."

With Grandpa's bucket singing its rhythmic song, imaginary villains would keep their distance, so I ruled that possibility out.

I heard the straw being rustled in the corner beyond the mews. There was a space between the manger and the barn wall used to hang old harness, equipment and other treasures that were never thrown away on a farm. The resulting space in that corner of the barn floor contained a heap of straw. I stopped milking and looked closely, leaning right under the cow. My heart stopped. Almost covered by the straw was a hint of fur. A very still piece of black and white fur lay unmoving. A curled up black and white piece of fur ... SPOT!

I didn't even move the bucket of milk. I went right under Hilda. It was Spot. Unmoving but breathing her black eyes rolled upward, looking deeply into mine. She wasn't alone. Her tail flopped cautiously in recognition, but her head covered six squealing little bundles as she possessively licked them one more time. Miniature black and white reproductions were vibrantly milking Spot and not one of them had a bucket. Good sense, rare for me, said let them be for now, but I knew a pan of fresh milk would be more than welcomed by the new mother. It was.

Summer Storms

Heavy Air, Blackening Sky
Gusts — Flash, Boom, Shudder
Squishy Mud — New Life

Threatening weather seldom catches a farmer by surprise. Most men of the soil are attuned to the vagaries of nature, as closely as the plants of the earth and the birds of the sky. Like those flowers that know when to signal spring with a splash of color, the farmer seems to sense when to plow, plant, or cut the hay.

To err is human, for a farmer it can be disaster. Plant too early and seeds may not germinate, or if they do, get killed by a late frost. Plant too late and the heat of summer, combined with the lack of rain, may wilt the crop like bacon on a hot griddle. If it rains on cut hay, it's probably wasted. The Farmer's Almanac, a source of laughter to some, is nature's bible for the gentlemen of country.

This interaction between men and nature was taken so seriously, in Salem, Massachusetts in the 17th century, that some farmers were burned as witches, because their crops failed. The good Pilgrim forefathers believed that the farmers who suffered crop failures had sinned and that crop failures were God's punishment on them. Therefore, if God saws fit to punish these farmers, the ruling class, called

Didja' Ever Make Butter?

the Elect, must punish them as well, to curry favor and show their support of God's wishes.

On a small family farm during the Great Depression and World War II, a successful main crop every two years was hoped for. These farmers would have been real nervous back in Massachusetts. Usually three main crops were planted; wheat and soybeans for cash and corn to feed the stock. Grandpa called soybeans "cowpeas," by the way. Rain always determined which crops produced in any given year. Too much could be as bad as too little. Rain in June ruined the wheat. Too little in August hurt the corn. Too much in the Spring or Fall could make it too muddy to plant or harvest. Thus was the arm's length relation between the farmer and nature.

Winter wheat was planted in the late fall, hopefully on an already harvested corn field. The wheat would sprout, developed a root system and then be nourished by the winter's snow. In the spring, it grew like a teenage boy and by the fourth of July, had gone to market. Corn was planted as soon as the frost danger went north. The idea was to catch the early summer rains and establish the crop before the summer dry spell. Harvesting started in late September and continued until Thanksgiving.

Missouri is fortunately rich in water resources. The state is blessed with a lot of springs, many of which break the surface, others of which are underground rivers, tapped by deep wells.

Grandpa relied on faith and rainfall. We had a deep, spring fed cistern that supplied water for all the animals, humans included. The fields were on their own. If it rained the correct amounts and at the right times, he prospered. Too much, or too little and it was like losing a baseball pennant race — wait till next year.

It was one of those days that promised to settle the dust, make the creek rise and fill every pond to brimming. A magnificent sunset the day before had outlined towering thunderheads in every shade from orange to purple. The purple deepened into a menacing charcoal gray. Sometime during the night, the attic rattled with the first rumbling vibrations of thunder. Lightning flashes projected eerie, jagged shapes on the walls. Imaginations were activated. A dead, bare limb was silhouetted by lightning, flashing like a strobe light, outside the window of my bedroom. The branch tapped a tune of the west wind and imagination forged for it a new identity. The unearthly image, projected onto the wall, might have been the wildly galloping Ichabod Crane, or angry witches stretching sinewy thin arms in their spectral attempt to steal a frightened young child.

The safe cocoon of the heavy featherbed gave warmth and shelter beyond imagination, at these times. The bulk alone of the downy mass seemed like a guardian angel, firmly surrounding me with heavenly security. Pull it over your head, and it silenced the crashing thunder into hypnotic rumblings. It shut out the witches and the flashes of space creatures that rode into your dreams chasing Buck Rogers. It became...

"You boy, last call for breakfast. I have been calling you for over an hour," Grandma's decibels level finally penetrated sleep and the featherbed. Totally refreshed after being rocked into deep sleep, I sprang from the bed and saw the dull gray sky. The incessant hum of rain played its mournful melody on the roof. Liquid life was returning to the soil. There would be no field work this day.

All day, Kate and Pete would rest, eat and swish their tails. The cows would munch the newly washed grass and stand, or lie under a huge tree to chew their cuds. The chickens feasted on the half drowned worms seeking higher ground. The cats stalked vermin in the barn. The rain on the tin roof muffled the deadly game of cat and mouse. The gloom and the noise tilted the advantage to the cat. Spot would ignore all of it, curling into a tight ball in some dry straw and rejuvenate for the next dry day. A half-hearted wave of her tail would acknowledge your presence.

Grandpa would sharpen, fix, oil, rivet, saw, nail, or help Grandma straighten the porch, clean out the wood stove, or rearrange the cellar. The temperature had a great deal to do with decisions. Fall, winter and spring usually meant keeping dry. You got too cold, too soon to get wet then. The summer was a different story. Once the lightning went east, I couldn't wait to get outside, rain and all.

Huge warm drops would soon plaster your hair. Rivulets of new born water would run down your face. A contorted twist of the mouth,

Didja' Ever Make Butter?

a projected lower lip would yield a sip of rain water. In minutes you were wetter than a Monday wash.

Craters of water in the grass were more than my toes could resist. Each magnificent droplet splashed a similar, but different round pock mark. My feet strained to join them. We did. Standing water two inches deep, level with the top of the yard grass was like walking in the plushiest carpet ever made. Soon walking became a merry jig with crystalline water flying up from the ground, almost as fast as it fell down from the gray clouds.

Once this exhilaration of youth slackened, the yard gate to the barnyard beckoned. The barnyard offered feels and textures not found in the grassy yard. Rain splattered on the bare rocks of the driveway. Some boulders bigger than a watermelon, other rounded like eggs. Years and traffic had compressed them into an aggregate of almost level surface able to support any machinery capable of fording the creek to reach the farm.

The barnyard oozed with a magnificent blend of colors. Rich browns, yellows, ochers ran in palette drenched hues. The area was deep in mud and slippery footing. It was irresistible, of course, for me. The silken slime gushing between your toes massaged your feet. It provided an exhilarating challenge, the slipping and sliding, barely being able to balance on the unknown footing.

Rarely objects were encountered that punctured the feet. Everyone did a good job of picking up any nails, glass or other dangers to the hooves of the stock. Mysterious objects did flash momentary signals of dread from foot to brain often enough to thrill the most avid horror movie devotee. All were handled with prevailing intelligence, unless it moved. Boom boxes can't begin to equal the decibels emitted by the bare foot, supported by a wiggling unseen object, usually harmless, but only found to be so after the scream of terror had alerted most of the county to my momentary state of terror.

Inevitably, my soaked body would reach the stable. Kate would turn her head and stare. I would snitch an ear of corn and she would eagerly reach out for it. The powerful crunch of her teeth echoed

Summer Storms

from the feed box. The hard corn popped and ground noisily. The sounds seemed to focus the brute power she possessed.

While she munched, I would take the brush and currycomb to her broad back. I commiserated over the lumps in her skin caused by the ever hungry horseflies. I smeared a pungent black salve on each bite. A few strokes from the hand sprayer would cast a fly killing mist over her back and shoulders. Even Pete behaved when the sprayer came out. His haughty arrogance melted into a pleading "me, too, please" look.

Lastly, I would unwind each of Kate's hairs tangled around the many cockleburrs in her long tail. The offending relatives of the thistle plants were a plague for man and beast. They were the inevitable unwelcome guest of any hike, hunt, or berry picking expedition. The mules picked up these hitchhikers at the ends of the rows of corn while pulling the cultivator through the corn fields. The inch long, spine covered, miniature porcupines asked for no mercy and certainly offered none, as they lurked at the ends of the rows, hitching a ride on any host that brushed by them.

Once, on such a rainy day, Helga gave birth to a calf. I almost missed a meal that day. Within hours, the calf and I curled in the straw, side by side. His huge brown eyes seemed to look at me in adoration. Maybe he thought that I was his brother. I would stroke his soft coat while he lurched time and again, making connection with and trying to drain his mother from one of the four, randomly chosen, feeding stations. Helga licked him from time to time. I made sure that Helga had plenty of water and an extra cup of bran. The calf tried to suck my fingers from time to time. After a few frustrating tugs, he discovered that nourishment wasn't forthcoming. The calf's head would bob and tug, clamped onto the flavorless fingers. His frustration level would rise until he rediscovered his nearby mother. A clumsy lurch and his mouth would reconnect to the nearest feeding station. If true hunger persisted, he would hang on until satiated. Later I helped wean him from Helga by having him suck on my fingers while I dipped them into a bucket of milk. He quickly learned to let go of the fingers and noisily slurp up the milk, directly from the bucket.

Didja' Ever Make Butter?

A sudden cooling would signal the passing storm. Sometimes the rains slashed wildly in a fury that lasted minutes. Mostly though, storms huffed and puffed to a furious beginning, then settled in for an all day love affair with the soil. Grandpa always prayed for the latter. When the cool dry air rushed in, it was over. Now it was time to explain the mud and the wet clothes, the smell of the barn and my disappearance. Did Grandmas really have to ask where you were, or was it just their way of saying, "I missed you."

The Hunt

Leaves crunch; chattering squirrels
White dust from Jack Frost
Branches or antlers?

There's a picture, carefully posed, showing a young boy with a shotgun in one hand and the ears of a cotton tail rabbit clenched in the other. The shotgun dwarfs the alleged hunter and the rabbit hangs to the ground. Each time the boy viewed that picture, his desire to go hunting grew as much as he did. He also learned that you only hunted what you ate, or that which was about to eat you. There was no exception to that rule on Grandpa's farm.

At what age you got bullets for your gun depended upon certain mysterious unwritten criteria. No one ever spelled out the criteria, therefore it was a vexing thing to learn. It involved skills not commonly heard of in youth, things like common sense, responsibility and listening. When the older hunters thought you were ready, you were invited to play "tag along."

My oldest daughter, for example, hunted at a younger age than did my boys. She was more responsible, listened and didn't argue about everything she was told. I'm not sure of my exact age when I got to "tag along" but my hair hadn't turned gray yet.

Didja' Ever Make Butter?

"We're going to the deer stand. Ya' can't talk and ya' have to sit still if ya' want to tag along," Grandpa said those magic words, as we finished eating our hot rolled oats slathered with brown sugar and cream.

"Be still, my heart," I thought to myself. The pounding excitement inside my chest would surely disqualify me from being quiet. I wanted to jump and yell, but outwardly I remained as tranquil as a poker player with a full house. He checked my clothes, pocketed a handful of deer slugs for the shotgun, put four apples in his jacket and headed for the door. Hot on his heels, I wolfed down my last piece of buttered toast. Outside, it was pitch dark and cold enough to read the words in your breath.

"Carry this hickory walking stick. This year it's your gun. Maybe next year..." The rest hung in the crisp morning air like a frosty breath.

Grandpa set a brisk pace, as he headed up the dirt road leading toward the back pasture. He had scouted all summer first while plowing and then during the harvesting. The deer had left consistent, well defined trails in their meandering. Grandpa had his spot picked out. It was a spot that revealed spoor from not only deer, but rabbit, wood chucks, coon and other woods dweller, as well. 'Possum had wandered by. Bird tracks of many sizes abounded. It was like a small game preserve. Grandpa expected to have venison on the table tonight.

A gently sloping hill overlooked the trickling creek. Water pooled on slabs of white limestone that formed the creek bed. Cedar brakes gave shelter from the northwest wind. A corner of the corn field was visible to the right. With food, water and shelter close at hand, the small herd of deer visited this paradise daily. The sharp hooves had churned an arrow like path to the creek. Grandpa choose this spot to capture his deer. It was time to harvest the meat crop.

There was no resentment of the few crops that the deer ate. During the depression, few farm budgets could afford meat from the store. We ate deer and rabbits, so we could sell the chickens and hogs for much needed cash. Surely, our holiday dinner would include a venison roast.

The Hunt

Keeping the wind in our face, checking each step, we slowly, made our way down the hill. The cold breeze brought tears to my eyes and drip to my nose. Halfway down the hill we carefully sat amongst the cedars to watch and wait. The cedar thicket stood between us and the corn field. The corn field narrowed to eight rows between the cedars and the creek. We each took a few bites from an apple. Grandpa tossed the cores into the corn field. I remember him saying, "It helps to mask our smell from the deer. They love apples."

It was silent time now. The sky had turned from black to dark gray. Black silhouettes surrounded us. The eerie quiet was interrupted by things seldom heard while we were moving and talking. Oak leaves held a whispered conversation with the breeze. A bird flew noisily from its cedar roost. A dog barked in the distance. A rooster issued a tentative invitation to the sun. Cows mooed. Each sound caused muscles to twitch. My hand tightened on my hickory stick gun, but not one stitch of my clothing moved.

My nose itched. Slowly, I brushed it with my wool glove and was rewarded with a glare from Grandpa. A piece of wool fiber stuck to my nose. That itched worse than the itch. My eyes watered from the new irritation, but no way was I going to move again. Now, each time I breathed that thread of wool wiggled and tickled a little more. I was in agony.

Desperately trying to take my mind off the powerful itch, I looked for rabbits in the nearby lush grass. I saw spots where they had burrowed, making a small rounded cave in which to hide. One was decorated with small brown pellets. I spotted a wide eyed hare, remembered the picture of the dead hare and felt a rush of sympathy. My preoccupation was jangled once again by the reality of that unrelenting itch.

"I..will..not..move," I steeled myself with grim determination. Hopefully, I stuck out my lower lip, trying to force my breath upward and blow that damnable wisp of wool off my nose. Bad move — earned another glare. Worse, "it" still itchingly clung.

"Grandpa..." I whispered, almost silently. No answer, but I felt his glare as if it were a hammer.

Didja' Ever Make Butter?

Bare trees reached skyward like gnarled fingers on the opposite hill. Soon the dazzling sun was sliced into shafts of lights by the barren hardwoods. Then one by one the birds chirped a cheery greeting.

Walking to the stand, beads of sweat had moistened my hat band. Now sitting quietly, the sweat turned to ice as the insidious cold sneaked inside my clothes, heading for my bones. My butt was cold. Soon my marrow would quit working. My blood would freeze. Grandpa would be sorry then.

A gust of air reminded the piece of wool to move. A sneeze gave notice. Isn't it awful, a sneeze that can't be consummated? I wanted desperately to sneeze, but because of the circumstances, instead I called on every reservoir of self-discipline to stifle it. You know, like having to sneeze with a mouth full of mashed potatoes. But I said nothing. I did nothing. Grandpa didn't glare. I was learning the rules.

In an awesome heartbeat three, no, four does and two yearling fawns separated from the shadows. They were on the far side of the creek, a long way out of shotgun range. I stopped breathing and momentarily forgot the sheep shaving that was tormenting my nose. Grandpa stirred ever so slightly, as if checking each muscle. I heard the hammers click back on the shotgun. The small herd grazed toward the creek. They would be out of sight while they watered, but would then head for the cedars to bed down for the morning. My heart was pounding with anticipation. The cold wasn't as cold. My marrow had a chance, but the irritation from that devil wool continued to torment my nose.

A loud crunch sounded to our left. Grandpa's head turned ever so slowly. Imperceptibly, the shotgun slowly moved to the ready position across his chest. I heard movement in the creek, then saw a branch shudder. It was the only branch moving. Now the branch was two feet to the left. It wasn't a branch. It was a buck! Silently, Grandpa lifted the shotgun to his shoulder. Patiently he waited. Then, as if in slow motion, a head took shape. It was a huge buck! At least six visible points showed on his right antler. A twelve point buck!

A saucer like brown eye accented the buck's beautiful tan face. His ebony nose gleamed like patent leather in the growing light. His

The Hunt

white ears twitched hither and yon, searching for the sounds of danger. Muscles rippled as he rose majestically from the creek. Tufts of black tipped, tan hair shuddered in a gust of November air. His white stomach hair faded from sight as he stepped into the waist high brush at the top of the creek bank. He presented a perfect side shot. At fifteen yards Grandpa couldn't miss. It would be a swift, instant kill. I watched Grandpa's finger slowly squeeze the trigger.

The explosive sound caused pandemonium. My ears rang painfully from the force of the blast. The buck leaped straight up, before he landed and vanished from sight. I watched the does and fawns clatter across the field and disappear into the far woods. As my ears stopped ringing, I heard Grandpa uttering unfamiliar words as he unloaded his unfired gun. The buck was nowhere to be seen. That long-contained, but irrepressible sneeze had ended the hunt.

Didja' Ever Make Blood Sausage?

Pigs squealing as if they knew
Kettles on the fire
Hams in the smokehouse

Sometimes the farm isn't pretty. It's kind of like a microcosm of life at large. Butchering day is probably the most gruesome, but to a young pre-adolescent it's fascinating beyond belief, an educational show and tell that will never be seen in school.

Long before breakfast, hot oak fires roared under the huge black kettles. I remember there being at least three, brim full thirty gallon cauldrons, heating the "scalding" water. Ideally, there would be a touch of frost in the air, making heat from the fires was welcome in the pre-dawn chill. The children were kept busy hauling wood to feed the blazes.

The odor of hickory from the smokehouse blended with the burning oak heating the black pots. The hint of bacon sizzling in the kitchen wafted into the yard. A few yards away a nervous snuffling from the pig pen made you wonder about the foresight of the porcine victims. Perhaps it was the empty troughs. Maybe the presence of extra hands milling around. Maybe it was the chatter of the women rolling biscuits. By nightfall these 200 pound food machines would be smoked,

Didja' Ever Make Blood Sausage?

boiled, cured, salted or stuffed. Almost nothing would be wasted. Pound for pound, Mr. Pig was the most edible creature on the farm.

Long wooden tables, hastily constructed for events like butchering and thrashing, were lined up and the morning feast began to assemble. Coffee and cream, biscuits and gravy, bacon and eggs, sausage and homemade bread were deposited by the women. Freshly dug potatoes fried in what else, bacon grease, were mounded alongside yeast rolls, coffee cakes and other assorted special treats. Each farm lady showed off her best recipe on these days. After all, the extra helpers were friends and neighbors.

After consuming the epicurean breakfast, the last steaming cup of coffee was carried to the farm yard in tin cups with rolled soldered handles. They held at least a pint of coffee or beer we found out at day's end. Robbie Berger was the best shot. He was the executioner, but nobody even teased him about that. We knew it was time. He carried his .22 caliber rifle into the pig pen. The sty churned like a busted anthill with cloven feet dashing hither and yon. Grunts punctuated by puffs of vapor from the snorting noses seemed like steam from train engines spinning their wheels on a slick track. Squeals filled the air as the frightened pigs plied for traction on the slick semi-frozen ground. Robbie and his brothers, Ott and Paul, herded the nervous pack of pigs nearer the gate. The less distance they had to carry the dead animals the better. They worked quietly without talking. Everyone watched with fascination except some of the women who went into the house to clean up the dirty breakfast dishes.

Crack! The first hog dropped instantly, without a sound. It was dead before it hit the ground. Bob carefully planned to shoot each one between the eyes in order to kill it quickly and mercifully. And so it went. Within minutes, seven of the chosen eight hogs were dead. Only one pig remained alive. Sometimes the best laid plans go astray. At the last instant, that last hog dodged and the crack of the rifle was followed by a terrified scream. The bullet hit off center and only wounded the now panicked pig. It ran away from all three men with Robert in hot pursuit. He fired, less carefully now, desperately trying

Didja' Ever Make Butter?

to put the anguished animal out of its misery — anguish, caused more by fright than from pain, Grandpa explained to me later.

"Attaboy, run!" one of the older boys cheered for the pig. There was a nervous laugh or two from the men as Bob ran slipping and shooting at the wildly careening critter. Suddenly Robbie's feet went right; the rest of him went left and his gun went off, thankfully straight up. The pigeons on the barn roof, thinking they were part of the harvest, flapped crazily for the safety of the sky. One flew over Bob with an expected result, in what had become a chinese fire drill.

As Robbie gouged the pigeon dropping from his head he laughed and said, "It a darned good thing cows don't fly." Laying flat on his back in the rich aromatic mud of the pig sty, Robbie howled with laughter, as did the whole crowd. Just then the pig dropped dead. To this day it's argued whether that last pig died from a lucky shot, pure fright or a very bad joke.

Any where from eight to a dozen hogs could end up on the ground. Today they slaughtered eight. The three brothers called for the porcelain wash basins that had been sterilized by the women. From here on the lady readers should cover their eyes as it get pretty messy. Each pig was faced downhill, head held over the pan and the jugular vein punctured. The blood was drained into the pans and taken to the very table upon which we had eaten breakfast. By nightfall it would be delicious blood sausage, stuffed into the large intestine of the pig and simmered in the huge pots of hot water.

In the doorway of the barn, a dipping barrel had been filled with scalding water. Each hog was lifted on a chain hoist and lowered into the water. It was washed and scraped, even the hooves and the nose in order to prevent contamination during the next steps. When thoroughly clean, the carcass was slit carefully up the belly so as not to puncture the intestines. Ideally the intestines were removed intact to be cleaned for making sausage. I don't know how many feet of intestines a pig has but every inch had a use. The stomach was used for the head cheese, the small intestines for link sausage, the large intestine for liver sausage and the colon for blood sausage.

Didja' Ever Make Blood Sausage?

An always engrossing sight was the skill with which these men wielded the sharp knives and meat saws. Whet stones hissed across steel blades. The shush, shush, shush of saw blades gnawed through bone, muffled by the surrounding flesh. After the carcass had been gutted and cleaned they ceased to be animals and were meat; food for the table. After that it wasn't so bad to watch any more except...

...Grandpa had the recipe. He also was an expert at dicing the fat back. Actually the fat back was really the sow's belly, the part with no meat, just fat. The fat with meat in it, you got it, bacon. The bacon went straight to the smoke house still wearing its clean shaven skin, now to become rind. Grandpa laid that fat belly on the table and sliced neat, straight lines exactly one-quarter of an inch apart all the way across. Then he turned it 90 degrees and did the same thing the other way. Now came the skill part. He turned that knife parallel to the tabletop and cut the fat a quarter of an inch down, all the way across the top, resulting in hundreds of quarter inch squares of pork fat. These were then dumped into the pig blood.

Grandpa had his sleeves rolled as high as he could get them and broad elastic bands were in place as skid insurance. He always ended up to his elbows in that bloody mix. Salt, pepper and several other spices were added in large quantities and he mixed and mixed until he resembled jack the ripper more than my quiet old grandfather. He pulled his forefinger one final swipe through the mixture, unhesitatingly plopped it into his mouth, sucked it completely clean, rolled his eyes heavenward and sighed, "Perfect."

He then looked straight at me and said, "Here boy, have some."

Just like Grandpa, I rolled my eyes heavenward and that was the last I remembered, as I sagged unconscious to the ground. I had taken Robbie Berger off the hook. Everyone had a new chump at whom to laugh. Next year I tasted the mix without batting an eye. By the way, I still like blood sausage, but that first time, raw, did me in. Most people get bothered more by the head cheese.

In the kettles were put the de-brained heads and various other scraps. The feet and tails were also used if not wanted for pickling.

Didja' Ever Make Butter?

Usually some were held aside to be cooked with sauerkraut for dinner. The heads were boiled for most of the day into a thick rich soup. The solids were pulled from the soup, cooled and only the bones removed. Everything else was then chopped coarsely and returned to the soup. Spices were added and the mixture was poured into the pig's stomach. It jelled and became head cheese. Add corn meal to the mixture, pour it into a shallow pan, let it cool, voilá, scrapple. The natural gelatin comes from boiling the bones and cartilage. Both delicacies were dearly treasured. Sometimes it was hard to get the feet into the pot, as pig's feet boiled with home made sauerkraut dumped on mashed potatoes was a favorite meal for these first generation German farmers.

Unlike thrashing time when the main meal was at noon, the big meal for butchering was at breakfast. Sandwiches and buttermilk were always waiting, however. Near the end of the day, when the cleaning up was being done, a celebratory act was customary. The small kids walked to the tavern near the Berger's farm and trudged back with full buckets of beer. The buckets had better arrive full. Suddenly would appear the tin cups, home baked rye and white bread. Mr. Robert Berger Sr. then served some of the freshly cooked sausages.

Already the hams and the bacon, skewered on iron hooks in the smokehouse, were curing in pure hickory smoke. My lifetime love for beer has never matched the taste of a cold draft sipped from those old tin cups while watching the sun sink lower with each bite of supper. Even fifty years can't dim the memory.

Wash Day

Cistern water, warmed by sun
Lye from the ashes
Fatback from the pigs

Big round galvanized tubs that I could move, empty. As soon as the new day advertised its value, the tubs were set on the old capped cistern and filled with water from the new one. It was at least sixty feet from one to the other. At eight pounds a gallon, those two gallon buckets got heavy.

'Course, Grandpa always said, "It's best to carry two at time so as to be balanced."

Grandma would always give the go, "Sun's up! Not a cloud in sight. Reckon I'll need you to crank up the machine, Pa." She always called it the machine and what a machine it was. The only thing that fascinated me more was the thrashing machine that came once a summer to spray golden gales of straw into rich, yellow piles while collecting the bounty from the winter wheat crop ... but that's another story.

Turn left when you skipped down the four steps from the screened in back porch and you were confronted by a bare board shed twenty feet away. The most common of country locks fastened the door. A clasp hinge with a carved wooden pin secured the door from wind,

Didja' Ever Make Butter?

weather and stray animals larger than a cat. Mice abounded, in spite of spring traps and careful sentry duty by the cats. Once upon a rarity, Grandpa killed a copperhead inside the seldom used building.

Just inside the door was a natural shelf formed by the old studding spanners. Those familiar with farm sheds realize that no space is unused in a covered shelter. Only the contents varied from farm to farm. This particular space was memorable to me because that is where the turpentine bottle resided. That brings to mind a harrowing incident, but that too, is another story.

I would gaze for a moment upon entering the shed. My eyes tried desperately to distinguish the gloom from the cobwebs. A three foot path zigged and zagged down the approximate center of the sixteen foot, by twenty foot building. On the right, occupying half of the twenty foot side sat "the machine." The first thing to catch your eye was a round massive flywheel, resembling a railroad wheel. The black four cycle engine sat squat and powerful looking, with a glass bulb of gasoline attached above the carburetor. Grandpa opened the petcocks. After fiddling with some doodads here and a thingamabob there, he breathed deeply in preparation for his battle with the rope. A quarter inch piece of hemp with a wooden handle was wrapped around the hub of the flywheel. It was pulled to start the motor. In cool damp weather, it was a learning experience to hear the rich phrases he could utter in praise of the machine's obstinance.

A loud bang would signal that its interest was awakening. A chug, chug, bam; then a much smoother ka-chug, ka-chug, ka-chug evidenced that it was ready to work. A lever engaged the power shaft to a six inch wide leather belt. Two equally wide pulleys transferred the energy from the engine to the washer which groaned and wiggled as the clothes had the hard earned country dirt wrenched out of them by the violent action of the primitive agitator. The "Spray n Wash" of the country set, a wood framed brass washboard and piece of Fels Naptha soap took care of the stubborn stains. There was no gentle cycle, nor was one needed. When clothes get washed in the country, they were so dirty some of them walked to shed by themselves.

Wash Day

Load after load went from wash to rinse. The noise was deafening — the odor of smoke from the engine, worse. Although the exhaust was aimed at a hole in the wall, much of the blue white smoke seemed to hang inside the wash house. Bucket after bucket of water from the warming tubs were carried by stoop shouldered boys, namely me and dumped into the washer tub or the rinse tub. Grandma was never idle. Over seventy years of age, she fed garment after garment through hand cranked wringer. Those white rubber rollers were her pride and joy.

By noon time she had everything in baskets, or hung on the long clothes lines that ran between the elm and the sycamore in the back yard. The hanging sheets always blocked the path to the outhouse. Long clothes props were inserted at opposing angles to keep the line elevated from the grass. As the last sail was hoisted, she announced lunch.

Usually we had our big meal at noon, but on wash day there was no time to cook and we settled for slabs of homemade bread with butter and last year's grape jelly, or sausage from the smokehouse.

I could smell the freshness coming in the window, as I sipped my buttermilk. The fresh clean air wafted in the windows from the damp, fresh washed sheets. I licked a moustache of fresh buttermilk from my lip and tasted a fleck of butter. This was one day the afternoon nap sounded just fine. Sleep that night came easy on the fresh smelling bed clothes.

Wash days got further apart, as grandpa and grandma got older. Now, twenty years younger than they were then, I no longer wonder why.

A Harrowing Experience

Two furrow spiked toothed harrow
A singletree hitch
Giddyap, Kate! Haw!

"Boy, do ya' want to harrow the corn field?" The question sliced into my half listening mind and exploded into an unbelieving, fully conscious brain.

"You'd let me harrow the field ... by myself?" Suddenly, totally focused on Grandpa, I searched his eyes and face for the signs of a first rate scam.

"He would never let me," I thought, waiting hopefully for his reply. "Come on, I'll hitch up Kate if you want to try." He smiled, but that telltale, mischief exposing twinkle wasn't there. Optimistically, I headed for the stable.

"Want me to brush her, Grandpa?" My thoughts were racing. I remembered that first time, it was on the hay wagon that Grandpa handed me the reins. We had our legs hooked on the rack that supported the hay. It wasn't easy to stand on a hay wagon, pitching and rolling unpredictably, over the rough farm land. Until I had mastered standing up without holding on, I now realize, there would have been no holding the reins.

A Harrowing Experience

I had the reins, one in each hand, and proudly straightened imperceptibly. The team, unaware of the change in drivers, plodded onward toward the barn. The wagon was filled with hay, cut two days before. Near the barn, Grandpa spoke in his quiet, yet firm way, "Haw, Pete, haw. Whoa team, whoa." Pete and Kate pulled a little toward the left and stopped right under the hayloft door.

Several times afterwards, Grandpa would hand me the reins upon coming from, or going to the fields. A few times he had me move the wagon while he stayed on the ground, but never before had he let me solo.

I was almost afraid to breathe, as we harnessed the gentle Kate, I saw him reach for and hook up the singletree. The bare gray piece of oak had an iron fitting in the middle that attached to the harrow and two iron fittings on the ends used to connect to the harness.

Grandpa led Kate from the stable, handed over the reins, pointed and said, "I'll meet you over there." I knew he meant by the rocky hill, where we parked the plows, planters and other mule pulled implements.

"Giddyap, Kate." She immediately hit top speed, a steady three miles per hour that wouldn't slacken or hasten till sundown, or whoa, whichever came first. The singletree dragged and bumped a dusty path, then slid as we reached the grass, bouncing occasionally to identify the larger clumps. Whoa came first, as I stopped within hitching distance of the harrow. Grandpa was waiting, ready to hook the singletree to the harrow. He let me gently stop his hand and demonstrate my proficiency.

I was about to pop the reins when Grandpa, gently said, "Whoa boy. Lower the lever."

The lever moved forward and backwards when a ratchet, spring handle was squeezed. The lever caused the harrow teeth to point where needed. When the points of the teeth slanted rearward, the harrow slipped over the ground allowing easy travel to and from the field. The lever was lowered all the way forward to achieve this setting.

"Pull it all the way back the first time around the field, you hear." It really wasn't a question. This shallow setting would break up the

Didja' Ever Make Butter?

big clods from the plowing and level the top of the ground for the second pass.

I had watched the day before when Grandpa, in the hot sun, had looped the reins across his back, spit on his hands and followed the plow that Pete had pulled all day in the creek bottom field.

A small, wet, dark patch in the north corner yielded forty pound watermelons. The rest was devoted to corn, field corn, the corn that fed the stock. Horse corn, as it was most often called, provided fodder for the cows and the mules. The stalks were burned as kindling, or were carved into fiddles on a rainy day. After shelling, the cobs were burned in the wood stove, or in a moment of foolishness, hollowed into a corncob pipe. Grandpa wasn't good at that, so mostly they were the fake kind that never smoked. I never did hear of a corn cob being used in the outhouse, one touch would tell you why. That probably was a city rumor, or a hill billy joke.

Kate got me to the field and "whoaed" long enough for me to raise the lever and get her moving again at her steady three per. My bare feet hopped on the rough board, wired across the metal harrow frame. My weight and that of two heavy stones helped the teeth dig into the ground and break up the clumps. Proud enough to bust, I pretended this day to be Grandpa. I was him, sweating under a straw hat, plowing behind the mule. I remember how I watched him the day before. His bare shoulders glistened under his bib overalls. His muscles bulged and stretched, even when he was seventy years old. He fought the plow, which became a living writhing monster, turning a ten inch deep furrow of thick bottom land gumbo. An infrequent rock would cause a halt. He would bend and pitch the intruder to the nearest edge of the field. In the winter, we pitched the rocks into the manure wagon and dumped them into the creek.

My knees flexed in juvenile imitation of Grandpa, as I rode the harrow. The steady hypnotic rhythm of Kate's swaying rump soon took me far away.

The harrow became my chariot. Kate, the mule became Katherine the Great, my regal war horse. The creek lay along one side of the

A Harrowing Experience

field and its trickle of water from small springs encouraged the growth of sycamores, elms and oaks along its banks. The shadows from the trees contained foes and dangers introduced by my imagination. Each pass of the harrow was fraught with newly imagined dangers. Filled with pride from this first solo, as well as the arrogance of youth, I knew not the meaning of fear.

My flights of fancy made the hours pass quickly. Already I had lowered the levers for the second raking of the soil. This time Kate and I started in the middle of the field and worked our way outward. Each trip brought us closer to the creek. The shadows were lengthening and the imaginary enemies gathering. The sun had long since crested the hill. Doves were cooing their melancholy call from dusk's early shadows. Crickets added their clatter to the cacophony of country sounds. A mockingbird imitated and teased from high in a creek side tree. I was relieved to be on the last furrow, the furrow closest to the creek.

All at once, loud sounds exploded from a dark tangle of brush and weeds next to the creek. A black shape led by bared, slashing teeth hurtled at us out of the shadows. A terrifying, fluttering, whirring sound chilled my heart to a stand still. Brown missiles hurtled one after another, right at me, missing my face by inches. Even Kate deviated from her steady three per and bolted ten feet, in a deer like leap. I was pitched like a rag doll from the harrow, toward the creek, losing my balance. Tan and white pieces of flint approached me at a dizzying speed from 10 feet below. We met half way — it seemed.

Spot, also in the creek, was licking my face. Taking inventory of my aching body, an uninvited rock stuck out from the heel of my hand. Tears started, then just as quickly, stopped. "You can't cry and be a man, too," I reasoned. I looked for a place to scramble up the bank.

Dear, sweet Kate was patiently waiting. Crossing the field at an awfully fast clip, was Grandpa. I hadn't even seen him pretending not to watch.

He checked me over and concluded as I had, that I had an extra rock in my hand. There was little blood, as the two inch wide piece of

Didja' Ever Make Butter?

flint was jammed deeply, but tightly into the heel of my left hand. Grandpa assured himself that I could walk and headed Kate for the barn. Gentle Kate sensing an emergency, sped along at four miles per hour. What a sacrifice she made that day. Just for me. She never hit that speed before, or since. For the first time in my memory, Grandpa turned her into the corral and just threw the harness over the fence.

We headed for the wash house and out came the bottle of turpentine. I'm not sure to this day whether it was really turpentine, or coal oil, as Grandpa called it both. Call it what you will, on that farm it was penicillin, sulfa, alcohol, aspirin and bandaid. Not able to pull the rock out with his fingers, Grandpa liberally doused my hand from the dust covered bottle and using a nearby pair of pliers, gave a quick tug and pulled the offending piece of flint from my hand.

I now experienced first hand the expression, "blood and tears." A flood of both appeared. The blood slowed as Grandpa liberally splashed more bottled fire on the wound. The bleeding soon stopped. It burned so badly, I think it cauterized the wound. Didn't do a whole lot for pain or fear, though. He wrapped the hand in a clean, by farm standards, handkerchief and we went in to supper. I sure got out of mucking the barn that night.

My self-deluded mind had been looking for imaginary enemies and had overlooked the real culprits. Dear Spot, our version of man's best friend, had exploded a covey of quail into Kate and me, scaring the bejesus out of both of us. To this day, I jump when those birds take flight anywhere near me.

Seat in The Garden

Bare bleached wood, odor so rare
Flies hum, wasps can sting
The wealthy sat two

About a hundred feet behind the house, at the rear of the garden, sat an inelegant gray wood structure with an oversized, sloping roof. Taller in the front than in the rear, it could accommodate a standing man. It was well ventilated, of the same construction as the hen house, come to think of it. The bare boards were of the roughest grade of lumber, although the seat boards inside had the high polish of the finest furniture, having been rubbed smooth by daily use.

The view through the cracks in the boards changed seasonally. You could watch string beans grow in the spring, leaves fall in autumn, or snowflakes convene to press dead foliage into mulch, while you encountered gluteal frostbite in the winter. Many a list of chores was contemplated from this rustic throne.

There was a certain tranquillity surrounding this four by six foot building. Farm animals tended to graze in other vicinities. The cats and dogs had developed no fondness for the area, either. Other than the hum of flies and not too particular mud-daubers, it was quiet enough to listen to the rustling of the growing corn. I remember the first time Grandpa asked me, "Do ya' hear the corn growing?"

Didja' Ever Make Butter?

I didn't answer. It surely was another of those wonderful stories that people substituted for television in those days. I was getting a little too old to fall for his tricks anyway. "Listen to corn grow, does he really expect me to buy that?"

I said nothing and neither did he. We sat quietly thinking our own thoughts. It was windless night. Bright stars and an iridescent moon cast pale illumination, interrupted by the massive, stygian silhouettes of the barn, the house and the stable. Then came one of those rare, silent minutes, when even the insects were napping. A strange, rustling whisper became persistently evident. It began as a quiet, almost inaudible hiss, then a "woosh," that produced a whispered blend of the two sounds. I listened to it off and on for the better part of an hour. Grandpa remained silent. Several times I tried to speak. He only said, "Listen and remember."

I learned much later in life that on warm, humid summer nights, following a summer rain, corn can grow so fast that the leaves actually brush against each other, causing the whispering phenomenon. You really can listen to the corn grow. Yes, Grandpa, I heard it and I remembered.

Wire was an indispensable item on a farm. A piece usually hung from a nail on each side wall of the outhouse. A nail hole through an old Montgomery Ward catalog provided an opening to string a wire. Violá, hanging reading materials and tear out pages for the necessities at hand.

Flush was a foreign word in the outhouse. The only deference to sanitation was a sprinkling of lime, periodically. Only once did I see the outhouse emptied and that was manually. A board was pried loose and the wheel barrel was odoriferously filled and transported, as far from the house, as the property line would permit. It got scattered on the alfalfa field. That field did grow fast and green when you think about it.

Stifling in the summer and frigid to a bare behind in the winter, the outdoor toilet was commonly found well past World War II in that area. From what I read, the serviceable old sheds are yet in vogue

Seat in The Garden

away from the bustle of the interstate highways. Modern versions, the kind we find at outdoor events and construction sites are called "Johnny on the Spots". They lack in the charm and naturalness of their country cousins, although they remain competitive, aromatically.

Complaints about rough paper, bad odors, etc. regarding the shady shack, would bring a quick reminder from Grandpa about the spot in the woods with the broad green poison ivy leaves. Does everyone learn about poison ivy the hard way? With all of its negatives, coping with the quaint privy was quite easy. You soon learned to talk not, breathe through your mouth, as little as possible, and then, only in shallow gasps.

Pickin' Berries

Purple fingers, itchy hands
Backs tired, buckets full
Crisp crust cobbler, ummm.

Blackberries, dewberries, raspberries are all fragile nuggets that Mom Nature made difficult to harvest. The competition for this delectable is quite fierce. Along with us, the bears eat them, as do the birds. I always thought the birds had the best go. They are armed with a sharp, hard beak to cope with the guardian thorns. Those same prickly spines lie waiting to sting our soft flesh. Bears seem impervious to the hazard. Stands to reason that if a swarm of bees can't discourage a bear's penchant for golden sweet honey, what chance does a mere thorn have?

Everyone is familiar with the results of the mid-July harvest. Every small town that features seasonal fruit cobbler on the menu managed to serve a fresh blackberry cobbler. The berry season is begun by the strawberry. The raspberry continues all summer depending on the variety and in Missouri, the blackberries appear in time for the Fourth of July. Dewberries make it a few weeks earlier, by the middle of June. It all makes for a berry nice summer.

Strawberry shortcake with thick cream, beaten just shy of butter, is enough to overwhelm the palate. This treat is no challenge to ac-

Pickin' Berries

quire, except in keeping the beds free from weeds. The picking can be back breaking, but it's easy compared with harvesting the rare jewels of the wild. I wouldn't include them in the story, except that strawberry shortcake is as irresistible as apple pie.

Raspberries have likewise been domesticated. Straight rows, wire guides and easy heights to pick. The careless picker may hit a sticker, but by and large the raspberry was the easiest of the berries to pick on our farm. Blueberries, huckleberries and boysenberries did not do well on our place. I have had the pleasure of picking blueberries in the Minnesota woods and the pie made in my summer camp kitchen at Lake Hubert has never been equalled. All things, in which we have a hand in the making, seem better, don't they?

This story is leading to memories of seeking and enjoying the jewels of the wild, dewberries and blackberries. A horticulturalist friend once told me that these deep purple gems are related, but they certainly grow in vastly different habitats. The dewberry matures much earlier, growing in open pasture land, alfalfa fields or any where the birds have dropped the seeds. Those birds better keep eating the berries, or the berry will soon disappear from the earth. By eating and pass-ing the seeds with bits of phosphate, the bird plants and scatters the low lying green vines all over the farm. Grandpa kept his eyes peeled for their white flowers in the spring in order to find the berries later.

Calling upon his mental notes from the spring plowing, Grandpa would unerringly lead the bucket brigade to the thickest spots in order to find the biggest clusters of juice bursting berries. Invariably, it was a hot day. In order to preserve the skin, long pants, high top shoes, socks and long sleeves were recommended amidst a chorus of grumbling. The tin quart buckets remained empty until the picker's greed was satiated to a degree. Leather gloves with the finger cut off helped protect the back of the hand from the attacking thorns.

Grandpa and Grandma always seemed to pick faster. Their buckets filled twice as fast as mine. I guess they had better self control and their buckets received the bounty before their stomachs. I was amazed the way these so called older folks could glide across a sunny hillside.

Didja' Ever Make Butter?

Their hands would be seeking, fingers plucking and bucket slowly rising with the purple bounty. In no time they were working on the second bucket and mine would be barely covered on the bottom. Of course, my mouth was kept tightly closed for fear of displaying the purple mouth of a berry thief. Grandma and Grandpa were incredibly easy to fool. All those years of berry picking and they never caught me eating my way through the patch. Naturally, their comments came suspiciously close at times. They referred often to my purple mouth and my extended and the frequent visits to the outhouse.

My one fear in picking dewberries was to occupy the exact same spot in a sunny field that Mr. Copperhead picked for his morning snooze. It only happened once and both of us set farm sprint records. He in one direction and me in the totally opposite other. More common were encounters with black snakes and blue racers. Grandpa also thrilled us — thrilled, my foot — he scared the daylights out of us with his tales of the legendary hoop snake. According to Grandpa, the ferocious skinny reptile attacked berry thieves. It smelled the berry juice on the thief's breath and attacked by swallowing its tail and rolling like a hoop across the field toward its intended victim. It would bite to paralyze then squeeze to break all of its victim's bones before unhinging its jaw and swallowing the remains. If he didn't want me to eat those berries ... why didn't he say something?

Blackberries were my favorites. The picking art, as learned from Grandpa, I passed on to my children. My success in teaching them was obvious; they came to hate blackberry picking, as much as I hated dewberry picking. By the time my kids were old enough, the land was rapidly filling with subdivisions. The locations of the remaining patches were carefully kept secrets. Two such patches existed into the early 1970's. One patch grew on a power line right of way. The other near a fenced in sewage lagoon. The conditions in both places produced the finest berries I have ever seen. Some berry crops from those spots would have filled a quart with six berries. Well, they tend to get a little larger every time I think about them. I learned to tell stories like that from Grandpa, too.

Pickin' Berries

The plants grew about eight feet tall and that was no exaggeration. I wore heavy leather gloves to pull them down in order to reach the berries. I wore rabbit hunting clothes in order to belly up and break trails for the kids through the spiny patch. The kids followed and gleaned the lower hanging berries into their baskets. I refused to tell them about hoop snakes. Children shouldn't have nightmares. Instead I told them about pollution and pesticides.

The patch with the biggest berries of all spanned a wet weather stream. The berries grew in a hanging arch intertwined with poison ivy vines. The long curved blackberry spines supported the ivy and the ivy weaved a lattice work that supported the added weight of the huge fruit. Completely grown in shadows and shade, the birds never found them and the fruit was always perfectly formed, never sunburned, grade A prime. It was the easiest to pick, too. I walked in the bed of the stream between the arches and just reached up and dropped the plump purples into my waiting basket.

My kids were city kids. I always managed to lose one each trip. A distraction, a wrong turn in heavy growth a minute or two out of sight and a panic stricken scream would alert us to the brief dilemma. Much worse was when one got entangled so badly in the stickers that we would have to carefully extricate them. Were blackberries worth all that effort?

Check the price of blackberry jam in the store. Better still taste it, smear it on a knife. Smear grape jam on another knife. Spread both on bread. The grape jam knife comes clean. The blackberry jam knife will have a coat of purple. You can't even lick off with one pass. That demonstrates better than anything I know, the extra rich flavor of the grandest of wild berries. My secret patches inevitably yielded to the expanding boundaries of civilization. I don't pick blackberries any more. I envy those that do.

Thrashing Day

Golden cascade of fresh straw
Incessant chug chug
Creaking wagon wheels

Excitement, as tingling as an electric current, pumped energy into the pre-dawn hours. Alive with a bustle of activity, the kitchen hummed with the sound of swishing calico dresses. The incessant drone of the voices of our neighbors and our friends invoked images of a beehive in springtime. Every available inch of shelf space was stacked with baskets, pies, porcelain buckets and jars. The stove top popped and crackled with hissing pots and rattling lids. Outside, Spot sporadically barked to alleviate his over wrought nerves, stimulated to bursting by the endless arrival of unfamiliar teams, wagons and drivers. The men intermingled, sipping cups of scalding coffee, while munching buttermillk biscuits, crisp smokehouse bacon and fruit coffee cakes. Others practiced their aim with fresh issues of chewing tobacco juice. It was "thrashing" day and it started early.

Grandpa and the crew chief were checking the moisture in the fields. If the dew was light, the crew soon headed for the field. A heavy dew and everyone would await the drying power of the hot, summer sun. This day, the chaff would be separated from the wheat. I heard the phrase in church and by day's end, I would understand its origin.

Thrashing Day

"Crank 'em up!" The word echoed across the barnyard bringing renewed barking from Spot. Cups were drained of coffee. The cistern cranked out some final cool splashes of water. Men and boys climbed the wagons for the short trip to the field. Two to a wagon, they "giddyapped" from the barnyard. One man drove and stacked, the other forked the shocks of wheat from the ground to the wagon. The rhythm of a pitcher and catcher developed, as bundle after bundle was lifted to, then caught by the driver and swiftly tucked into the most desirable spot to assure balance and continuity of the quickly growing load. How high the wheat could be stacked in defiance of physical laws, was part of the fun. It was a total loss of face for even one bundle to drop from the wagon before being unloaded into the maw of the thrasher.

The chug of the steam engine had been heard in years past, but this year the muffled clamor of a gasoline powered engine resounded over the fields. A huge leather belt connected the engine to the thrasher. One final check of the gauges and a lever was engaged, allowing the drive wheel to slowly begin turning. In moments the huge leather belt added its song to the hum of activity. The shaking, clattering thrashing machine became the main orchestra for the discordant, unnatural sounds, shattering the farm's tranquillity. It had taken over two hours to level, assemble and adjust the magnificent machine. Now the star of the day awaited its first wagon load of ripe grain.

I walked along the right side of the wagon next to Kate. Pete, the nasty member of the mule team, wouldn't tolerate anyone near him, unless Grandpa was leading him with a halter. My pitchfork was in the wagon. There were two, one for Grandpa and one for me. Mine had a long handle, was surprisingly light and had three graceful tines curving from the handle to the sharpened points. With it I would toss the bundles of wheat up on the wagon.

Several days before, Kate and Pete pulled the ancient combine through the field. Today's combines cut, separate and bag the wheat, while driving through the fields like an over grown lawnmower. Those early models cut the wheat, gathered it into uniformly sized bundles

Didja' Ever Make Butter?

and tied it with a piece of twine. It was fascinating to walk behind the combine and watch it gracefully sculpt an eight foot path through the golden field. It had a slowly revolving paddle wheel not unlike that of a river boat. The paddle circled slowly, pushing the wheat against the sickle bar, insuring that the wheat fell upon the cradle. The cradle gathered, bundled and bound the fresh cut crop. The bundles rolled out the back and the trailing women and kids collected and stacked the bundles into shocks for drying. The sickle bar left the field sporting a four inch stubble. Today, thrashing day, these shocks were loaded, bundle by bundle onto the wagons, for the brief trip to the thrashing machine.

Most farmers couldn't afford to own a thrashing machine. Some didn't even own a binder-combine. In order to harvest the wheat, one of the farmers would buy the thrasher and the others would pay him for its use. Everyone joined together to help with the labor. The women, in unspoken competition, cooked a meal that made Christmas, Easter and Thanksgiving seem like a Monday brunch.

Our wagon was at last full. I could barely reach high enough with the bundles. Grandpa reached down, speared them with his pitchfork and boosted them the rest of the way. For an old man and a squirt we did pretty good. Our wagon was piled as high as any other, thanks to Grandpa's ability to stack a load sky high. At last he urged Kate and Pete toward the trashing machine. Already most of the wagons were lined up and tossing bundle after bundle into the insatiable maw at the top of the thresher. Golden streams of straw were spewing on the ground forming the beginnings of a shimmering pile.

"All right, boy, you can head for the lunch bucket." Grandpa had no doubt that I would hurry. He would get the team in line for the thrasher and we would eat our lunch after we emptied the wagon. The sun was high over head and we were coated with dust from head to toe. A quick stop at the cistern yielded a drink from the gods. A splash of cool water helped the worst of the dust run off as mud. A dark brown line clearly delineated the dusty zone. Another slosh of crystalline water and my eyes once again opened without blinking.

Thrashing Day

Grandma handed me a huge cylindrical, metal bucket. It had a tightly fitted lid with a black knob handle.

"You walk now. Don't spill the buttermilk," she cautioned. I did walk, but let me tell you, it was a brisk pace.

Lunch was simple fare. Inside the covered bucket was a quart of buttermilk, that had been chilled in the cistern. Grandpa swigged deeply to cut the dust from his throat. I gave him a wet rag and he smeared the dust around his weathered face. Also inside the bucket were stacks of sandwiches. Slices of homemade bread, fresh and plain. Generous slatherings of butter accompanied the variety of homemade sausage, slabbed between the uneven hand sliced bread. Bacon, liverwort, blood sausage, head cheese; it was a delicatessen of the best each family had to offer. It was recipe show off time and it seemed like only the best was offered. Amazing quantities of sandwiches disappeared in minutes. Then it was back to the fields for another load of wheat.

Eating in shifts was necessary to keep the thrashing machine working. Sometimes two farms were done in the same day. Speed was essential, as rain was a dreaded enemy once the grain had ripened. Wheat got rust if exposed to too much water during the ripening and rotted quickly if excessive rain fell during the harvesting. Our farm had the crew for the entire day. That meant we hosted the harvest dinner, an unforgettable feast. Dinner would be served when the machine shut down, not before. Silence was the signal for the women to begin filling the specially constructed outdoor table.

The sun sliced through a western stand of trees. In a couple of hours it would be dark. Grandpa's was one of the last wagons in line. We made three loads that day. It had been fully five hours since lunch. I was on the top with Grandpa this last trip. I was dead tired. I perked up when we reached the thrashing machine. Grandpa was throwing bundles of wheat into the still hungry opening. The shaking, rattling and grinding continued without let up. The end result was quite plain. Kernels of wheat, the staff of life poured like a small spring into sacks attached to the machine. As one filled, a lever switched the flow to another sack. The full sacks were tied shut and tossed onto a truck for transport to the mill.

Didja' Ever Make Butter?

A long tube, not unlike a giraffe's neck, stretched off to one side and angled upward, peaking about fifteen feet in the air. Chaff and straw were blown out in a continuous stream to form straw piles. If the wind was steady from the west, as it usually was, most of us could avoid the worst of the thick dust. Trying to avoid all of the powdered air was an act of futility in that it coated everyone and everything eventually. Poor Kate and Pete looked like twins. Kate and Pete were the same dusty brown color, as Grandpa and me. Cleaning them and the harness would take days. The two mules would roll some of it off in the corral tonight and get a good curry combing in the morning.

At last, the final bundle was thrown into the hopper. The straw thinned its stream then stopped. The crew chief hollered, "Shut it down!"

The metallic cacophony dwindled to a pianissimo, as the giant machine died in segments. A moment of total silence swept across the field. Almost gently, the creak of wagons, snort of mules and dust choked voices crescendoed happily with the sounds of leather harness straining the wagons homeward. Everyone headed expectantly toward the house by way of the cistern.

Soap, towels and wash basins had been placed around the cistern by the women and girls. The men watered the teams, then washed thoroughly and some splashed each other, as spirits surged upward with the long day's ending. Thoughts turned now, toward the feast at hand. Already, the overwhelming aromas from the meal were tugging us, relentlessly, toward the repast.

Inside the fenced in yard, the women had covered a table thirty feet in length. I've never forgotten the cornucopia that greeted our eyes. Waiting were mounded platters of fried chicken, boiled chicken and dumplings, slabs of ham, red eye gravy, biscuit, breads and rolls. Mountains of mashed potatoes, tubs of butter and bowls of cream gravy dared you to empty them. Greens, beans and tomatoes splashed color about the table. Cucumbers in sour cream, pickled beets, corn relish, pickled onions and senf gherkins added their spice to the festivity. Spare ribs and sauerkraut pungently drifted into each breath.

Thrashing Day

Tea, buttermilk and coffee did their best to wash each palate clean for the next heavenly bite. Heaven wasn't forgotten. Someone always gave thanks for the bountiful harvest and the asked His blessing on those who helped their neighbors.

As plates emptied for the last time, desserts infiltrated the scene. Pies and cakes were proudly presented by the women who cornered the blue ribbons at the county fair. Money couldn't buy anything on that table. It was freely given and shared in this unforgettable event, thrashing day on a midwestern farm.

Hoein' Rows

Jungles hid the enemy
Machete chopped path
Imagination

Sweat and top soil drizzled in muddy streaks down my cheeks and neck. The dust swirled and bit acridly into my nostrils. It was search and destroy time. The mission — seek the enemy infiltrators and destroy them. There were to be no friendly losses. It would not be easy. It was a mission impossible. In the jungle out there, the enemy had been burrowing in for weeks. He was well camouflaged and greatly outnumbered our allies.

We had been on the move since early morning. The hot yellow orb stood high in the sky, scorching everything in its hellish glare. Thankfully, our water supplies were good. Thirst was the enemies problem, not ours. Crystalline cool water, stashed close by in the nearby shade, slaked the unending thirst developed by the continual hacking of the machetes. The luxurious chill from a cup of the precious liquid, poured on my head, brought relief from that ball of fire hanging at its zenith. It was almost chow time. We had successfully engaged many of the enemy and left them wilting and dying in the bright July sunshine. We chopped them down by the hundreds. It was a massacre.

Hoein' Rows

"Dinner!" Great-grandma's welcome, prolonged invitation echoed from the house. The shattered reverie of the military fantasy faded from view. The reality of the cleansed rows of beans stood in proud salute. The weeds lay curled in the dust, dying. My machete was no more. In its place was a brown handled hoe. I straightened and walked toward the house. Grandma Weniger slowly straightened with considerable effort. I could never understand why old people got stiff so easily and why their backs always seemed to be in pain. I guess that's why Mr. Doane sold so many of those little round pills. Fifty years later, I understand. Grandma was older then, than I am now. I don't hoe any more. I don't garden any more. Her arthritis was surely, as bad, as mine is. Are we as tough today, as the old folks were then? She didn't even take Carter's Little Liver Pills. Me, I've got a half dozen prescriptions.

I loved to day dream about the military. Rommel was usually the time worn enemy and Patton always won each and every imaginary encounter. It mattered little that today's jungle full of greenery was dusty. The convenience of imagination can fit any scenario to a childhood fantasy.

You know, when it came to hoeing, I never could keep up with Grandma Weniger. She flicked that hoe in and out of the beans faster than the eye could follow. Seemingly, she never missed a weed, nor ever nicked a young green bean plant. Occasionally, I would stoop and prop a sagging bean plant that I had wounded with "friendly fire." A pile of dirt pulled around the plant with the hoe, usually hid the damage from my careless "machete." My dexterity wasn't fine tuned at age nine and once in a while a "friendly" became a casualty. By sundown the wounded and dying bean plants would droop showing their curling leaves. Grandma would cluck her irritation, as she spotted my examples of bad aim.

I hated hoeing, but I have since spent many hours using the wicked instrument in my own gardens. I rarely nick any of the young plants that I start from seeds. My aim hasn't improved an iota, but my attitude has. My loathing for the hoe was only surpassed by the torment-

Didja' Ever Make Butter?

ing ache brought on by the picking of the ripened green beans. In spite of the relish with which I regard the tender green pods when boiled for hours with fat back and onions, this kid never volunteers for the pickin' or the hoein'.

Canning

Aromatic scents
Wooden spoons and wax
Bounty preserved in green jars

It began in July. Warm weather would turn hot for the occasion. The straw piles had barely settled and the noise from the departing threshing machines barely faded before the waiting began. The outhouse, conveniently located at the back of the garden, became the medium for the messages. Each trip would bring an optimistic foreboding.

"They are pushing up the soil."

"A tinge of red shows through the leaves."

"Some are almost six inches long." The appointed day was rapidly approaching.

Grandpa would increase the time attending to the pile of stove wood. The rasp of the buck saw and chunk of the axe could be heard any time during the daylight hours. The uninitiated don't realize that firewood and stove wood are quite different. Those of us that light a fireplace enraptured by its beauty and toasted by its warmth, enjoy a luxury descended from an ancient tradition. Until very recently, the fireplace, the wood stove and the cook stove were a cherished necessity. They traced their ancestry to the damp caves of our pre-historic

Didja' Ever Make Butter?

forefathers. As recently as the current century, the wood stove was the only way to cook and to heat most rural kitchens. It burned smaller pieces of wood than the big mouthed fireplaces. I'm certain that somewhere out there are people, who by necessity, or choice, yet enjoy the unforgettable experience of living with a wood stove.

Tending the wood stove was the first chore of the morning and the last task at night, save extinguishing the flickering coal oil lamp. Poets and urban cowboys may wax eloquent in their praise of the crowing cock, as the harbinger of morning. In actuality, the alarm clock of the hinterlands were the rattling iron lids and grates of the cast iron stove.

When properly banked at night and aroused in the morning by a gentle shaking of the grate, the careful placing of finely chopped dry wood and a jet of warm breath, the stove would bring a whisper of smoke, promising warmth and satiation to still sleeping noses. Eyes gritty with sleep were greeted by the glowing metal giant.

With the damper wide open to assure a good draw of air past the reviving coals of yesterday, Grandpa would add selected splinters to create a roaring blaze that sucked the chill night air into the hungry innards of that friendly iron beast. Droplets of water clinging to the bottom of the coffee pot would pop and sizzle, as Grandpa set it on the hot stove top. His first chore of a long day was completed. With a final adjustment of the damper, he headed outdoors, tackling the mental list of chores that charted his day from pre-dawn to pitch dark, seven days a week. Today would be an exception. He would begin earlier and labor at a heart pumping pace till long after dark. I wouldn't have to rationalize my way out of a nap today. It was the first day of the canning. A nap would be a lost luxury.

My first clue should have registered the day before. The freshly washed green jars, standing at attention on the table, gleamed like rare emeralds in the slanting light of young sol. Their matching zinc lids, white porcelain inserts and sterilized rubber rings invoked images of troops on parade. Dates on some of the hand blown jars provoked images of the Civil War. One such jar was labelled *"Ball*

Canning

MASON'S, PATENT 1858." It had mold number 323 in raised letters on its concave bottom. I shall remember that jar forever. I still have it today. It's a prized possession along with others I have salvaged from the farm. Another of these antique works of art has a fly preserved for eternity, trapped many years before in a hot bubble of glass. Or was it a bee attracted by the honey like scents of sweet fruit, stewing on the stove? No, it couldn't have gotten in that wall of glass during canning. Did farms make their own jars long ago? My thoughts, in those days, would range across the unlimited expanse of the mind. It was a fertile environment for thought. Conversation was sparse, talk took energy, of which there was little to spare on canning day.

Both of my grandmothers, grand and great, from my mother's side of the family were there today. Another hint of the arrival of that portentous day that should have registered. Stiffness and kinks in the sore backs earned by gleaning the rows of string beans the day before were loosened by the end of breakfast. Several baskets sat on the porch, over flowing with long green tendrils. Two bushels of tomatoes kept them company amidst the cornucopia of colors accented by the deep purple bunches of beets, bleeding on the bare wood floor.

Two huge kettles of water were beginning to steam. Grandpa carried the first buckets of an apparent fire brigade of water from the cistern, before the coffee even perked. He filled to the brim almost every large container in the house. Breakfast, this day was a rare, eat-on-the-run affair. Bread, churned butter and a glass of milk laced frugally with coffee. Dinner, always served at noon, would be green beans, fresh pulled onions and potatoes, cooked all morning with a piece of fatback. Luscious tomatoes, too ripe to can, would be thickly sandwiched between slices of homemade bread and butter. It was a tough life, full of many hardships, but someone had to do it.

The spatter of water droplets diving suicidally from the huge cauldrons to the top of the red hot stove, signalled the beginning of the canning. Into one vat were carefully placed the sparkling clean jars and lids. A pot of amber colored sealing wax and another of white paraffin were heating on the side burners, next to the simmering pot

Didja' Ever Make Butter?

of beans. It was time for the tomatoes, the crown jewels of the crop. More jars would be filled with tomatoes than all the rest of the vegetables put together. Hardly a winter day went by that these plump red beauties didn't grace the table in some fashion. The two women, both ancient by my measure, carried with apparent ease, the heaping bushel of bright crimson colored globes to the kitchen table. Washed the night before, they were ready to to be skinned alive in the boiling water. Eight at a time they were gently dipped for a few seconds then lifted to colanders. In no time the basket disgorged its bounty. Huge tongs lifted the scalding hot emerald jars to receive their red jewels of fruit. With knife in hand, great-grandma sat and dropped limp skins into the bucket at her feet. A flick of her wrist and a remnant of stem fell into the bucket, as one ripe ruby after another plopped into the waiting sterile bottles. How quickly they filled, were salted then covered by loose fitting lids. A rack of eight jars would then plunge into the boiling cauldron for 30 minutes. This is called cold packing. In an hour the baskets were empty and the jars brim full. The first eight jars, with now tightened lids, stood proudly cooling in the pantry.

Almost forgotten was the process that gave the name canning to food preservation. Squat shiny tin cans filled the table in the fall. Into these sterile receptacles were plopped plump, ripe fruit; blanched, peeled and cored. Amply tasted, they melded with the thick sugar syrup and disappeared as the tin lids clicked into the waiting grooves. Announced by its pungent odor, hot red sealing wax was then carefully poured into the channel at the top of the can effectively sealing the contents from air, contamination and impatient appetites. Later a sharp rap or two on the wax would crack it sufficiently to dig it out. The pieces were carefully washed, melted and saved for the following year.

Repetition aside, canning green beans presented an altered challenge. In the days before genetic engineering, beans came with tough strings. I believe that the promise of Eden was sold out for the string bean, not an apple. Erroneously, in my opinion, we were taught that it was the apple to which Adam succumbed. As maturity and sophisti-

Canning

cation honed our judgement, we preferred to blame the wiles of woman. Logic certainly dictates that woman was involved, but in my opinion the apple got a bad rap. You see, I think that beans originally grew wild. Their bushes were waist high, perpetually decorated with succulent, ready to eat morsels. Pick 'em and eat 'em. Weeds did not clog the plants or the pathways between them. The soil was perpetually loose and loamy, never in need of cultivation. Rain fell at propitious moments, leaving the ground neither arid nor muddy. Adam and Eve walked by the plants and a perfect portion of the stringless pods would fall right onto their dinner plates. Look what Adam "blew" succumbing to one act of disobedience. Adam, my revered fore-father, how could you have ruined this paradise? Because of this ancient indiscretion it now took hours for Grandma to cut the ends and carefully convince the strings of each bean to release its prisoner. In time, the green jars filled with green edibles.

In our family, a major portion of the bean crop was diverted from the blanching. Spared from the steaming kettle, half the bean crop was sentenced to the guillotine. Well, it was a really sharp knife. We didn't have a bean snippler then. Be assured, I do. The ante-snippler task consisted of two or more women with calloused fingers, sitting patiently, discussing the weather, family and neighbors, while reducing a pile of tender beans into one-sixteenth of an inch diagonally cut slivers. These slivers were fed into a jar in one inch layers. Canning salt, that coarse relative of the shaker family, was sprinkled liberally on each layer. After several layers, a flat bottomed length of wood was used to tamp the beans tightly. I always figured the more beans packed in a jar, the fewer jars you would need. I have since found that it was important to get the air out of beans. They simply preserve much more satisfactorily without air. It must work, I've used jars of beans grown nine years earlier that were perfectly edible, but that's another story.

Later in the day, the jars would fill, the baskets empty and the stove grow cooler. The last drops of paraffin would harden, sealing the tops of the jelly jars. The tops of the cans cooled under an amber

Didja' Ever Make Butter?

rim of sealing wax. The hogs had feasted on the buckets of skins, peels and tops. The humans had slabbed salami and cheese on home baked bread and guzzled a cold cup of buttermilk. Grandpa and I had lugged the last bucket of frothy milk from the barn to the cellar and the day's eggs rested on the sink ready to be wiped before going into the ice box. The dishes were put away for the night and the many coned separator was washed and dried in the last kettle of hot water. Flour sack towels hung around, as if bearing witness to the limply exhausted workers. The coal oil lamps were extinguished one by one. I snuggled nakedly under a thin sheet. Hopefully, a cool evening breeze would sneak through my upstairs room. Sleepily, I heard the soft clanking of the stove being banked for the night. As I sank into my dreams, I heard Grandpa blow out the last lamp.

Tractors

Bang, clang, rumble, lurch
Antithesis to nature
Godsend to old mules

"WE EAT CORN, SOME WE MILL, ALL THE REST, GOES IN THE STILL, BURMA SHAVE." Dusty country "highways" were infested with the catchy sloganed small red signs. They always ended with a single sign reading, "BURMA SHAVE." When cars traveled thirty miles per hour and less, it was possible to enjoy the scenery and even read the well spaced, clever jingles. Soon Old McDonald's barn had REDMAN TOBACCO painted on its side. STATE FARM INSURANCE and BUICK ROADMASTER soon added their names to the logo stained out buildings. The unobtrusive ways of yore were yielding to a new lifestyle. The urbane modern world began its irresistible march into the hinterlands.

In order to appreciate the degree of isolation experienced by farms prior to World War II, consider the differences in communications technology of then and now. By 1945, many farms had party line telephones; most did not. Many farms had AM radio receivers; most did not. Some received a weekly or bi-weekly local newspaper; most did not. Fewer than one per cent of all households had television and

Didja' Ever Make Butter?

these were concentrated in the northeastern seaboard cities. Today, it is an exception not to find each of the above in every home.

Conversation was integral to life back then. Conversation was communication. People talked at the barbershop, the grocery, the feed store, the blacksmith's, the ice house, Church and any where else they broke their solitude. Two farmers meeting at the ends of their furrows led to a brow wiping breather and an exchange of comments about the weather, crop prices or politics. Collective harvesting was a tremendous opportunity to converse. Rallies and town meetings were important. Quilting bees, ice cream socials and holidays like the Fourth of July stimulated the garrulous glands. The most likely phrase to enter a conversation beyond the basic cordialities was, "Didja' hear about...?"

Some sophisticated city cousins erroneously considered farmers to be ignorant, or at best backwards. A more accurate description would have called them, "out of touch." For years the farmer was subjected to contempt and derision by the rude slickers and exploitative comedians. There were more farmer jokes than vice-presidential jokes in those days.

One source of information merits special consideration, namely, the mail order catalogue. Montgomery-Ward and Sears Roebuck were the chief dispensers of the gaudy books, as well as rivals for the country based markets. Depending on allegiances or purchasing power, most farmers had at least one of the multi-paged volumes. Status in the country was displaying a copy of each publication on opposite walls of a two-holed outhouse. Most, if not all of the out-dated catalogues ended — no pun intended — hung by a wire, ignominiously prepared to sacrifice their last page for the good of mankind.

These voluminous merchandising marts contained an array of goods designed to fascinate every member of the farm family. Husbands coveted the latest guns, newest tools and modern equipment. Wives lusted for the button up shoes with the french curved heels. Calico, taffeta and exotic silk whetted their latent appetites for buttons and bows. Poke bonnets tempted many a fair hand to reach for the hard earned butter and egg money. I yearned for the pocket knives

Tractors

and dreamt of owning one of the huge Bowie knives. Of course, no lad past nine could fail to browse the risque sketches of pantaloons and corsets adorning the headless bare shouldered nameless women.

The Sears Catalog is now history, but worry not, mail order ain't dead. It's stronger then ever. In one of these fascinating tomes an idea germinated in Grandpa's head. It began at 8:30 one evening long after the supper dishes has been put to rest.

"Maw, Kate's been lookin' poorly of late," he opened cautiously.

"She just needs a tonic," Grandma murmured. Fully thirty seconds of silence rushed into the void before Grandpa began anew.

"Pete's almost 18 years old and getting more contrary every year. Can't dodge his kicks, as fast as I use ta." At 8:32 with bedtime approaching, silence again blankets the room, but Grandpa wouldn't let it rest.

"Takes a lot longer to plow with the team. Fred Price gets done days ahead of me." He pauses significantly for a full thirty seconds. Grandma continues to give her undivided attention to her stitching.

"Half my crop goes to feed those mules."

"Isn't that why you grow the corn?" Another uncomfortable silence as Grandpa rethinks his position. Grandma's needle rhythm is as steadfast as a metronome.

"Half my day is used currying those two mules." Her eyes flicker, seen only by me, as she darts a glance at him over her bifocals.

"Hmmph, you exaggerate, Phillip." Calling him Phillip was certainly significant.

"I'm too old to drag harness every day." It was 8:35. It was past my bedtime, a highly unusual occurrence, brought on by the duel of agendas between Grandma and Grandpa.

"Half my day is spent cleaning the stable." A pregnant pause ensues. I sincerely believe that this is the longest I ever heard Grandpa talk since the last retelling of his snowball story. "Half my day is spent cleaning the stable."

Having run out of fresh material, he repeated himself in a last heroic effort to get a reaction out of Grandma.

Didja' Ever Make Butter?

Grandma's snigger, unheard by her long suffering husband was a clue to her sagacity in being able to penetrate Grandpa's ruse. His mind had been made up months before. He wanted to buy a tractor. Like most men, he did not know what reaction to expect from his mate. After all, ladies could be quite unreasonable when a man wanted to spend scarce funds on necessities, when a catalog full of luxuries was tempting the feminine eye. Any way, that is how those old fashioned, chauvinistic men saw it.

"Are you going to buy the same tractor as Fred Price?" Grandma gently inquired. Grandpa was rendered speechless. Not so much that she saw right through him, but at his wasting such well planned deviousness.

It wasn't the first tractor Grandpa had owned. It was the first one I saw run. A very old, rusted heap of iron sat alongside the barn. It was beyond question a tractor. I would spend hours struggling to turn the steering wheel an inch or so either way to see the almost imperceptible movement of the metal front wheels long since welded to the sod. I must have plowed the entire farm a hundred times in my mind's eye. The throaty sound of its engine kept me company. I pretended so much at times I got a sore throat after making that engine sound for hours. The comfortable rounded metal seat still bounced satisfactorily when I dropped my full weight into it. I would bounce up and down, as if driving over a rough field. The odor of gasoline still emanated from the tank when the screw top was opened. A whiff now and then kept the imagination working. The rear wheels were most fascinating. Taller than me, they were huge iron cylinders with cross straps radiating from each hub. Welded to the outer circumference were triangular metals cleats called lugs. Highways signs noted their existence by the "Lugged Vehicles Prohibited" signs. The four inch high metal cleats were spaced around the wheel in two staggered rows. There would be no slipping with this well engineered piece of equipment.

Why then, did this behemoth labor saver sit idly rusting in the weather? For reasons not yet admitted by Grandpa, those first can-

Tractors

tankerous beasts just didn't run well. Farming is dirty. They were invented before efficient oil and gasoline filters. When the gas line got plugged, it didn't run. Plowing was dusty. When the carburetor got plugged, it didn't run. When the oil line clogged, the engine would overheat, complain and seize up. Always in the middle of a row. Most certainly in the farthest field from the barn.

Kate and Pete had laboriously pulled the outdated rival to its present location. Their smiles clearly indicated that they understood that Grandpa's occasional oath was not meant for them. The extra ear of corn in the feed box meant a working day tomorrow, but that was their life.

Memories of past tribulations faded in the light of the seductive promises of the new advertisements. The catalog listed all the new improvements. A battery operated starter. No dangerous kick backs from a cantankerous starting crank. Lights for plowing at night. A real glass sediment bowl on the carburetor that let you see when the dirt was accumulating. An oil bath air filter for the carburetor. Fram had invented a new filter for the oil line. A gauge told the farmer if the engine was too hot. Radiators were guaranteed for 1 full year against leaks. A new product called anti-freeze could be put in the water to keep it from freezing. It was expensive, but kept the farmer from having to drain and refill the radiator every day. Purchases made by March first would get, at no additional cost, a tool kit, a grease gun, a funnel, a five gallon gas can and a six foot rubber siphoning hose. For a frugal farmer those extras proved to be irresistible.

My smile was preserved for posterity in the photograph that shows me clinging to Grandpa and the metal monster. I stood on the axle housing holding onto the rim of the seat and the fender. Grandpa had that tolerating look that he conjured for the box cameras brought by the "city-slicker" relatives on weekends. Grandpa was ever anxious to end these "photo-op" sessions. He had chores to perform in direct proportion to the number of visiting relatives. Like many taciturn men of his day, he preferred the company of mules, cows and children to the incessant prattling of the urbanites.

Didja' Ever Make Butter?

In order to start his new McCormick Tractor, he carefully checked the gas and oil with a dip stick. Within a week the dip stick vibrated off the tractor and was lost. After that, a clean dry twig was substituted. He would open the petcock from the gravity feed tank to the carburetor. After assuring that the carburetor glass was full of gas, he would set the choke and gas feed levers. Grandpa was ready to fire the starter. Usually stiff from cold oil, the cranking would begin slowly and laboriously. As inertia and friction surrendered to electricity and leverage, the engine would turn with increasing rapidity. Soon hints of a cylinder, or two, firing were detected. (Two cylinders firing on a John Deere and you had 'em all.) With a chug, chug, pop, pop, bang, the motor would roar into action. A two minute warm up, several choke adjustments and the behemoth was ready to lurch into service.

A straight one inch by two inch iron tow bar extended to the rear. It had three half inch holes drilled through it. Various implements could be attached with a pin or any ½ inch bolt from the scrap pile. The modern mule substitute would effortlessly pull a two bottom plow or a four row harrow across the fields. The face of farming was changed forever. This would mean leisure time on the farm. Right? Wrong.

Grandpa was now busier than ever. The plowing and harrowing were done by the tractor, but Kate and Pete still pulled the wagons and cultivators. The mower and rake were still considered light work and the mules were cheaper than gasoline to operate. Gasoline was rationed during the war. Corn was still cut with a corn knife and left to dry in large vertical stacks called shocks. Harness was still hauled, curry combing still attended to and two spoiled mules got better treatment than ever. The tractor did the heavy work, but it too needed constant cleaning, greasing, adjusting and pampering to keep it chugging along. Was Grandpa unhappy? No way, we men know that every kid needs a new toy once in a while.

The Model A

Stubborn as a mule it stood
Dressed in lustrous black
Would it go to town?

Bright, shiny and proud, it stood outside the gate to the yard, a gleaming Model A Ford. Like a knight's charger it stood, in my imagination poised defiantly, awaiting its next crusade. My attention was drawn to the updated tin lizzie, our modern steed, when I heard Grandma and Grandpa talking during breakfast. I munched on oven toast, made from homemade yeast bread while they talked. Grandma had on another of her cotton dresses, the kind that could pass for a kimono or a night gown, except for all the buttons down the front. Grandpa wore a blue denim shirt, sleeves rolled up, tucked inside his bib overalls. Both were stocking footed in the house. The shoes were neatly lined by the porch door. The morning milking was finished and the stock had been fed and watered.

Shivers of anticipation washed over me when she said, "Pa, let's make ice cream this afternoon."

Now those were not her exact words. Grandma actually said, "Pa, we need ice, sugar, rock salt, vanilla and some other things from town."

Didja' Ever Make Butter?

"It's as good a day as any, Boss," Grandpa replied with a twinkle in his eye, as he glanced my way. He always called Grandma, Boss. It sounded like the most respectful, loving term in his vocabulary. Most men held women in high regard back then. It made good sense to me. After all, women could cook like you wouldn't believe. They did all the housework, except for the children' chores. Heck, they even tended to the garden and could milk a cow if they had to. Nowadays, it seems that women want all the respect, but most can't even cook.

Men did have the fun jobs. We operated the machinery, handled the mules, swung the axes, walked the fields, butchered the hogs, hunted the game. None of that women's drudgery for us!

I knew I was going to town with Grandpa. Grandma gave my clothes the once over, combed my hair and scrubbed my ears pink. Even with the irritations, the chance for adventure would be worth it.

After making sure that Rommel the rooster was out of sight, I darted for our horse in black, armor, jumped on her running board and popped inside. Of course, in my mind, the running board became a stirrup and the squeaky seat, a saddle. Grandpa smiled covertly, aware of my obvious discomfort at having to venture across Rommel's barnyard domain. I didn't realize his good humor was at my expense. The older folks discussed those things when kids were asleep under the feather bed.

Some of my fund was speculating on how many cranks it would take Grandpa to start the "old lizzie." She was a complicated, high-tech device, full of wonders for someone like me, who marveled at the complexity of a flat iron. I would climb on the running boards and peer in the windows, eyes filling in wonderment at the mysterious knobs, levers, gauges and pedals. No matter how many times I watched Grandpa operate them, I could never quite understand what the throttle and spark retarder levers on the steering column controlled. Of course, I had no idea what electricity was at age eight, either.

In those days, most gasoline engines had a petcock on the fuel line that had to be turned on to allow the gasoline to flow. It was pulled by gravity from the tank to the carburetor. I smugly anticipated

The Model A

how many times Grandpa would try to start that balky beast, before remembering to turn on that petcock. He always disappointed me and remembered, just like today. Actually, the only time he forgot was the day I learned about it. I watched him set the spark lever, as he mumbled to no one in particular, "Too much, it fires prematurely; too little and the danged thing will flood."

He next manipulated the gas lever. His eye had an imaginary spot for the best setting for this device, too. I think that Grandpa was like a modern day computer, able to call all that knowledge from his head at will. His storehouse of information about things on that farm, seemed more vast than a set of encyclopedias.

The choke knob was on the dash. Pull it out and it shut off air from the carburetor and fed a jet of vaporized gasoline directly into the engine. Again that wondrous brain told him just how far out to pull it. Think of all the possible permutations and combinations with those levers and knobs. I have often wondered if Grandpa considered the effects of temperature and humidity in his mental calculations.

A final wiggle of the gear shift lever to insure that the car wasn't in gear and Grandpa tugged his sleeves once more, as he moved to the front of the car. A test of wills was about to commence. He engaged the crank onto the crankshaft, gave a preliminary tug and braced himself for the back wrenching fast turn of the handle that might result in ignition. No, I forgot a step. He always turned the handle slowly, all the way around a couple of times. He told me why, too. Two slow revolutions got the oil moving onto the parts and some gasoline on the way to the cylinders.

Before I knew it, he spun the crank, grunting in tempo, while growing red in the fact. Nothing. Absolutely nothing. Undeterred, Grandpa straightened, spit juice from his wad of Redman off to one side and made an imperceptible adjustment of the levers and knobs. He said some things kind of low voiced that didn't resembled any words I knew. I reasoned that the words probably didn't sound right, because of the tobacco in his mouth. In later summers, when the words became old acquaintances, I realized why he spoke quietly.

85

Didja' Ever Make Butter?

Then, another gut wrenching spin of the crank and the cantankerous auto sputtered, then growled into an uneven putt-putt-sputter. Grandpa quickly went to the driver's side and fiddled once again with the spark and gas levers. Within seconds, he had the black beast purring contentedly on all four cylinders. That day's start-up was almost perfect. You wouldn't want to hear about the hard ones.

The two knights left their castle on their adventurous crusade for ice, sugar and vanilla. I could almost visualize the Holy Grail, filled to the brimming with buttery yellow hand churned ice cream. "Charge! Black Beauty, charge!"

The Crusade

Four cylinders roar
Black steed carries bold, brave knight
Infidels await

Dust clouds billowing behind the ancient Model A, competed with the storm clouds convening above. The old farm driveway split the corn field from the orchard, then joined a section line before it meandered nearly half a mile to the paved Wiedman road. The well defined dirt and rock pathways were negotiated with respect. In places the hump between the two wheel paths rose high enough to scrape the oil pan. In most places it was only rim deep into the rock packed Missouri clay. Top speed was dictated by nerve, washouts and exposed rocks. As often as skill permitted, the wheels were expertly balanced on the ridges, much safer for the oil pan, vulnerably exposed under the car. The rest of the time Grandpa chose his rut wisely, it was his likely companion for the next mile or so

At the first tee intersection in the road we turned left. Heading east on the rocky property line road, I saw the lush green corn field still to our left.(Most county roads and many private roads, like ours, in rural areas were originally built on the survey lines dividing one section of land from another.) To our right was a fallow field of brush and grass that sheltered this winter's hasenpfeffer crop. The smooth

Didja' Ever Make Butter?

round tunnels the rabbits formed in the grassy undergrowth always fascinated me. Their superhighway system provided speedy connections to the safety of the blackberry patches, that grew conveniently near the woods line.

The black charger poised above the barely trickling wet weather creek whose banks had been carved to allow vehicles to roll safely down to the ford. Some of our wealthier neighbors pour a concrete low water bridge for a smoother crossing. On country roads, bridges were a luxury. The shallow ford served us well and provided a standard for judgement, courage and excitement in wet weather. When needed, Grandpa would stop and move a migratory rock or two to ease passage. Grandpa never experienced a need great enough to tempt him into crossing that creek if the water was deeper then a foot. It never stayed high more than a few hours anyway. That day the rough bottom only shook dust from the four wheeled horse.

Up the long sloping hill to Wiedman Road the black steed climbed and stopped near the mailbox. Grandpa pulled hard on the hand brake and ratcheted it into the set position.

"Always check for the mail on the way to town." He would say, "the ice will be melting on the way home." Our main reason for going to town was to get a 50 pound block of ice for the icebox. Wiedman Road wound south to Manchester Road. Nearby was the little hamlet of Manchester, a bustling example of a small, midwestern town.

"Can we stop for a drink?" I asked Grandpa as we approached the Rock House. The owners of the solid stone house built from carved granite blocks shared a deliciously cold spring with their neighbors. We always filled the water buckets with its icy water when thrashing wheat at the Wissman farm across the road. Long handled tin dippers hung by the round pool, an invitation to thirsty travelers. A unending supply of clear water boiled upward and over the edge of he round spring into a swimming pool edged with water lilies and croaking frogs. From the pool, the surplus water fed into a creek that wound for miles, eventually emptying into the Meramec River. Minnows swarmed in a deep pool of the creek in the shade of the bridge over Wiedman Road.

Crusade

"Make it fast, we're burning daylight."

As the cold water sluiced down my throat, I let my imaginary black horse share the spring with me. I jumped back into the saddle and yelled, "Giddiyup!"

Our first stop was a small gasoline station just east of town. I don't remember the brand and it has long since disappeared, but Grandpa always stopped there to get gas and renew his supply of Redman chewing tobacco. Naturally my active imagination checked every corner for hostile infidels. While I poked and nosed around, Grandpa discussed the hazards and conditions down the road. I soon learned the secret language in which they spoke. Example: "Is the Redman tobacco fresh?" Translation: "Have the indians been burning the wheat fields again?" I knew Redman was chewing tobacco, but at times I allowed it to stir visions of marauding indians into my fantasies.

I used to wonder if he sneaked his Redman. I don't remember seeing him flaunt the brown juicy wads in front of Grandma. He certainly never offered me a chaw in her presence. 'Course he only allowed me to chew once anyway. If begged, I would not have accepted a second time. Grandpa would pull out his worn black leather change purse, the kind that had metal snaps at the top that opened to show what coins were inside. He counted out the exact amount while he exchanged weather and crop reports with the man who owned the station. Transacting business in Manchester was like visiting old friends. Everyone was friendly and nice to each other. I sure miss that. A leisurely goodbye and we remounted to continue our quest.

Anticipation had me twitching. The next stop held an unimaginable potential of treasures. A two story bare board structure full of harness, tools, carriages, a forge and real men, exchanging views that ran the gamut from politics to the weather. The heavily muscled men in their overall uniforms gossiped by the forge. Heavy dollops of tobacco juice sluiced through the conversation, sizzling and dancing as it fought with the hot flames. The blacksmith, Mr. Hoehne, chest bare under his overalls, rang the hammer again and again as he formed yet another shoe for a waiting mule. Clack, clack, CLANG! The rhyth-

Didja' Ever Make Butter?

mic song of the anvil set the background for the laughter and hum of the conversation. I stared in awe, as tendons snapped tight under his brown skin, flicking rivulets of sweat from his powerful arms. His dark visage fluidly changed expressions in the dancing flames of the forge. He became my fantasy villain and the shop a Moorish fortress. It was a veritable Constantinople of the Occident.

Imagination took one look at the smithy and he was transmigrated. His red bandanna became a black kaffiyeh. His hammer was now the saracen's wickedly curved steel blade. He braced to meet the challenge of me and my black charger.

Fierce eyes glared, as the damascus steel ringingly clanged from my armor. I swung a heavy mace and knocked the threatening sharp edge from his hand. "Aha! You are at my mercy infidel! Die like a dog!" I reared my horse high above him, drawing my long sword and swinging heavily. A surge of victory coursed through my body, as his head tumbled to the ground. The crowd of moors gasped, as their leader writhed in the sand, legs twitching in paroxysms of pain. Then his brothers advanced toward me, fierce eyes burning hatred at the warrior who slew their caliph. The end was near, but God would save me from their wrath, or I would be with Him in paradise this very day. After all, this crusade was for him.

Grandpa grabbed the hoe from my hand. "I can't let you alone for a minute," he glared. The pile of harness around me bore testimony to the fierceness of the battle. My long sword had slaughtered the attacking hordes. Why was Grandpa so upset?

"You don't play with Mr Hoehne's tools! Who ever heard of swinging a hoe around like that. You've knocked every piece of harness in this shop on the floor!" Grandpa was a deep reddish-purple. The men were laughing uncontrollably ... except for Mr. Hoehne. "Get in the car. Now! And don't you budge."

In abject misery, I retired from the field of battle. Undaunted, my imagination quickly recovered, as I thought, "This day belongs to the infidels, but there will be others."

Today a yellow service station stands in place of the glorious blacksmith shop. Five twelve foot wide lanes of concrete squeeze an uncountable volume of four wheeled horses, bumper to bumper through a stoplight every two minutes. You know, I never see the immaculate Shell station without a fuzzy memory imposing the image of a grimy wooden harness and blacksmith shop. Shell with all its gleam and cleanliness can't inspire visions of unfound grails like its predecessor could. But those days were *my* good old days.

Is There Life After the Crusade?

Crashing chunks of crystal ice
Candy in a jar
Shopping Spree in Town

Undaunted after battling the imaginary saracen, the black charger rolled powerfully onward. The Model A, my mind's black charger was energized by the adrenaline left over from the battle at the blacksmith's shop. Thankful for my escape from the vengeful Moors, I sat quietly in the saddle allowing my courser to pick his own course to the next oasis.

Grandpa, with a somewhat tight smile, saluted the passing knights. Horse and buggies had long disappeared from Manchester's main thoroughfare, but to me each sputtering, barely muffled four cylinder engine was a snorting battle horse. My mind needed few clues to drift back in time to the romanticized days of knights, vassals and damsels in distress. Blue, white, yellow and maroon paint on the newer cars added to my sense of pageantry. The 1940 models were trying to leave behind the sombre colors and moods of the Great Depression.

Grandpa steered the steed into a dusty lot tucked between the street and the front of the General Merchandise Store. We dismounted. I watched the tiny puffs of dust from our shoes that announced our trespass.

Is There Life After The Crusade?

"Stomp your feet on the steps. I don't want you draggin' dirt inside," Grandpa reminded, "Use the foot scraper if you need to."

I looked where he pointed and saw what resembled an upside down ice skate nailed to the porch. "What are they for?"

"When it's muddy people clean their shoes before going into the store. When its dusty a good stomping is all you need."

When I visited this same store almost fifty years later it was a produce stand. Only three of the original buildings stand as testimony to those days gone by, this one, the Lyceum, a national landmark and a majestic old home. As I walked inside the produce market, I was disappointed. How small it was. In my youth it had seemed as huge as a modern day Wal-Mart. So much for the perspective of youth.

Vegetable bins were located on the porch in my trips with Grandpa, so that hadn't changed. Only hardy foods like onions, potatoes, carrots, apples were displayed then. From time to time, bananas, pears or other seasonal items made the line-up along with a smattering of excess crops from local farmers, like green beans, cucumbers, squash and tomatoes. To this day I have never tasted anything to match the juicy flavor of Missouri's July tomatoes.

Even in 1940, some store bread could be found from Wonder and Freund Bakeries. Only small quantities were stocked, as many of the women still baked their supply of the staff of life. Bread was baked twice a week in most households, as many of the modern preservatives were unavailable.

Grandma rarely accompanied Grandpa to town, but when so inclined, she was attracted to the aisle containing cloth, lace, buttons and thread. The peddler had since followed the horse drawn carriages into the past, or become Fuller Brush salesmen in the blossoming cities.

Tools, always fascinating, drew me to their corner. What new and ingenious weapons could I construe from these shiny pieces of steel and hickory. Buying wasn't necessary. Burning the points and sharp edges into my mind was enough. That red buck saw became a guillotine. The exquisite double bit axe was a halberd. It looked just like

Didja' Ever Make Butter?

Grandpa's axe except the handle wasn't beat up and the blade had paint on it. Grandpa's blade was noticeably smaller from the constant filings needed to maintain its razor like edge. Maybe Grandpa would like a new one for Christmas.

"Would he give me the old one?" I wondered.

After the terrible battle at the Blacksmith's shop, the saracens were obviously avoiding me. Truthfully, I wasn't real anxious to encounter them either, after Grandpa's lecture. Besides, the sweets counter caught my eye. Large crystal clear jars held assorted temptations for the sweet tooth. To most people there were licorice sticks, peppermint sticks, lollipops, hard candies and peanut brittle. To me they were damsels in distress, imprisoned as colorful tidbits inside those jars. They needed to be liberated. I could almost hear them calling, "Help me. Take me."

Could an errant knight ignore these damsels? I approached Grandpa quietly then tugged on his coveralls, "Grandpa, help me save the captured princesses."

"Whaaat?"

"I mean, can I get some candy?"

"You want candy after what happened at Mr. Hoehne's blacksmith shop?"

"Aw Gramps, please, with sugar on it." Don't kids manipulate great? How is it they are so inherently expert in these techniques. Even kids raised alone know the techniques. Grandparents are even easier targets than parents. It's almost unfair.

"You eat this outside." I took the nickel bag of candy and ran for the door, ignoring the rest of the store. Had I looked back, I would have seen Grandpa noticeably relax and begin to enjoy the conversation with his friends. Whose manipulation was it?

Many times before, I had viewed the Fels Naphtha soap, clothespins, wash baskets and clothesline. The aroma of smoked sausages and cheeses were arrayed in prolific confusion. Absent was fresh milk, lettuce, cottage cheese and butter (Canned milk, Bordens, was on the shelf). Oatmeal and cream of wheat were available, but Tom Mix hadn't corralled us kids into hot Ralston, yet.

Is There Life After The Crusade?

It was getting hot outside. Grandpa came out stuffing a fresh ball of curly Redman tobacco into his mouth. He cradled a bag containing salt and vanilla in his other arm. One experimental splat of brown juice and he popped the engine into a smooth putter with one twirl of the crank.

Down the road, the mill stood next to the ice house. There was a pleasant sweetish odor, not unlike that of freshly baked bread, originating from the mill. Bran for the cattle, chicken feed, flour, corn meal had all come from the giant water powered stones. Not even the milling was done here now. Huge silos of products cascaded into gunny sacks or barrels from dusty hoppers. Meal by the train car load was dumped at this distribution point. I walked over to the sagging old building and stared into the clear water that flowed beneath. Tadpoles swarmed in darting black clouds. Crawfish shared the crystalline water under the moss laden waterwheel. Some of the tadpoles had but a vestige of tail remaining as they neared completion of their odyssey to froghood. The submerged wood of the wheel was swollen and dark. It contrasted with the desiccated parts weathering in the hot sun. The wheel would turn no more. The creek was now diverted by construction needs. Only the millpond remained to evidence the trickling spring seeping from the nearby hillside. The ancient waterwheel had but a few years to exist. In 1972 it was torn down, condemned as a dangerous, attractive nuisance.

A young man in dusty bib overalls threw a sack of bran into the back seat of the Model A. His shock of corn colored hair wandered about his freckled face. I admired the way his arms bulged and he rewarded me with a dazzling smile, before hurrying to the next customer. The ice rack was needed on the rear bumper for ice, or he would have placed the sack there and secured it with binder twine.

Our last stop was at the blue and yellow City, Ice and Fuel building. They sold gasoline. kerosene and ice. We got our gasoline at the other end of town. At seventeen cents a gallon, it was a penny a gallon cheaper. The building stood thick and lonesome in the shade. It was the most solid looking building that I knew of. Surrounded by thickly foliated maples, the heavy walls easily fought off the few rays

Didja' Ever Make Butter?

of sun that leaked through the leaves. There was one door and no windows to protect the vulnerable contents. Grandpa said that it had been used for a jail one night when a bandit had been caught. It was the best place to hold him until the sheriff arrived. Grandpa said that is how the term "cooler" came to be used for a jail. To this day I don't know if he was pulling my leg. It makes sense.

The attendant opened the thick door, releasing a surge of cool air. Just as quickly, he pulled it closed behind him. I heard his ice pick slicing slickly into the thick blocks of ice. Huge two hundred pound blocks were deftly sectioned into what ever smaller size the customer needed. Grandpa always got a fifty pound block. I heard the fifty pound clump fall into the rollered chute. With a rumble to announce its arrival, the gleaming hunk of solid water brushed through the canvas opening. It halted, breathless, already sweating from its journey.

One time I got to go inside the ice house. Huge mounds of ice stood head high to a large man on an elevated heavy wood platform. A small 25 watt bulb cut a tentative hole in the dark. The wood interior, damp from the wet contents absorbed what little light escaped the center of the building. Gleaming blocks of crystal stood like clear granite rocks one upon the other. The cold quiet on a warm day invited a prolonged visit, but even the heat from our bodies was unwelcome. Quick in, quick out was the rule.

With a pair of tongs, the man lifted the ice onto the car. The black charger sagged, as the block of ice was laid on his rear saddle bags. Already drops were splashing in the dust. Grandpa handed him a dime and headed for the crank.

"Mount up little warrior, or whoever you are." Grandpa's humor seemed to be returning, as we started home from the crusade.

As Grandpa was seeming to lighten up, I ventured a question, timidly, "Is there enough ice to make ice cream?"

"Who said anything about ice cream?"

Player Piano

Hypnotizing Holes
Bellows Produced Sound
Voilá! Concert Pianist

Air, fresh and crisp from the lightning released ozone, blew softly across the porch. Crystalline droplets swelled slowly and stretched before leaping from the roof edge. Silently falling droplets created a musical plinking, as they dived onto the rocks below. Like the jingle of tiny tambourines, they melodiously harmonized with the squeaking of the porch swing. Birds chirped in celebration, as robins busily harvested worms, driven to the surface by the summer thundershower.

"Boy! Don't swing too hard," Grandma's admonishment was issued more in prevention than correction. Her favorite saying was, "A stitch in time saves nine."

She applied it to any situation fraught with the slightest element of danger. Undoubtedly, had she been a woman of the 1990's, she would have attained an executive position with OSHA. After all, the ancient swing hanging from its four swiveled supports could only move a few feet in each direction. The two slatted seats faced each other, separated by a treadle made of the same materials. A rigid wooden frame suspended the entire mechanism. Gentle pressure on

Didja' Ever Make Butter?

the treadle set up a swinging and swaying that was both addictive and hypnotizing. Amazing amounts of time could be invested while watching the pears grow in the adjacent orchard.

"I won't Gram."

"Sounds like it is squeaking real loud."

"Might need some oil, but I'll be careful." Whenever I pumped too hard, one of the legs rose from the wooden porch floor and would clump noisily down on the return swing. Grandma was never fooled. Like a clock striking the hour, she would alert me to the danger of rocking too hard. Of course, that only occurred during the midst of a vicious dogfight. When Messerschmitts and Zeros were jointly attacking my P-40 Flying Tiger, the adrenaline would flow, as the bullets spattered across the landscape. The only indication that it was active imagination, was the lack of debris in the orchard. Surely the there would be remnants of planes somewhere out there from the hundreds that had filled the sights of my wing mounted machine guns.

"Gram, can I go catch crawdads in the creek?"

"It's a little high now from the rain. You can go tomorrow if it doesn't rain any more."

Many times I had splashed and splattered into the barnyard following the down pouring gully washers, so common to Missouri weather. The contrast of grass stains from a flooded yard blended with a challenging grimy, multi-colored river of mud, produced clothing that would frustrate today's modern detergents. Fels naphtha soap and a copper scrubbin' board barely budged the soaked in dirt. Any way, I didn't see much problem with a dirty T-shirt and a worn out pair of shorts getting dirty. Grandma did. End of discussion.

Bright sunshine reflected from the standing pools of shimmering rain water. The brilliant light made the drops of water hanging on the wire fence seem like a jeweler's display of fine gems. Just as quickly another cloud snuffed the bright light and soft shadows surrounded the ancient porch. Fascination turned to restlessness. I declared a private war on the Axis Powers. When the entire German air force had been smashed and shattered, when all the worms had been harvested by the robins, when all the raindrops had fallen and when all the birds and insects once again settled into their mid-summer chorus of chirping, clacking and humming; appreciation and solace soon turned to boredom.

"Can I play the piano, Gram?"

"A little music might sound nice, at that," she replied, probably suspecting my boredom a second or two before I did. I was ecstatic. Usually the piano was reserved for Sunday afternoon, Saturday night, or visiting relatives. Like the Lotto game, it was a highly prized, rarely used possession. Like many possessions back then, it seemed more important to have one than to use it. For example, never did I see Grandma or Grandpa play the piano.

"Can you open the foot pedals?" Grandma asked. It was easy for me to scramble under the giant black block of wood and unfold the huge double foot pumps. Grandma pulled several rolls from the piano bench and loaded one. I had recently discovered I was finally tall enough to sit on the edge of the bench and reach the pedals with my outstretched feet. By shifting quickly from one side of my butt to the other, I could depress the pedals far enough to operate the prized music maker.

I was fascinated by the shining silver levers in front of the keyboard. I was certain they were just like the controls of my P-40. One made the piano roll rewind. Another made the keys depress just as if an invisible some one were playing the piano. Another made the keys stay still when the roller was playing. I preferred the setting where I could pretend to be playing the piano. In time, I actually learned to pick out tunes from memory. I can still pick out "Old Man River," "Coming in on a Wing and a Prayer" and "Abide With Me."

Next to the piano stood a hand crafted wood and glass case about three feet tall. It was brought from Germany by my grandmother's family. In it was a real china doll, exquisitely dressed in ruffles and lace. My aunt in California kidnaped this antique some years ago. She appreciates such things and has a daughter that will too. I would feel better if my daughter had it though.

Didja' Ever Make Butter?

It was hard work pumping the old roller piano. The bellows was hard to start. That first thrust of the foot took a great deal of strength for a pre-pubescent such as I. By the time I was bigger and stronger, the farm was history. I was thirteen years old in 1945, when Grandma died. I did not return to the farm again until well into adulthood. I took my oldest daughter. She was the last one of my family to see the old farm house standing. It is now a subdivision. Time and suburbia move relentlessly onward.

Peace and contentment inevitably followed five minutes or more of rocking gently to and fro on the porch. A monotonous rain shower, even a crashing thunderstorm provided accompaniment for the ancient swing. At other times, in the moonlight, crickets would sing their staccato melody in time with the slaps aimed at persistent mosquitoes seeking their evening feast. Having no OFF spray for protection then, the only "Off" was the one provided by Grandma, "Off the swing and up to bed."

Maggots

Quivering red and white mess
Nature's own horror
Maggots in a wound

A*uthor's note: Ignorance is not an excuse, but it can breed situations that unwittingly cause other creatures to suffer.* Grandpa would have never intentionally caused unnecessary pain or harm to any farm creature. *This particular description of life on a farm may be too severe for some people, as even today it brings to mind mixed feelings just in the remembering. It is presented not to shock, but to document what was.*

  The pears were out of reach. The twenty foot chain had defined the limits of her range, well short of the ripening pear trees. She stood, head lowered, front feet splayed, mooing plaintively, as if calling for help. The lightweight chain, looped around her horns, seemed to drag her head lower. The oversized liquid brown eyes were wet, as if from crying. Moist brown lines pointed downward from the corner of each eye. She seemed resigned to her fate. The scene called to mind pictures of slaves in the history books, abused, helpless and fatalistically awaiting the next degradation.

Didja' Ever Make Butter?

The iron stake at the circle's center stood straight. Like a tall metal mushroom, the top was rounded and curled from the daily pounding of the sledge hammer. Sometimes, while driving the stake into the ground, a blow of the hammer caused a piece to break off. Sometimes a spark would signal the randomly aimed bullet. Sometimes a piece of shrapnel hit your leg and drew blood. When the orchard grass got too high, the cows were staked out to serve as resident lawnmowers. This was always done just before the pears were ripe enough to pick. It's easier to see the snakes in short grass. Grandma didn't like snakes.

To grandfather's credit, he told me time and again that this horrible incident only happened once. I only saw it once. Once was a lifetime of being unable to forget. Milk cows are normally quite docile in small numbers, as on our farm. The daily, hands on contact, probably developed an intimacy of sorts. Milking a cow the old fashioned way is certainly intimate. They tend to stay close by. A minimum tether, of sorts, is usually sufficient to keep them confined. Cows should be tethered by a ring attached to the bottom of a halter, but halters cost money which was scarce on a Missouri depression farm of the late 1930's.

Maybe it was the scent of the ripening pears. Maybe it was an unusual thirst. Maybe it was a patch of extra desirable grass just out of reach, but the result was added chafing of the chain around the horns until a bloody abrasion was exposed to nature. Nature invaded with a fleet of flies.

My knowledge of biology can't tell you the time frame, but the flies nested and planted their eggs. The resulting larva soon infested the wound. When Grandpa and I went at milking time to bring the young cow to the barn, one glance upon loosening the chain was enough to etch an indelible scar in my mind.

Untethered, a six inch gash was revealed behind the horns. It was narrow enough that the chain and her hair had hidden it from view. Now the gore filled opening was angrily seething in pulsating red and white, as the maggots squirmed and twisted, fighting for space. Puffs of white appeared than sank once more into the bloody muck. I turned away

Maggots

nauseated at the sight of the seething parasites, inflicting their worst, inside another living organism. Well distanced from dinner, the nausea passed and my eyes were drawn back, in utter fascination, to the bizarre sight.

Grandpa slowly shook his head and muttered sympathetic sounds. I never saw him so gentle, except years later when Grandma had her stroke. He cleared his throat huskily, spat tobacco juice time after time, then raked the morass from the wound with his finger. I couldn't believe how deeply his finger penetrated the lesion. The cow patiently endured, as if accepting his help and apology at the same time. Time after time he gently probed the gash, extracting every last invasive nymph. Satisfied that he had removed the last invader from her head, we went for the bottle of turpentine. Grandpa cleansed the wound with our universal antiseptic, then smeared a generous dollop of creosote salve into the wound.

No odor seemed as noxious as that creosote salve, all shiny, black and greasy, but in several days there wasn't a sign of a problem with the good as new dairy cow.

Resentful, not that cow. She was more loving and gentler than before. Hilda became my protector in the barnyard. From that time forward no other farm creature could separate us. I remember a particular Jersey, one nasty minded cow, that bullied and intimidated any creature that knew fear; which of course, meant me. She would lower her head, shake her horns and trot after me any time I entered the corral, or the pasture. She seemed to take pleasure in my terror, as I ran for the fence. No longer did she succeed. My newly found friend would maneuver her bulk between me and the Jersey menace and with a shake of her horns warn her away. I would hang on her neck and rub around her ears and horns. Hilda became the first cow that I milked by myself.

The Calving

Huge brown eyes drown you with love
Spindly legs barely stand
Milk coats soft muzzle

"Grandpa! Grandpa! Hilda's dying!" I scurried for the house in a state of near panic. Hilda, my favorite cow, was bawling horribly in a tormented condition. Her mooing sounded like tremulous crying, as she lurched around in obvious discomfort. Her mouth was open, as she bawled pitifully. She twisted her head toward her tail almost bending herself double. I knew she was in horrible pain.

"Go in the house. She will be all right. She is going to have a calf," Grandpa calmly nudged me toward the house. Grandpa had taken off his shirt and was fastening his bib overalls on the way out the door. Grandma came to the door and put her hand on my shoulder. I tentatively pulled away from her to follow Grandpa, but she held tight. Terribly afraid for Hilda, I didn't move or argue. I stared after Grandpa, praying that he could help her.

"Stay here, its not a place for women and children," Grandma advised. In 1940, it wasn't proper but even then, many women helped a calving as capably as a man.

"Yes it is," I thought to myself, "Hilda needs me and here I stand like a namby pamby." The conversation was over but my determina-

The Calving

tion to be with Hilda wasn't. Within minutes, I saw my chance to bolt. A wood stove needs constant attention. When Grandma went to check her pots on the stove, I flew out the door. I might have even hit one of the six steps leading down to the yard.

Hilda and Grandpa were near the barn in a shady grassy spot. Hilda was still bawling and Grandpa was feeling all around her rump and belly. He stuck a hand inside of her, right under her tail.

I can't begin to tell you what my thoughts were. I was never so shocked in my life. It seemed so gross. I choked off question after question that started with what and why. One thing I knew for sure, if I got in the way, I was "history." How many times since that day have I wanted to relive that moment, knowing then what I know now. Knowing how much he was helping, by turning the calf that was poorly positioned inside of her. Instead, out of ignorance, I was hating him for hurting her, or so I thought in 1940.

It seemed like an eternity that Grandpa struggled, now with both arms inside the cow. They both ended up lying on the ground. Grandpa was pushing with his feet trying to reach further and further into Hilda. Blood and slime covered his upper body. It was even smeared on his face. He once again reached inside her with both hands and sat up, facing Hilda's hind end. He frantically tugged at a greyish sack, roughly the shape of a calf's head. The front of the placenta began to exit, coming right out of Hilda. One, or both of them were grunting a lot. A little at a time, the sack grew larger until it rolled onto the ground like an undulating, lumpy plastic trash bag.

Grandpa reached in his pocket and took out his ever present knife. Opening it to the sharpest blade, he slit the placenta and pulled it away from the calf's head. Already Hilda had struggled to her feet both to my relief and astonishment. She bawled loudly one more time, but not in pain this time. She seemed relieved but purposeful, almost as if saying, "All right, I can take from here, get out of my way."

Grandpa did just that. For the first time he acknowledged my presence and said, "Come on, as long as you're here, start cranking the cistern for me."

Didja' Ever Make Butter?

I ran to the cistern and began to spin the crank to bring the water up through the spout. Grandpa washed himself quickly. My eyes were riveted on Hilda and the newborn while I continued to crank. Hilda was eating the placenta right off the calf while she licked the calf in between her chewing. I vowed never to eat again, if I kept lunch down. Grandpa laughed when he saw my horror and explained that it was the natural thing to do. It cleaned up the calf, removed a source of disease, was nourishing for the cow and made the calf feel loved. I later learned it was the first step in bonding, the licking that is.

With everything gone, but the calf, Hilda and a few spots, Hilda turned her attention to licking the calf from head to tail. Grandpa's disappointment showed pretty quickly when he said, "It's a baby bull."

Unless registered from a good line of cows, the bull was just meat on the hoof. It would never produce cream or butter, therefore, it was only a matter of when it reached top price for veal. Naturally, I didn't know these things and wasn't told either. The little bull would just disappear when I went back to school.

But on that day, at that moment, my cow Hilda had a baby. That had to make me an Uncle, at least. Grandpa went inside to change clothes. I slowly walked over to my Hilda.

How was I to know that most animals became ferociously protective of their young. Hilda lowered her head and looked at me, but oblivious to all but my happiness of the event, I kept on coming.

By now Grandma was at the door of the house. Her hand flew to her mouth in frightening expectation, as she realized the danger I was in. She started to yell, but it froze in her throat. I was at arm's length from Hilda and reaching out to her.

Hilda sniffed once, licked my hand, as if to say welcome and I put my arm over her neck to rub her ears. The little calf butted into me and sucked on the fingers of my other hand. It scared me at first, not knowing what he wanted, but I soon directed him to a much more fulfilling appendage at the end of his mother's udder. He contentedly made his attachment and Hilda bent around to reassure herself that all was well. Both her bull calves were safe and content.

Betsy

Calico dress, eyes of blue
Skin like ripe peaches
Plump, cherry ripe lips

Her fingers were white from gripping the basket, laden with fresh baked coffee cakes. Her nervous blue eyes darted from person to person. Honey colored rivulets of shiny, soft hair cascaded over her round shoulders. A home made cotton flour sack dress was a miniature of her mother's. Sensible, high topped shoes peaked from under the hem. The girl's tiny feet shifted constantly, betraying her anxiety.
"She lives with her folks on the old Queeny place," Grandma quietly told me, "Go and make her welcome." Grandma's firm hand in my back left me the choices of moving forward, or falling on my face. My feet shuffled nervously forward.

"What do you say to a girl?" I wondered. Grandma and Grandpa had discussed the recent arrival of the Hutchison family, but didn't mention any girl. The dad farmed part time, while holding a job in town. The mother was pretty for a mother, with sky blue eyes and a plump, rounded figure.

I was a very shy ten year old at the time. The girl looked about seven. Girls, my age, at school were already flirting with the "mature"

Didja' Ever Make Butter?

boys. Thank goodness those girls hadn't directed their wiles toward me. I wasn't above, if circumstances permitted, noticing and appreciating feminine pulchritude, but I got real nervous up close to them.

Therefore, having the advantage of advanced years, I summoned from my supply of courage and shuffled toward her. I thought to myself, I will impress her right off, with a piercing question.

"HiI'mDougareyouhereforthethrashing?" Every word ran together in a totally unintelligible monotone. I sounded like an idiot and the question was about as dumb, as you could ask. Everybody in the county was here for the thrashing. My toes curled in the dust like some gnarled arthritic knuckles. Nervously, I jammed my hands deeply into my pockets. My eyes surveyed the ground, as if looking for approaching insects. The color of embarrassment crept visibly into my cheeks.

"Hello, I'm Elizabeth Hutchison. What is thrashing?" she asked in a voice that was sweet with promised friendship. She actually talked to me without a hint of scorn, or rejection, so commonly encountered from older girls. Tentatively, I looked her right in the face and grinned. Sweet innocence glowed from her smiling face. She really was asking me to tell her what thrashing was.

"We just moved here from St. Louis. I have never been on a farm before. Have you lived here long?"

"I spend a lot of time here with my grandparents. Every year when the wheat ripens, the thrashing..." As my voice gained confidence, my feet assumed a firm position and my posture greatly improved. Within minutes, this tongue tied introvert had blossomed into a barnyard rooster. I crowed on for minutes, expounding my worldly knowledge to this highly impressed lass.

"Want a drink of water, Elizabeth?"

"Yes thank you. My friends call me, Betsy."

"I'll pull you a cold drink at the cistern, come on." I set her basket on the porch, turned and started to run for the cistern. Then I stopped and waited for her. She was pretty for a little girl.

"You can sit here." I pointed to the cistern's rough board cover.

Betsy

With great ceremony and sophistication, I turned the crank masterfully, rinsed the tin cup several times, inspected each new cup of water until at last I was satisfied that no better cup of water existed in the cistern. I handed it to her, and truly wondered why I was carrying on this way. There weren't any other kids for miles. She is a girl, but at least she is company. I guess a guy can have a girl for a friend.

"Oh, Doug, that water is so good, thank you."

Every word she uttered was friendly. "Would you like to see the farm? I'll tell you all about it and show you the animals."

"Sure."

I carefully watched for "Rommel" the rooster, as we headed for the hen house. It was the closest building to the cistern. Alert to the barnyard perils, I was overly considerate where I led her, so as not to dirty her shoes. I boldly entered the coop and showed her the eggs in the nests, making no attempt to disturb the setting hen. Betsy was appropriately impressed.

Next we visited the wood shed. A stack of splits leaned like a big teepee close to the shed. Grandpa cut the trees into eight foot sections, then split the logs with wedges into sizes he could carry out of the woods and load onto the wagon. These splits were stacked into a teepee of firewood by the shed.

A well-used, weathered sawhorse lounged nearby. The rickety cradle held the wood, as it was sawed into stove size lengths. Betsy seemed fascinated, as I explained how to tighten the blade of the bucksaw by twisting the turnbuckle. Using the handy sawhorse, I cut a piece of stove wood and explained that it had to be split again, for use in the stove.

I wasn't allowed to use the razor sharp, double bit ax, but it was just inside the shed. Splitting a piece of wood would be impressive. I had watched Grandpa many times, hold the wood in one hand and the axe in his other. With two short rapid strokes, he could split it three ways in a blink. Betsy didn't know how good he was, so I just set it on the ground and whacked it once in half. From the look on her face, I could have been Paul Bunyan. (Grandpa would have never found

Didja' Ever Make Butter?

out that I had used the ax, if I had had sense enough to wipe the mud off before putting it away. Naturally, Grandpa never permitted the blade to touch to the ground.)

"Doug ... Doug, where are you?"

"That's Grandma calling, come on." I took her hand and we ran back toward the house. I shouted, "Here we are, Gram."

"Elizabeth, your mother said you can help Doug carry the lunch out to the field, if you would like to," Grandma expected a positive answer.

"Oh yes, I would like that. That way I can see more of the farm."

Grandma handed us three large, covered tin buckets. Betsy had the smallest, full of sandwiches. I had the other two, one also full of sandwiches and another heavy one, filled with buttermilk. We started for the wheat field.

The sounds from the thrashing machine grew louder and louder, as we approached. Betsy listened intently, as I told her all about it. What a magnificent sight it made clattering and clanking away. A huge leather belt racing around and around connected the thrashing machine to the powerful engine. Golden straw spewed high into the air, before gently settling into a golden mound on the stubble covered field.

Quickly, the sandwiches were devoured by the hardworking men. I gallantly found a grape jelly and butter sandwich.

"Try this, Betsy. My Grandma made the bread and the jelly and I helped churn the butter." It was absolutely amazing. No matter what I did that day pleased and impressed Miss Elizabeth Hutchison. I was happy beyond belief. I had a friend at the farm, so what if she is a girl. I could handle it.

World's Funnest Playground

Wide gray boards; rusty tin roof
Wide open doorways
Lofts full of hay bales

Silently, dark shadows sulked in the corners. Fiery motes performed pirouettes floating suspended in the shafts of sunlights. The bright beams sliced grooves through the weathered board walls. The barn still resembled the grand structure built many years before. Almost thirty feet high at its top beam, the two storied senile structure contained much of the machinery used on the farm. The lofts, split into two huge caverns, were piled high with baled hay. It seemed an immense structure to me.

It was a place for imagining. The rusting iron implements scattered over the dirt floor assumed shapes and roles never intended by Cyrus McCormick when brought face to face with a ten year old's imagination. Two bottom plows became a pair indian warriors, clamping naked knees to the backs of their galloping horses. The box like wagon beds blossomed with imaginary canvas covers to become the settlers' conestoga wagons. Of course, the indians would attack, the wagons would circle and I would become the quintessential hero.

Endlessly, new scenarios unfolded in my fantasy world. Sometimes I would be Tom Mix, other times the Lone Ranger, usually with

Didja' Ever Make Butter?

a touch of Jack Armstrong mixed in with the images of Ovaltine and hot Ralston. Such fun awaited me, if I could but escape the nap.

An afternoon nap for a septuagenarian is a necessity that can stretch right into a luxury. When the weather is such to produce harmonious sleep rhythms, a phenomenon brought on by low humidity and a cool breeze, the young got restless and the old slept soundly. Low humidity and a cool breeze in a Missouri July were as rare as hen's teeth. This was one of those days, a veritable blessing from on high.

Naps were taken on the only floors with rugs. The living room and formal dining room were only used on holidays like Christmas and Thanksgiving, except for daily naps. Its cool shuttered darkness sheltered the fine furniture and a player piano. A rare Dresden Doll, that grandma had brought with her from Darmstadt, Germany, stood sedately in her handmade glass case next to the piano. On a huge quilt, the three of us would nap peacefully. To levitate from the quilt to the door, soundlessly, was an often practiced, but seldom successfully undertaken event. That day of the cool breeze and low humidity, I was successful.

The kitchen floor sighed, freezing my passage, momentarily. Unlike the traitorous kitchen floor, I had the indiscrete porch boards identified and easily negotiated that peril. Pulling gently on the screen door spring, I disconnected it from the hook and let it gently hang down from the door jamb. Without its screech-like blabbering to give me away, I was out the door, down the steps, free as a bird.

Having successfully escaped, it was big decision time. Where to go? The dusty shade by the rabbit tree was always used. It was close to the house and I played there, so Grandma could see me. My friend Kate, the mule, was tired from the morning's cultivating, so I let her be. Hilda was in the back pasture, so it was just Spot and me.

"Come on, Spot, let's go girl," I quietly urged, inviting her unnecessarily. There was no way I could have left without her following. In a cloud of dust, we ran up the wagon track toward the big barn.

Cirrus clouds raced across the sky from the west. Thin fingers probed the bright, pale blue sky. The sun was already plunging into

World's Funnest Playground

the clutches of the advancing scouts of darkness still four hours away.

The barn no longer had doors on its south side. The building was twice as wide, as it was long with broad doors opening on the wide sides. The west side of the barn was "companioned" by the rusty remains of the ancient steam engine. It had died before I was born. The primitive engine had been used to power the thrashing machine before the newer gasoline powered models. Now it was useless scrap, too far from a factory to be used in the war effort. To me it was a glamorous remnant that took many forms in my mental manipulations; train engine, tank, river boat, the possibilities were limited, only by my childlike abberations.

The doors on the near side had become part of a scrap pile of lumber. The huge board doors had been hung by rollers that could be slid open on tracks along the outer wall of the barn. Now, without doors, the south side of the barn was a cavernous hole of shifting shadows inviting adventurous minds, hypnotically onward.

"Whoo...coo, coo." The haunting mournful sound from the doves created sound effects unmatched by Hollywood's best efforts. The scurry of critters could be heard throughout the structure. Field mice, farm rats, cats, ground squirrels all whisper walked in their never ending game of survival.

The center of the barn sheltered a golden pile of straw that had been shot in the barn from the big spout on the thrashing machine in June. Its twin stood a hundred yards away in the middle of the wheat field.

"Don't ever climb on the straw pile." Grandpa's stern warning was still remembered. "Your foot prints will make pockets and the rain will collect and make the straw rot."

Rotten straw had no use except to fill washouts and gullies on a farm in those days.

"It don't rain in the barn," I gleefully reasoned. Straight up a board ladder, I scrambled. Nailed right to the barn's wall, handmade from scrap lumber, the smooth board rungs connected the first floor to the loft. The ground floor, in the middle of the barn, was literally dirt. To

Didja' Ever Make Butter?

each side, rough flooring for stacking small tools, or hay was nailed to huge beams, two feet above the dirt. This allowed the hay to breathe and kept iron tools from rusting. Ten feet up was a solidly floored loft for additional hay storage. There was my refuge.

Hay was baled on our farm in long heavy rectangles sixteen inches square. Just a few years earlier it had been pitched in huge, loose forks full into the hay loft. On other farms it was rolled into huge six foot wide cylinders. The rectangular bales were natural building blocks in an isolated hay loft. A push here, a shove there and tunnels were formed that a supple ten year old could scout for hours. A minute's boredom led to alterations, as the combinations were endless. It was like having life sized building blocks.

From the top of the ladder, a narrow defile led ever upward with steps carefully crafted from shifting the bales. Then a tunnel plunged downward. A bridge was formed by turning the hay bales sideways to span others. At last, in the remotest upper reaches of the loft, a hidden opening allowed me to enter my sanctuary. Walls two bales high formed, what else, a fort. I had been fascinated by forts since I saw my first black and white cowboy and indian motion picture. In the Hollywood traditions of the day, all indians were sinister and all the cowboys were good. It took almost forty years for me to untangle all those early misconceptions. In the course of play, I had made forts from cord wood, horseweeds, snow and countless other materials — always that which was most conveniently handy. Hay bales were a natural.

Spot fretted uneasily on the dirt floor of the barn way below. Until the first floor was filled with hay, she couldn't get up to the second floor. I spoke to her and she answered with a plaintive bark, as if to say, "Come down here. If you think this is fun, let me show you some rabbits."

The whirring buzz of wasps stole my attention. The dark blue insects hummed incessantly, building tan, mud nests in the corners. Every winter we knocked the mud huts down. Every summer newly designed replacements reappeared. Spot, her energy level primed by the cool day, tired of waiting and rambled off to her own designs. On hot days, she would find a dust bowl under the raised floor and curl up for a peaceful nap.

A pigeon flapped out of the barn through a window sized opening near the eaves. A block and tackle was suspended from a two by six in the opening. It was used to haul bales into the loft. A solitary white feather gently floated to my feet inside the walls of my fort. My thoughts floated in harmony with the feather, back into time. Back to the days of good and evil. Back to the reverie that conjured heroes and villains. I was the hero.

"That white feathered arrow is their final warning. Surrender the fort, or face a diabolical death at the hands of the dreaded Comanches." Sometimes these conversations were out loud and in different voices. I peered cautiously over the wall of the fort. I could see the indians, today Comanches, tomorrow Apaches, with the Sioux always skulking about in the advancing shadows.

"We will fight to the death, but surrender — never!" I shouted my defiance. I smiled arrogantly, as they melted back into the darkness. Looking down, I saw a burned out conestoga enduring defeat, half in the light and half in shadows, next to the hill of straw. I scurried through the tunnels scouting and shouting orders to my ethereal colleagues. Confident of fending off any attack, we nevertheless, had our escape route well planned. Coincidentally with the completion of our defenses, an arrow thumped into the the wall of the fort, narrowly missing my head.

"That was close, you scoundrels, but take this!" My weapons were cornstalks, denuded of leaves. Spears, rifles, clubs, all of the same golden brown material that adapted immediately at my slightest whim. I slashed a brave with my sword. Another took aim at me from the top of the wall. I fired. His feather headdress spread like a turkey tail, as the bullet burrowed into his painted brow. His arms flung wide, as a dying scream was wrenched from his lips. Seconds after he disappeared from the high wall, I heard him thump into the hard earth. Two others immediately took his place. I ducked a crushing toma-

Didja' Ever Make Butter?

hawk blow aimed for my head and countered with a thrust of my sword to his stomach. He joined his fellow braves in the dirt. The second indian released a flaming arrow. I caught it in my hand, comtemptuously broke it in half and threw it into his face. The flint arrowhead stuck deeply into his eye. One shot from my revolver opened a hole, .44 caliber sized, in his other eye.

Eerily, the howling painted savages poured over the wall in overwhelming numbers. It was time to escape. I leaped over the wall, ran to the edge of the loft and with one final defiant shot over my shoulder, leaped over the cliff into the straw below. A five foot drop in reality, was twenty to over three hundred feet, distance determined only by my mood of the moment. I slid quickly down the straw to the ground and ran to the ladder for another circuit. A new tribe of indians was snarling at my heels, forcing endless repetitions of the battle. The fun would be interrupted only by exhaustion, dry throat, or darkness.

Intermittent glimpses of reality would remind me of the lengthening shadows. I did watch for Grandpa from the loft window. If I saw him walk by heading for the back pasture, I quickly dispatched one last indian and ran off to join him. It was time to milk Hilda and obey my one cardinal rule — never miss a meal.

Herbie

Blotchy freckles on pale skin
Hanging head alert
Penetrating eyes

Muddy toes leaked from the remnants of a once proud pair of mail order brogues. Concentrated observation revealed a group of pedal digits that comprised a matched set. The two feet blended well, half buried in copious amounts of construction mud. White fringe hung like disheveled hair from a pair of bleached out denims, like a row of scruffy mock hair, it delineated the bottoms of a barely wearable pair of levis. Scrutiny could not determine accurately if the patches held the material together or vice versa. A sleeveless rag of a shirt hung half in, half out of the waistband. A nondescript pair of oversized suspenders prevented the entire outfit from flapping like a luffed sail. Acres of freckles fused into patches of pigment. A grin glowed warmly from amidst the blotchy pattern. Dark gaps in his pearly grin showed him to be younger than my once again solid white smile. Ruffled, mousy brown hair wrestled with sun bleached tips, in an apparent effort to evade any semblance of order. His feet ground slowly onto each other attempting to conceal his dead, but not buried shoes. The mire left by the autumn rain had painted the world below a foot in height, a rich creamy brown. His hands clasp lightly on some object unseen by his blue-gray eyes.

Didja' Ever Make Butter?

"Hi, I'm Herbie. Who are you?" Herbie's shy, soft voice was pure innocence, reaching out in midwestern friendliness.

I stood transfixed by this unintentional bizarre vision. Having not as yet read Huckleberry Finn, how was I to recognize this preposterous impersonator. I was a city kid invading the country. Indians I expected, extraterrestrials I did not.

But here he was, free, independent from any apparent adult control. I felt more self conscious than usual of my department store suit. The tweed pants, jacket and matching billed cap, were termed "darling" by my mother, ever alert to the dictates of haut couture. Nervously, I shuffled my shiny leather shoes, taking great care not to soil them. My mother's last reminder had been to stay neat and clean. This obvious deterrent was fading rapidly in Herbie's spritely presence. All things considered fun by a six year old boy were obstructed by that neatness admonition. I told Herbie my name.

"I live in the last house, up there." He swept his hand toward the west. "Wanna' play cowboys and indians? I'll be the indian."

"Can't, my mother told me not to get dirty." I eyed the inviting trenches, piles of dirt, invitingly open doors and walls that were emerging into a house on the half acre wooded lot. Guns, hidden as scraps of lumber and broken sticks, lay everywhere. It was very difficult to remember cleanliness reminders demanded to protect my overly dressed persona, under such overly tempting circumstances. The seduction of cowboys and indians was much too powerful for my frail self-discipline.

"We'll be careful. You can use the house for a fort. Is this going to be your house?" Can you spot the phrase composed of famous last words? We used those same words before every adventure on the farm. Grandma never seemed to detect our quickness in telling her exactly what she wanted to hear. You know something, I really think we meant it at the time.

"Yeah, it is. I can't leave the yard," but eyed the inviting patch of woods and weeds on the overgrown next door lot. That lot remained natural for several years after WWII had ended. Our house was the

Herbie

last one built before the war. Today was late fall, 1940. Hitler had already introduced Europe to the blitzkrieg. In Missouri, kids our age still thought indians were the real enemy.

"The vacant lot, high with weeds would make perfect cover," I thought.

"This is a sharp looking rifle. You can use it," Herbie offered, handing me a broken limb from an oak tree that did resemble a rifle. "Count to twenty, slowly then find me."

I watched him disappear over a pile of dirt and heard him scrambling through the trenches that were ready for the laying of the septic field. The clay pipes were stacked and ready. Many of the trenches already had rounded river rock in the bottom. What was a six year old boy to do?

"One, two, three..."

The last syllable of twenty had barely been whispered when I tore over the dirt piles, noting the challenge that leather shoes presented in seeking traction on wet clay. I veered impulsively toward the weeded lot. My pace slowed to a dangerous half walk, half run. The first shot, that breathy blast of the "p" sound followed by a whistling "s" rush of air that signified an imaginary bullet was winging on its way, shattering reality and sucking me inexorably into the illusory world of children. I dove for the nearest pile of dirt and returned rifle fire at the attacking renegade indian.

"Gotcha!" Herbie hollered in the universal language of kids.

"Missed me." I replied with the only acceptable answer. The war was on. In less than fifteen minutes, we explored every trench, every pile of dirt, every board and every room of the half constructed house. We leaped fell, resurrected and died innumerable times while my mother and step father conducted their business across the street. They were in a sanitized office. Herbie and I were in childhood heaven.

"Herrrbieeee!" The drawn out call to supper chased visions of indians back into the recess of imagination. It echoed across the quiet neighborhood beckoning my new found friend.

"Coming!" He bellowed his answer, "Gotta' go. See ya when you move in. Bye." In a flash he was gone. The new house was look-

Didja' Ever Make Butter?

ing great. I had found a friend. I watched him disappear then turned just in time to see three adults coming in my direction from the builder's office. My appearance seemed suddenly inappropriate for the circumstances. We were on our way to Schoeber's Restaurant and my appearance didn't quite complement my step father's Brooks Brother's suit, vest and matching tie. My mother was dressed to the nines in her latest outfit from Stix, Baer & Fuller. I watched her grow short of breath and exhibit an extremely unhealthy appearing color, as she approached me in obvious irritation. The contractor, Mr. Cole, hid his amusement by covering his face and faking a cough to hide his laughter.

I was in deep "doo doo" and it was all over me. My shoes were shiny. The glisten of fresh mud even covered the cloth laces. The cuffs of my tweed pants bulged outward with an oversized load of wet muck. It could be said that the colors did not clash greatly, as the basic brown mud merely dimmed the lines of the herringbone tweed. Only my billed beanie seem spared from the grotesque mess. Naturally, I blamed it all on Herbie.

"Herbie, who?" The shrill voiced inquisitor demanded. It was produce a Herbie, or die. Herbie no longer existed, not that it mattered. My punishment would now include lying.

Whenever this first meeting with Herbie is recalled, I wonder if the seedy little son of a gun had snookered me purposefully, or if my longing for a friend had created this onerous disaster. I asked Herbie many times, even after he earned a doctorate from Harvard and always got the same enigmatic grin.

The Queen Mary

Screws, glue, ancient wood
Paddles cut to size
Look out catfish, here we come!

In the silent dark, before dawn on certain days, aficionados can hear it. Its persistent pleading pulled me from sweet slumber accompanied by occasional chirping, that pierced the silence. The pre-dawn twilight silhouetted broad cotton wood leaves, creating gentle shadows, wavering across my upstairs bedroom window. I wasn't still dreaming. Today was such a morning. There, I heard it again. The catfish were calling. Do visions of worms flash through a bird's brain, like visions of catfish sweep through mine?

I clearly listened to the plop of a huge fish after leaping for a plump insect. It was a deep, resonant splashing sound, made by an object falling into deep water. The sound made by a lead weight, or a wad of dough bait "splooshing" into the wet. It harmonized with the memories of that slow grinding buzz of the drag. A unique noise, it animated the tug of war between land and water creatures. Those aural images pried open my eyes long before normal waking time. That I heard them is beyond question. It was summer. The catfish were calling.

We started about a week ago and it was ready for the water. The last coat of spar varnish had been applied last night. The impatience

Didja' Ever Make Butter?

of youth made waiting twenty-four hours between coats an almost unbearable torture. Seal and sand. Clean and apply. Finally, coat after coat hugged the wood, firmly assuring dry feet.

Measuring roughly four feet by eight feet, the dinghy was dainty and box-like, but to me it was the Queen Mary. The *Queen Mary*. Yes, I did name her that. Several small lakes abounded on nearby farms including the magnificent tooth shaped lake on the Queeny farm. When cattails and water lilies extended their influence into the waters, fishing from the shorelines became impossible. The little boat gave us access to otherwise inaccessible hot spots. Not only was she perfectly designed for fishing, but she proved faultless for shallow water venturing to snag mesmerized bull frogs, frozen by an after dark flashlight. But that's another story.

Two, one by twelve boards and a sheet of quarter inch plywood bent carefully over a frame of one by two inch slats were used in her construction. A flat bow board and transom, glued and screwed to the one by twelves formed the outline. The transom was a full twelve inches deep, but the bow board was half that measure. It was also six inches narrower than the four foot sheet of plywood that would eventually form the outer skin. The twelve inch boards that formed the side of the craft were bent gently to meet the narrower bow. Two large radius curves began amidships to slant the bottom gently toward its union with the bow. We got that far the first night.

"Grandpa, will we be able to stand on that thin piece of plywood?"

"Won't be standin' on that. Hand me one of those." Grandpa pointed at a pile of one by twos usually reserved for tomato stakes. He carefully made a mental calculation and cut the little board to match the length of the boat. It looked a little too long to me. The cut wasn't square either.

"Looks a little long, Grandpa," I ventured. Without looking up or acknowledging me in any fashion, he fitted the "too long" piece against the transom, bent it carefully and rested the other end against the inside of the bow board. The resulting bow in the slender spar conformed perfectly to the narrowing side boards. The "crooked" cut on

The Queen Mary

the one end lay flat against the bow board, as well. Quickly, using the first cut spar as a pattern, he cut six more identical siblings. When glued in place they made a strong frame for the thin bottom skin. A rasp and a plane smoothed all the saw marks from the finished exterior. The entire inside was caulked and then brushed with a coat of sealer. That took us two more nights.

As far as I was concerned, it was finished. Evidently, the gleam of anticipation in my eyes was more glaringly bright than the shiny coat of sealer. As always, Grandpa was eons ahead of me and told me that another couple of nights might have it finished. I lived with my disappointment.

The next evening he installed three seats, six inch boards across the bow, stern and midships. He carefully explained these nautical terms at the time. Hopefully, I haven't lost their correct meanings, as I chipped the rust and barnacles off my memory to recall them. The hardest ones were port and starboard. I could never apply them to the correct side of the boat until he told me, "Johnny left port."

I have ever since remembered that left and port go together the same as ham and eggs. Of course, I still think all Johnnys are left handed, too.

One whole night we sanded. We started with the rough stuff and worked our way down to the finest grit he could find. It felt softer than a day old kitten when we got through. After we swept out the shed and wiped the wood, he splashed on a coat of sealer on the outside of the hull. The next night we sanded lightly once again and applied the first coat of varnish. The varnishing seemed like it took forever. In reality, it took only a day or two. The Queen Mary was finished.

The two of us carried her easily. Grandpa attached four screen door handles, two on each end. She sat easily on the roof of the car and we carried her from there to the ponds. Some times it was quite a hike, but that boat never seemed heavy. The adventures could now begin.

Watermelon Time

Verdant, rotund balls
Bursting with juicy delights
Painted sticky pink

Like huge land mines they cluttered the field. Unlike those devices of war, they lay exposed and harmless. For weeks the swell of their pregnant bellies expanded in ever increasing girth. The dark green vines wove a pattern of cooling shade for life at ground level. Tendrils had long since knotted into proud entanglements. The plants exchanged clasps as if to congratulate each other on their maturing broods. The bare earth, beneath the plants was as dry as the nearby creek. The bordering corn field whispered softly, painted a lush green by the humid summer days. The tranquil air rested briefly in this small corner tucked between the corn, the small stream and a hillside. When rested, the breeze drifted slowly, gently massaging the elm and oak leaves along the creek bank. Grandpa and I entered the scene, as the result of a summer walk about.

"Are they big enough yet?" I implored, hopefully. The question had become reflexive each time we came within sight of the patch. The patch lay central to many other places on the farm. Consequently, Grandpa was subjected to this inquiry several times daily since the green globs had exceeded the size of a grapefruit.

Watermelon Time

"Yep, it's time to thump 'em." Grandpa responded to my pleasure. His anxiety to taste the sweet red fruit nearly always matched mine. Except for dewberries, sweet pears, yellow apples, grapes and persimmons ... oh, let's face it, he liked anything that was in season on the farm. Who can wait for that first bite of bounty of each new, eagerly awaited season. Even desolate winter had the delight of picking morsels of hickory and walnut meat from those casings so reluctant to surrender their prize.

Grandpa lovingly perused each and every melon. In most, the dark black stripes had faded as they expanded, like the lettering on a balloon. Some exposed whitish spots where they had been carefully rotated while they grew. I watched while he kneeled and rapped the front of his knuckles against an imposing brute. The deep, resonant thump, thump promised a choice, deliciously juicy interior. Satisfied that his ears confirmed what his eyes had chosen, he deftly snapped the stem, hefted the green gourd to his shoulder and took three steps toward home before I had moved one foot.

"Can we have some for lunch?" My thoughts quickly caught up with my appetite. The sun was nearing its mid-morning check point. Breakfast had surely been an eternity ago. Thirsty or not, my mouth ran juicy at the thought of the huge globe of seed filled, red fruit.

"No, but it should be cooled down by supper." I knew the routine as well as he did, but each year, at each harvest, my secret desire was to devour an entire melon right in the field. Didja' ever want to break one open and just dig the heart right out of it? You know, pack delicious chunk after deliciously flowing red chunk into that maw we call mouth. To feel the sticky sweetness escaping our lips and dribbling downward in a shirt staining flood. Do I alone crave the glorious excess of avoiding those inconvenient seeds and just one time, stuffing ourselves with chunk after watery chunk of the red ripe fruit? It was one of the few fantasies in my life that I actually fulfilled. It's the only one I will tell you about, as well.

Didja' ever think about the fondness that watermelons hold in our minds? It has always been a special fruit in our family. Was there ever

Didja' Ever Make Butter?

a July Fourth celebration without watermelon, fried chicken and corn on the cob? Can't you still hear the raucous hilarity of giggling immature voices, punctuated by slurps and spitting? Efforts seemed equally divided between gulping cool morsels of melon and chasing the nearest child relative, in order to splatter them with seeds. Extraneous bits of half chewed goodness splattered into hair, skin and clothes along with the seeds. Spot would join excitedly, chasing and nipping the heels of the combatant cousins.

Inevitably, Grandma would, "Tsk, tsk," at the behaviors. Young mothers reassured the aging sentinels of propriety that washing the clothes was much easier now and the play continued. It was the highlight of every summer, the migration back to the farm roots. The watermelon was always the catalyst of blithe spirits. It even exceeded the after dark fireworks. Giant sparklers overshadowed the fireflies one night of the year. Rockets were sent skyward from a piece of drain pipe braced against the fence, but that's another story.

Aside from the holiday melons, July and August usually were noted for the daily appearance of the ruby colored fruit. It was always available from the icebox for snacks. Once cut, the big fruit was sectioned into pieces that fit in the tiny "keep cool" receptacle. It occurs to me now why I enjoyed those farm melons so much. Melons cooled in today's refrigerators get too cold. Those cooled in a deep cistern were always refreshing, but never hurt your teeth. Of course, the rosy glow of memory adds luster to those sweet days.

Grandpa's increasingly noticeable huffing and puffing returned my thoughts to the present. I thought of the big bad wolf in the story of the three pigs, as he climbed the hill going from the watermelon patch to the cistern in the barnyard. I don't ever remember weighing one, but I think that fifty pounds would not be an exaggeration for some of larger ones. That's a lot of weight to carry uphill for almost two hundred yards.

Grandpa had a gunny sack secured to a rope for cooling things in the cistern. A couple of boards would shift sideways to provide an opening to the shady cool water. By late afternoon, the melon would be just right.

Watermelon Time

My expectations were heightened by a long thought out plan. I had carefully worked it out in my head all summer long. It was perfect. I was, at last, going to get my revenge on Rommel, the rooster. We usually ate the melon outside, sans plates and silver ware. The round wedges were designed for finger to mouth processing. Unfortunately, the first bite was always the best. Eating watermelon is a downhill procedure. The best bite is the first and each succeeding bite is less sweet and more seed filled. Somehow, I always fought off the depression.

Unless Grandma was saving the rinds for pickles, we would throw the green and white pieces over the fence into the barnyard. This quickly produced a flock of hard pecking chickens, followed by the strutting bully, Rommel. He delayed his entry until the hens had lanced heartily into the rinds, then with arrogant purpose, he would crow pompously, flap his wings threateningly and scatter the cowed flock with thrusts of his rapier like beak. Having re-established his primacy in the pecking order, the rascal would select the choicest morsels for himself.

By now, being well into my second wedge, I had carefully hoarded a hand full of shiny, black seeds. By dropping the rinds ever closer to the fence, the chickens and Rommel were lured nearer my position. I sidled slowly, ever closer to the fence, nearing Rommel. His beady red eyes stared menacingly, in spite of the fact that he could not reach me through the fence. His arrogance left him vulnerable. Glancing quickly at Grandma and Grandpa, who appeared pre-occupied, I jammed the entire handful of still slick elliptical black missiles into my mouth. Now full with seeds and pink juice, I inhaled a gigantic lung full of air through my nose. Grabbing the top strand of the fence I slowly moved my head and upper torso backward, as if drawing a bowstring, then propelled myself forward to get maximum velocity behind the seeds. As I slammed against the fence, I unleashed a machine gun like stream of syrupy seeds directly at, and unerringly upon, the jaunty rooster. Oh my, it was worth any trouble Grandma or Grandpa could bring on.

Didja' Ever Make Butter?

He squawked like a coward, jumped straight up, wildly flapping his wings and landed with his feet scratching gravel to distance himself from the attack. He stopped about thirty feet away and attempted to recover his dignity, but I knew my laughter continued to wound his pride. Somehow, his head didn't stand as tall. His comb didn't bounce jauntily when he walked. He now walked. He used to strut. His approach to the remaining rinds was wary and his pecking tentative. He even deferred to some of the hens. His humiliation was complete. Black seeds continued to slide and fall from his previously unsullied plumage. His ignominious defeat was total. My ambush was as successful as the Sioux's surprise party for George Armstrong Custer. It was the Pearl Harbor of the barnyard. It was my surrender of Cornwallis. Best of all, his chastening was forever. He never chased me from the barnyard again. From that momentous day on, **I** owned the barnyard. **He** sneaked away when **I** approached. That night was born a new, "cock of the walk."

The Flood

Roaring wild water
Layer of new life
Rain's thundering symphony

Heavy winter snows assured a high water table. A nearly perfect spring had permitted expedient planting. Steady, soil soaking rains had nourished the young plants and maintained high water tables. The creek ran steadily, pouring foot deep, fast water over the ford. The creek's deep pools were indistinguishable under the rolling surface. Excess water gathered in the shallow ditches at the edges of the fields. Low spots in the fields hosted shiny black mud that never quite dried. Plants turned yellow and white from lack of sunshine. It was a race for survival between crops and weeds. Morning glories were smothering corn stalks with their love. Chokeweed flared like a jealous rival. Cockleburrs bristled with pale green determination. Green was in. It was as green an early summer, as anyone remembered. It was a little too wet, but of course, that's better then a little too dry.

The clouds were a long way off, as we came back from the evening milking. The western sky was more hazy than cloudy. The heat was oppressive. The humidity was worse. The air was as quiet, as a can of night crawlers. For days a flood of warm wet air had been slowly

Didja' Ever Make Butter?

flowing north toward the farm from the Gulf of Mexico. Record rain falls were flooding parts of Texas and Oklahoma.

"If that cold front gets here tomorrow, we will see a bundle of water, let me tell you," Grandpa mused at the supper table. Weather had been the topic at the store that afternoon. Grandpa liked to appear informed and relayed these tidbits for Grandma's edification. Grandma knew that adverse weather talk would be followed by complaints about his knees and the "rheumatiz."

"My 'rheumatiz' says it could rain more than two inches tomorrow." A discussion on the relative merits of Doane's and Carter's Little Liver Pills would follow. Those stalwart remedies, turpentine and Sloane's liniment were about the only medications available on the farm. By age sixteen, I knew that weather and knees were part of farm lore — old wives tales. By age fifty, when my own knees became an accurate barometer in detecting those approaching thunder storms, my beliefs underwent refinement. Of course, no one is silly enough to use Sloane's liniment any more, not when we have WD-40.

Anyway, as I remember it, we went to bed early, but sleep didn't come easy, surrounded by that warm blanket of humid air. I probably drifted off just in time for the first cracks of lightning that jarred me from a too short night's sleep. What a racket. What a display. Flashes brightened my upstairs room. Cracks of ear-splitting explosions vibrated the windows, causing them to rattle within their casements, with each rumble of thunder. Long, loud rumbles that wandered off into the distance. Wildly waving branches produced spectacular shadow shows throughout the room. After an initial tantrum, the storm dumped sheets of water mixed with hail. The drops of rain were so big that we couldn't distinguish them from the hail. When I looked outside and saw the ground glaring an eerie white, I knew. In between rumbles and flashes, I heard Grandpa up and about.

"What time is it, Grandpa?"

"Only about 5:30, go on back to sleep." But I was wide awake and in need of the security of adult company. I quickly padded down stairs and stood close while Grandpa started the wood stove. His

The Flood

ritual was the same every day, winter or summer, rain or shine. Crumpled paper, shave sticks followed by stove wood. One match, a wide open damper and soon the blaze was roaring to do battle with the harshest invading elements conjured up by nature. I thought of Mother Nature as the enemy during storms. At those times the roaring fire, either in a stove, a fireplace, or a kerosene lamp gave off more than warmth, or light, it provided mind comforting security.

The hot water kettle began to sizzle and rock metallically. We walked to the porch to watch the outdoor display. The first lashing sheets of rain had blown by. Now the water was pouring straight down. It was certainly a gully washer. The sky, a leaden gray, was beginning to lighten imperceptibly in the east. The uniformity of its color gave a hint of the all day nature of the rain.

Hours later with no let up in sight, Grandpa "slickered" up and headed for the barn. Regardless of the vagaries of the weather, the cows had to be milked. It was one of the rare days I was left behind. There was work enough without having to clean me up too. In a while he returned with wooden lids covering both milk buckets. Slicker or not Grandpa was soaked. Grandma soon had him steaming dry by the stove, talking woman talk to him in an endless prattle.

"Phillip, you will catch a death ... wait till it quits ... look at the puddles ... your hat will never dry." She had her own way to display her concern.

Grandpa, through it all, just murmured, "Yes boss, you're right boss, of course, boss."

It was fully light. When I looked, there seemed to be a lake of water in the yard. The house was fully six feet up from the ground, so I wasn't worried. We stood on the crest of a hill up from the creek and cornfield. There was a lot of water out there in the bottoms today.

By noon, there had been no abatement. Already the water in the creek could be seen, brimmed, rushing by in a brown torrent. This happened frequently. Such a storm could put four feet of water over the ford. We were briefly cut off from Wideman Road and the mail. In a few hours it would run off and we could safely wade the foot

Didja' Ever Make Butter?

deep water at the ford. This time the rain persisted. It slacked off to almost a drizzle by late afternoon, but after a brief respite, seemed to invigorate itself and storm anew throughout the night. Grandpa chose the slack period to feed the chickens, mules and milk the cows once again. He still got wet. He carried several loads of stove wood into the house.

By the next day we had the awesome sight of seeing the entire cornfield under water. The creek was a lake. The barnyard was lake. The front yard was a lake. Have you ever seen water four inches deep on the TOP of a hill? Well, actually any spot with a semblance of level had standing water. Anyway, the water that kept pouring off that hundred yard long slope behind the barn was incredible.

After more than twenty-four hours inside the house, I was stir crazy and rapidly driving Grandma in the same direction. Since the lightning had departed, she relented to allow me to go outside and splash in the water. It was still raining, but not enough that you needed to duck inside for a breath any more. Wearing just a pair of old jeans, out I went. Spot wouldn't even come out from under the porch. She twice wagged her tail lazily and widened her eyes, but that was it.

It was heaven. Each step was like treading on luxuriously padded carpet. I was ankle deep in water and soft grass. In the yard, the water was clear. In the barnyard it ran multi-colored, from red to yellow, from dark brown to beige. I splashed in every color I could find. I was so wet, I looked like a drowning survivor. I waded and splashed to the crest of the hill to listen to and observe the creek. Don't ever doubt the power of water. That day you could hear the power.

Without warning a new front sneaked up. Suddenly fresh torrents of rain began falling amidst crashing lightning and reverberating claps of thunder. The wind blew ferociously. The sky blackened almost as if a blast of wind had extinguished the sun. I ran for the house, even before I heard Grandpa's holler. As I neared the house, the strangest experience I ever had, happened. It started with loud, dull thumps coming from the roof. Grandpa must have heard them, as well, because he came outside to investigate and together we watched amazed,

The Flood

as several live fish flopped off the roof. Several more were flopping in the grass. It was raining fish. None was more than four inches long, and all about the same size. Mesmerized by the unexplainable occurrence we went inside and left the mystery to mother nature.

It rained almost a week that summer. The water eventually covered the two foot high corn in the bottoms. In time the creek went down, the ground dried and cracked. Bent plants shook the mud and grew straight and tall. The hay crop was never better. Some corn was lost, potatoes washed out and the wheat was a disaster, every acre lost. The blackberries grew huge The bountiful mast crop fattened many a squirrel that graced our table. The plump rabbits made hasenpfeffer supreme that winter. The cisterns were brimming and swimming hole was never deeper. Man and nature coexisting as usual, on her terms. She may be a dictator, but her terms aren't all one sided. Don't have to worry about her successor, either.

Learning to Frog

Beady eyes Alert
Heart pounding like a tom tom
Escape, or capture

Raucous, high energy barking quickly became a gurgling, water soaked imitation. The forty pound bundle of fur sent water splashing in every direction. Only the black shiny nose remained visible, as she all but completely submerged following her running leap into the lake. Powerfully flailing forepaws forced her upward and toward the stern of the Queen Mary. A vee shaped waked trailed her approach. It was a game of tag and Spot had chosen herself to be "it." She confidently expected to catch us. My worst fear was that she would.

The long awaited launching of our better than an air mattress floating device was planned for an idle Sunday afternoon. Grandpa, the ever present Spot and me headed for a nearby piece of water big enough to test the miniature ship for leaks and navigability. The spirit of adventure and two short, homemade canoe paddles accompanied the trio of fun seekers.

"Will she float? Will she hold us? Why didn't we bring the fishing poles?" With more questions than bullets in a machine gun, I tested Grandpa's patience more than he tested the Queen Mary. Calling upon his long perfected stress coping techniques, Grandpa merely grunted

Learning to Frog

appropriately. To the best of my memory, the grunts answered my queries quite satisfactorily. It is quite likely that neither of us heard a single word uttered by the other. But it passed the time getting to the pond.

"This spot will do just fine." We set the small boat on the shallow bank. The Model A stood less than fifty feet away observing us with contempt for deserting her for a flimsy wooden boat. Grandpa chose a spot where the bank sloped gently into the water and a minimum of aquatic growth impeded the launch. Holding the painter in one hand, he pushed the Queen Mary into the water. Like a poorly loaded canoe, she rode high in the water at the stern and low in the bow. Her bottom was visible under the bow, but just barely. The empty boat, ungainly as she may have seemed, floated like a cork. Grandpa gave her the once over, checking for uninvited water in the dry interior. His smug, satisfied demeanor confirmed that she was as dry, as a Carrie Nation family reunion. He pulled the bow back onto the grassy bank by the painter.

"Hold on to the painter," he directed, as he handed me the short piece of rope tied to one of the front handles, "When I get seated, push her out and jump in at the same time."

I choked off the immediate response that came to mind, "What if I miss?"

Grandpa sat in the stern seat and the front of boat rose sharply upward like a giant hippopotamus yawning in the Congo river. I leaped nimbly into her. I didn't need to shove the boat into the pond at all. Grandpa's weight in the stern made her bow float free. The fact is, she came even closer to shore and my nimble leap was really no more than a quick step. In any case, we were successfully launched. Spot, stranded on the shore, was nervously dancing around, barking spiritedly. From Spot's point of view, we were about to desert her, never to be seen again, although she could easily see us anywhere on that pond from any where on the shore. At its widest, the small lake wasn't more than two hundred feet across. Nevertheless, Spot determined that she was not going to be stranded while we ventured upon the waters.

Didja' Ever Make Butter?

The navigation strategy was for each of us to wield an oar and propel the boat like a canoe. Lacking the trim lines of a canoe, it required an inordinate amount of work and she proved difficult to steer. After a little practice and coordination, Grandpa and I moved her in an approximate direction. We weren't ready to attempt an Atlantic crossing, but we remained high and dry with four inches of sideboard above the water line.

About this time the frenetic Spot created a mini-tsunami. Her only concession to discretion was that after about three water logged attempts, she gave up on the idea of barking, in favor of breathing. Always an exuberant swimmer (a marked difference in her attitude prevailed, however, if the water was in proximity to soap), Spot seemed determined to intercept and board us. The size of her wake, as compared to the Queen's, conveyed creditability regarding her chances for success. The Queen could hold her, but having her scramble aboard could upset the tiny craft. Furthermore, the spectre of a forty pound dog spraying twenty pounds of water in all directions was as appealing as being confined in the four by eight foot boat with a rattlesnake, but that's another story. Surely, you have seen the rock and roll dance of a water soaked dog, vibrating their body in order to send torrents of water onto everything except themselves. The wet might have been welcome, but the odor can linger for hours, especially from a farm dog.

"No, Spot!" Grandpa said it once just as Spot was within striking distance. I often wondered what the next minute would have brought had she been less obedient. Another of those unanswered mysteries of life. From that moment on, if the mood and the temperature were to her liking, Spot swam as if attached to a tow line six to eight feet behind us. When we turned, she turned. When we quit she quit. I have never seen such long distance swimming by any dog before or since. Living to be almost 15 years old, I like to think her hours in the water added greatly to her longevity. The only temperature water she wanted no part of occurred briefly when the ice was too thin to walk on and too thick to swim through. It can be safely assumed that she had a strong affinity for swimming.

Learning to Frog

"Head back to the bank. We'll leave her here for now and give her a night test later." Grandpa's taste buds were actively attuned to the presence of some plump green bullfrogs appearing as statuesque lumps around the waterline of the pond. Catchable during the day with stealth, a long gig and a lot of luck, they presented an easier target at night when mesmerized with a flashlight and caught by hand. Having never before hunted frogs, that night was to be my virgin venture.

"Walk quietly and don't talk, whisper." Didja' ever wonder if "no talking rules" was a convenient way adults invented to get kids to shut up? I wanted to go, so except for occasional lapses, I muffled my mouth.

By the light of a half moon, we gingerly embarked and paddled onto the pond. Spot? She was last seen pouting, displaying her best hang dog demeanor, securely inside the fenced in yard. Grandpa told her to watch over Grandma, but I don't think Spot believed a word of it.

Grandpa had explained to me how to scan the bank with the flashlight beam and look for the glistening beady eyes of the bullfrogs. When I spotted one, I was to hold the light steadily on the frog while he slowly and quietly guided us into grabbing range, which of course, was very close. He had to paddle without splashing. One inadvertent noise from the paddle and the frog would kerplunk out of sight.

When within reach of the quarry, I had to hold the light, focused on the amphibian, while carefully reaching up and over the intended victim. I had to keep my hand and arm out of the flashlight beam. One hint of a shadow on the frog and kerplunk. When poised to strike, I then, in theory, would firmly grab the frog behind head, then plunge him kicking and squirming into the wet gunny sack on the floor of the boat. Sounds easy. Actually, with practice, it is. There are, however, some things that can go astray. Flashlights flicker, kerplunk. Paddles splash, kerplunk. Boats drift off course when Grandpa loses sight of the frog, kerplunk. Frogs submerge, silently. Water is too shallow to get close enough, frog laughs. You get a bug in your mouth, Grandpa laughs.

"I think that one is a snake," Grandpa says seriously. You get scared and hesitate, kerplunk. He laughs at his own joke. The good

Didja' Ever Make Butter?

news was that we eventually got it right. The bad news was that one frog did not make a meal. The undoubtedly frightened, but still lively frog was returned to the water and two sleepy, slow moving humans headed for home.

"It was great Grandpa. Can we go again tomorrow night?" My excitement was enough to overload a small boat. Now that the hunt was over and I could talk, I was determined to make up for lost time. I would never forget the hammering of my heart, as my hand approached that first frog. Excitement and fear triggered enough adrenaline for me to run a marathon. There I was having to bottle all that energy while sneaking quietly up on a suspicious frog. I really followed directions perfectly until the last instant. My grab should have been decisive and dartingly quick. Instead I moved a tad too slowly, hesitating out of fear of the frog's ferocious teeth. Grandpa had told me all about those ferocious teeth, in order to assure I grabbed the frog behind the head. Little did he know what results his graphic illustration and my fertile imagination would bring.

Coping with the reality of a cold slimy Mr. Frog and his imagined, crocodile like mouth, was more than my unsophisticated mind could handle. When the giant croaker leaped through my grip, straight at my face, his reality scared me worse than my imagination. With a solid splash, he disappeared into the depths. In the ensuing hours he was followed by untold numbers of his brethren, who easily survived my ineptitude.

The second frog earned his escapee label when Grandpa lost sight of the target and I grabbed before we were in range. I got a hand full of mud and a face full of water when the critter dived right under my chin. Luckily, the flashlight fell into the bottom of the boat, although I later discovered that it was easy to find in shallow water if you grabbed it before the light shorted out. We didn't have those dandy waterproof, floating things back then.

The one frog we caught, actually got scared and leaped into the boat. Grandpa plopped him into the bag just before he gathered himself for a second, freedom winning leap. This first time frog hunt,

Learning to Frog

taught me why frog legs were an expensive delicacy. I actually touched several of the slick critters, learned that they didn't have teeth, in spite of Grandpa's testimony and in fact, had absolutely no possible way to harm a human. With this bit of knowledge building confidence, I was certain that another try tomorrow night would yield a worthy meal. Then I begin to think about actually eating one of those squirmy slimy things and the meal part didn't sound nearly as good. As it turned out, the first bite of Grandma's fried frog legs dispelled the negatives, as quickly as reality chased Grandpa's frog teeth tale.

Of worse consequence, the Queen Mary had proven unreliable for frogging, but the called-for modifications were made. Grandpa installed a used pair of oar locks the next evening. The stability of the paddles, now located in the middle of the ship allowed either passenger to row and guide the Queen any where we wanted. The paddles, now oars, permitted quieter maneuverability and the capability to spin in a full circle, if need be. We could power the little dinghy with efficiency of effort and go backwards and forwards in a straight line. The last modification installed three one by two runners on the bottom. These protected the smooth flat bottom from small stones on the banks and allowed the craft to slide on the grass, as dragging her cross country proved easier than carrying. We were well pleased with the newly configured boat. She proved lethal to fish and frogs.

Grape Coffeecake

Purple clusters on the vine
Yeast making bubbles
Come home from the fields

"Come, boy. Carry the basket for me." In her later years, Grandma had trouble with names. This was the third generation she had raised over the past forty summers. First was my grandmother, her daughter. Then came my mother, aunt and uncle. I would be the last. Now all of us were boy or girl, but no one minded. Sharp in many areas yet, names were confusing. I suppose there were too many memories of too many look alike kids.

She tied on her bonnet, picked up her field scissors and moved out the door. She knew I would follow. We'd just gotten up from the mid-day nap. I was ready to run, but going with Grandma would be just fine. "Be sure to close the gate, boy."

Her stride was purposeful, no wasted detours. Carrying all those years seemed an additional chore. I dashed here and there, called Spot, wiped off his "sloshy" kiss while generally following Grandma. She headed between the barn and the stable. Kate and Pete, our mules were pulling the mower for Grandpa in the upper hay field. Grandpa called it lespedeza. It looked like alfalfa and smelled wonderful. Tomorrow Grandpa would rake it into wind rows to dry the other side.

Grape Coffeecake

The sweet odor from the manure pile crossed our path. On cold wintry days the pile of aging fertilizer would steam aromatically into the frosty air. On our right, the wood rail fence of the corral led us to the nearby straw potato patch. The dried vines from the harvested potatoes lay on the brown, rich earth. This fall the disc would chop them into compost to feed next year's crop.

The corral turned abruptly away from us and joined with the barbed wire pasture fence. Three strand barbed wire fences were always difficult to negotiate unless Grandpa was there to "step down" the bottom strand and hold the middle one up for us kids to climb through. Fortunately, Grandma and I didn't have to cross it to get to the grapes.

The orchard was on our left. Behind the big barn, on the hill, stood trees, heavy with ripening red apples. The yellow apples had already been picked in early August. The weeds were knee high once again. Rabbits were thicker then fleas on a hounds back in the orchard. They feasted on apples dropped by the passing thunder storms. We collected the rabbit's rent in hasenpfeffer. Many a dinner came from the orchard during the fall hunting season. Didn't need ration stamps during the war for that delicious meat.

A quick bark from Spot, a flash of white tail, even Grandma stopped to watch the futile chase. We glanced at each other and smiled. Spot would be gone for at least an hour, chasing that rabbit. The rabbit would circle and be nested and rested long before Spot gave up the chase. Somehow Spot never learned that he was a step too slow and lacked the nose of the neighboring beagles. Like most dogs, I think she just enjoyed the chase.

Past the orchard about a hundred yards from the big barn was our two row stand of concord grapes. When I saw the bulging clumps, I realized school was just around the corner. Summer was at an end. Labor Day and grapes, agony and ecstasy.

Gram took the stick at the end of the row and tapped it quickly into the grass along the vines. Then she banged it against the metal posts. Seems that snakes like to lie in the shade there. She cleared a section, then began to cut the bunches of royal purple, carefully put-

Didja' Ever Make Butter?

ting them into the basket. The peck sized basket gained weight as the "ready to burst with sweet goodness grapes" quickly mounded.

"I'll cut enough for coffeecake and make sure that we have plenty to eat, too." She knew I loved to eat the tangy sweet grapes one after another. I do to this day. I can hardly wait for the Concords to show up in the markets, each year. My thumb and forefinger turned purple from squeezing each seed filled morsel into my mouth. Then the tart chew of the skin released yet another flavor sensation. I wasn't allowed to devour belly achin' quantities, but with a quick hand and sneak trips to the arbor, I managed to get close several times.

We stopped at the cistern and ran cool water over the freshly picked fruit. The water took off the heat and the field dust, but most of the white spider webs clung tight. We always found the white webs, but seldom spotted a spider. hey loved to feed on the other insects attracted by the sweet nectar from the clustered purple fruit.

Back in the house, Grandma kneaded the yeast dough one last time. The dough, covered by a towel, had been rising in the pantry since before lunch. She filled several coffeecake pans while I pulled each grape from the stem and dropped them in a bowl. Most of them made it, but the skins from the "sneakies" probably would stain my underwear right through the pockets. Butter was brushed on the dough and then the luscious fruit was spread side by side to cover the top with a blanket of purple. White sugar was sprinkled like a blizzard to create a frosted mural.

The wood stove was crackling in the background, driving back the fall chill trying to sneak into the airy old house. In a little while, irresistible odors would sneak around the farm and call grandpa home from the fields.

Rodeo!

Cowboys for an afternoon
Wash line in ruins
Angry grandfather

Westerly breezes brushed tendrils of white clouds on an azure canvas. It was a rare spring day, held in reserve until mid-July. A day that God knew we would need to separate one, steamy mid-summer day's heat spell from another. Everyone was charged with a new found energy. Spot was frisky. She and the cat played a rare game of tag. The chickens were busily pecking in the gravel. Kate and Pete could be heard stamping and snorting in the stable. The cows, milked and fed, were waiting by the gate ready to head for the lush, green grass of the back pasture. Minotaur, Hilda's weaned but frisky calf, was making a nuisance of himself by trying to grab free drinks from any available spigot. Herb and I laughed at his comical hops and allusive skips, as he avoided the menacing horns thrust at him by the annoyed adult bovines.

The brisk day's effect wasn't lost on the young humans. Relieved from the necessity of seeking cooler activities in the shade of the creek, hyperactive brain cells were free to devise more creative forms of self destruction. The fates seem to contrive with coincidence, in order to assist boys in their efforts to devise nefarious bits of mischief. The

Didja' Ever Make Butter?

first coincidence was the temptation of Grandma's clothes line hanging neatly coiled, like a lariat on a fence post. Coincidence number two was the weather being stimulatingly perfect. Herbie, my prime catalyst for mischief, was spending a week on the farm. He was coincidence number three. If all these coincidences hadn't happened simultaneously, the idea for a back pasture rodeo might never have happened. But they did.

"Herbie, stuff the rope in your shirt and head for the woods."

"You grab it, I'm still in trouble for the egg fight." His long forlorn face grew a little longer with the burden of advance guilt. Neither of us remembers who first had the idea.

"I would, but I've got to find Grandpa and tell him where we are going, if he sees the rope that will be the end of it," I reasoned, rather reasonably.

"If I get caught, it was your idea," he mumbled, stuffing the soft cotton strands into the top of his overall.

Grandpa was in the garden, deftly chopping the hoe in that back breaking ritual used to eliminate foreign growth from a long row of almost ready to pick beans. He barely paused, as I volunteered to walk the cows to the back pasture.

"Where's Herbie?" he asked. My brain, edgy with newly forming guilt, wondered if he ever missed anything.

"Oh, uh, he's by the gate watching Minotaur mess around."

"I guess you guys will keep busy chasing snakes, or something, huh?" He had wry smile on his face, suspecting that two boys had some form of mischief planned.

When the crops are growing and the cultivating is finished, a lot of time is spent waiting for rain and catching up with minor chores. Grandpa probably figured he could get more done without two frisky colts under his feet than with the assistance of two reluctant go-fers.

"Make sure you're back by dinner time," he murmured in dismissal.

I sprinted for the pasture with Spot in hot pursuit. In about three shakes she was in the lead, glancing back from time to time for a

Rodeo!

direction check. I shielded my eyes and glanced at the sun. We had about three hours until it would be straight up indicating dinner time.

"Open the pasture gate! Let 'em go!" I shouted to Herbie, as soon as I got within range of his hearing. He responded by climbing up the gate post to lift the wire loop that held the gate shut. By then I had caught up and pushed open the creaking gate. No second opportunity was needed for the cows to escape Minotaur, the bothersome. His antics, comparable to those of a young human, earned him the name Minotaur after the mythological half man, half bull creatures. The minuscule mixed herd headed for the peace and expanded room of the pasture.

A few steps took us out of sight of the farm house and into the woods. We heard the squirrels, hidden by the dense summer foliage, chattering to the accompaniment of the drum beat of hooves on the hard clay path. The soprano songs of the jays, cardinals and sparrows blended with the alto melodies of the mockingbirds and the mournful calling to Bob-White by the quail. What a gloriously large day. What a day to be alive and full of devilment.

"Herb, how do you make a lariat?"

"Ya' make a knot, like this." He tied an overhand knot in the flexible cotton rope, then made a crude circle and coiled the rest. He tried to circle a small stump on his first throw. The loop refused to open. Instead, it wrapped frustratingly around the weed growth at the base of the stump. Retrieval proved a challenge. Some of the green things had stickers that hung on like today's velcro.

Between a too limp rope and an unyielding knot, making a working lariat didn't come easy. Experimentation yielded a more utilitarian knot with a larger loop that allowed the noose to close more quickly and the rope to coil uniformly. We found that a spinning motion kept the loop round and more inclined to circle and drop over the intended target. We discovered that a large loop was the most practical. All of this, of course, was like re-inventing the wheel. But then, we were Missouri boys, not Texans.

Now the swaggering, courageously incompetent cowboys were ready to rodeo. What we didn't realize, was how much we were about

Didja' Ever Make Butter?

to learn. Emotions like excitement cause you to forget concepts that you already knew, such as the fact that stumps, no matter how irritated, can't move — cows can and will.

Those we love the most seem to reap our worst ideas. Thus was Hilda, my favorite cow, the first object of our torment. Sweet, gentle Hilda, who had saved me time and again from the nasty Jersey, would be rewarded by starring in the first event. The first event in our rodeo was wild bull riding. Well, she did have horns.

Naturally, capturing the bull and getting aboard was the first order of the day. Herb kept Hilda's attention while she contentedly grazed. I approached on the other side from her rear. Hilda munched rapidly, cropping grass to chew later as cud. Unaware, at least, of our intentions, she grazed, paused, swallowed and chopped some more. When close enough to touch her flank, I circled the rope and gently looped it over her head. Unfortunately, the loop flattened during the toss and trickled between her horns scaring the flies from her head. She paused in her feeding long enough to give me a grateful glance. Practicality ascended over feigned bravado, so I walked up, looped the rope over her head and tightened it loosely around her neck. Herb came up on the other side and we led the docile Hilda to a nearby stump.

"You first," we simultaneously suggested.

"You're my guest," I uttered a by now, trite retort.

"No way, it's your cow."

Wasting time was always counter-productive in those too short summer days, and besides, Hilda was casting longing glances at the clover infested pasture grass. I climbed the stump, braced carefully against her broad back and swung my self aboard. Hilda's huge brown eyes widened in wonder, eventually becoming a doleful stare. Her body shuddered menacingly, as she adjusted to this old friend turned into a parasite. Her tail twitched excitedly. The horseflies, sensing a change in their environment, sought new hosts. With intense concentration, I nervously awaited the explosion of this "wild bull." Was it imagination, or did the sun choose that very moment to hide behind a

Rodeo!

cloud, casting a dark pall on the pasture? Herbie stepped nervously away and waited, hoping to watch me jolted upward into next never. My stomach churned, hoping that it would only hurt for a little while.

In wide eyed disappointment, Hilda took a tentative step away from the stump and dropped her head menacingly. Without warning she then terrorized the nearest clumps of grass, grabbing mouthful after mouthful, ignoring the intruder on her back. She apparently had decided that the extra weight was just compensation for protection from the ever annoying horseflies.

Doing eight seconds in perfect form on that wild bull was a cakewalk. Herbie, mumbling under his breath, led Hilda back to the stump and climbed on behind me. We, to the best of our knowledge, successfully pioneered the first double bareback bull ride in rodeo history. Shortly, boredom consumed our excitement and we slid down, happy to be unbruised, but still itching for excitement.

Old folks used to say that curiosity killed the cat, never extending that trait to include most young animals. That day it would almost turned a heifer into veal. Minotaur, his inquisitiveness whetted by our riding of Hilda, signified his presence by butting Herbie. Well, Minotaur's nose between Herbie's legs from behind was almost a butt. Minotaur was only looking for another udder. Herb didn't take kindly to the idea. His idea of pay backs was ...

"Calf roping!" Again concurrent conclusions were verbalized stereophonically. We retrieved the coiled lariat and continued flinging wild tosses at the now excited calf. After alternating throws at the prancing and dodging Minotaur, Herb finally made a successful toss while both of them were running at full speed. It was a magnificent roping to my way of thinking. For an instance, even Herbie flashed a glance of sheer glee at his success in roping the elusive beast. Minotaur had a somewhat altered view of the entire affair. Lacking the mature patience of Hilda, Minotaur became increasingly nettled with each unsuccessful toss. When the odious piece of rope finally settled over his head and tightened perceptively on his neck, his stampede instinct took over. Heels lashed rearward. His rump rose majestically. When

Didja' Ever Make Butter?

his four feet once again hit the ground, the terrorized calf bolted.

Like rodeo wranglers before him, Herbie had wrapped the rope around his wrist to better hang on. His strength, unfortunately, was no match for the now berserk, two hundred pound calf. Herbie's feet became a blur, as he negotiated a semi-balanced, staggered kind of dance until the first dewberry vine caught his bare ankles and pitched him forward into a perfect swan dive. Now, hopelessly entangled with the rope, he proceeded to plow the lush grass with his nose, creating a series of random furrows that rivalled the rabbit runs. The stickers and dewberry vines performed beyond the call of duty. With extra effort they effectively prevented chiggers and ticks from clinging to his bare parts. Ample evidence remained of their efficiency in scraping off the stubborn critters.

Why he hung on to the rope, I couldn't imagine at the time. He mumbled something about having to hang on for eight seconds. This proved to be a truly unfortunate choice. If he had released at six seconds, he would have avoided the ignominious happenstance of finding the largest, freshest cow flop in the pasture. But he didn't. At least he didn't see it coming and scream.

Face first he took the plunge. It must have greased his slide considerably, as he seemed to pick up speed, but a great deal of the manure was scooped down the front of his overalls in the process. I have since argued that it "squooshed" all the way down his trousers and came out the bottom like toothpaste out of a tube, but Herbie swears to this day that it merely fell through when he stood up. Nevertheless, he was a sorry sight and a far worse smell. He was a multi-sensory disaster. He never mentioned why, but I saw him brush his teeth real frequently for the next few days.

Grandma's wash line unfortunately preceded my buddy through the pasture fruit. It was never the same. From white to instant brown, the stain never came out. Neither did the smell. Herbie was more fortunate. The smell came right out of his jeans. Between scrubbing with Fels Naptha Soap and soaking in liquid bleach, he probably had the distinction of wearing the first stone washed denim in St. Louis,

Rodeo!

fully thirty years before it became an expensive fad. In those days, to his dismay, it branded him as an object of ridicule.

The whole incident had me so pumped with adrenaline that I considered for a moment riding the Jersey, but Herb's odor made rodeo seem less inviting than the nearest swimming hole.

We ate dinner on the porch. Grandma wasn't pleased with us. Grandma and Grandpa didn't seem to believe that we got that smelly playing rodeo, at least the way we told the story. Our version didn't mention the clothesline.

Grandpa's intuition filled in the gaps when he found Minotaur that evening and took the rope off the calmer, but grateful calf. I think from his silence that Grandpa had guiltily rejected lynching, as the logical course of action. I'm sure his decision was not based on kindness toward me and Herbie. He simply concluded that the rope was too weak for a double hanging.

Catfishin'

Complacent waters
Curved rod, taut stretched line
Moby Dick on six pound test

Thick algae choked fallen leaves, as it crawled across sparse pockets of water. A matched set of frog eyes bulged from the muck. A lonely, rock hard turtle head protruded to suck a breath of air. Discounting a few surviving crawdads and a speed skating water spider, the creek was severely dry and devoid of its usual plentiful life. Even the birds were conversing from afar.

    A plumper imitation of Huck Finn, had walked our creek's half mile length that day. A spear of grass, now mandated for this rustic setting, since mentioned by Mr. Twain, formed a jaunty angle with the corner of my mouth. A straw hat, too new for Huck, was squared on top of my sun bleached head of hair. Freckles were a solid brown tan. The rope belt was absent. The bare feet were authentically coated with native clay powder to complete the classic portrait. A seven foot hickory pole was balanced carefully over my shoulder. The fishing line's excess dangled around my neck like a necklace from Tiffany's. The line was a length of twine mated to a piece of leader. The hook, fastened to the end of the line, was stuck into the smooth handle of the pole. The mandatory cork bobber jiggled like a jeweled pendant, as I walked along. The bobber was a piece of cork through which the line had been threaded. The cork, salvaged from the rare opening of a wine bottle, was secured by a hand whittled peg jammed securely into the hole through which the line passed.

Thirst and the frustration of the fruitless wanderings led to the cooling waters of the cistern. I spun the handle and the precious liquid splashed out for Spot and me. Visions of fish unfound festered in my mind.

"Spot, there's more fish in the horse trough than the whole damn creek." I often practiced men's talk when alone with her. Spot understood and pushed her head under my hand. She lapped greedily at the cool water cranked from the creaking pump, then dried her tongue gratefully on my face. Like most dogs, she thought her kiss worthy, only if it left a large wet imprint. Such pure love she offered. Adults found this unbounded affection from dogs annoying. On the other hand, some diapered baby could slobber sour spit all over them and leave them in ecstasy. Who's to figure?

The steady rasp of the buck saw located Grandpa for me. I set the fishing pole by the skinning tree and followed Spot to the woodshed. Spot ran ahead to greet him and scout for Rommel. Rommel was never a threat to me when Spot was nearby. It was a Mexican standoff. Spot was forbidden to eat a live chicken, but defense of family was an appropriate way to acquire an edible dead chicken. As long as Rommel didn't attack me, Spot couldn't attack Rommel. The arrangement suited me just fine.

"There's not enough water in the creek to rust a hook." I planned my opening line carefully. I knew where I wanted the conversation to lead and wanted to begin subtlety.

"You don't say," Grandpa grunted without looking up. He sounded enthralled. I had his attention.

"Guess we'll eat beans and corn bread again tonight."

"Probably." Same tone, attention still on the saw. I sensed his grave concern about supper. Did I detect fear of starvation on his face? He continued sawing, pausing intermittently to move the length of wood into a new cutting position.

Didja' Ever Make Butter?

"Grandma's fried catfish would have been outstanding, but there isn't a enough water in the creek to keep the frogs wet." He continued sawing.

"Can I split some of that for you?" Of course, I wanted Grandpa favorably inclined to go fishing with me in a body of water big enough to hold fish. Logic whispered that if the wood box was full, the milking done early and the cantankerous Model A were to start quickly, we might have time to drown a worm in Mr. Queeny's lake. Obviously my plan was having zero effect on Grandpa. I turned in despair, surrendering to the cruel fates. His voice hit me in the back.

"Get the cows fed and watered. We'll milk early today. I'll finish the wood while you fetch the cows. Stop and let Grandma know that you and I are going to Queeny's and catch us some catfish." Grandpa didn't miss a stroke with the saw. I'll bet he didn't even look up, but I think I saw the fleeting glimpse of a grin dart across his face. How did he do it? All the way home I had conspired how to fool him into taking me to the best fishing lake in Missouri. As usual, he was five miles ahead of my best strategy. The good side was that we were going fishing, real honest to goodness, pole bending fishing.

The thick layer of foam on the milk buckets attested to the power of and rapidity with which the streams of milk had been extracted from the cows. We could strain and separate it after dark, but for now, the Sirens were calling from their shoals. The old Ford was sputtering eagerly. Grandpa grabbed some necessities and I saw two old, but real store bought, poles lying across the rear seat. Paradise to me was a huge lake two miles away. Grandpa was one of the privileged people permitted on our neighbor's fishing and hunting sanctuary. It seemed gigantic to me, but in reality, the lake was only five acres in size and probably no more than fifteen feet at its deepest part, that part being near the middle of earthen dam.

We drove right on the dam, twelve feet wide on top. Lush hardwoods surrounded the head of the lake. Blackberries covered the dry side of the dam that blocked off the valley between two small hills. Years of rain water had filled the dam enough to overflow the swales

Catfishin'

on each end of the dam. Two fingers knifed into the woods giving the lake the appearance of a tooth. Wild flowers decorated the homes of muskrats and native birds. Hunting was forbidden, but limited fishing, meaning family and a few selected friends, was allowed.

As soon as my foot touched the ground, I heard the splashing of huge bullfrogs leaping from the bank into the depths. Sparse lily pads at the corners of the dam, provided cover from marauders. Beady eyes could be seen investigating this latest menace to their environment. A bass jumped. I watched fascinated, as widening ripples marked his passing. Across the lake, birds and squirrels were heard cavorting in the trees. The woods walked right down to the water. Once before, I watched a doe and her fawn glide silently to the shore and drink deeply before melting once more into the shadows.

"Come on, let's do it." Grandpa intruded into my fascinating memories. He was already pressing dough bait onto a number six treble hook. The ancient rod and reels weren't fancy, but it wouldn't do to use a hickory pole in this lake. Grandpa gently arched the pole back over his head and gently started the whole rig forward in a smooth accelerating motion. At a precise point, high over his head, he released his thumb from the reel and I watched the baited hook sail gracefully out, before plopping into the water. While it settled slowly to the bottom, he explained that you had to be careful casting dough bait as it could easily be yanked off the hook. He took great care molding each bait into perfect teardrop shaped lumps that completely covered the deadly three pronged hooks. Satisfied that the bait had settled amongst the bottom feeding catfish, he tightened the line and set the pole against a forked stick jammed into the dam.

One of the attractions of catfishin' is the leisurely nature of the sport. Once the line was taut, all you did was wait until appetite and nose led the victim to what you hoped was an irresistible snack.

Crappie and sunfish, being of a voracious nature, greedily bite incessantly, if at all. So long as a remnant of worm remains on the hook, they methodically seek to remove it. They demand an inordinate amount of attention for their size, but if one feels energetic, the

Didja' Ever Make Butter?

lively denizens can provide unlimited action. With a hickory pole and a can of worms, it was all business and absolutely no challenge to bring home a bucketful in a couple of hours.

Bass required huge amounts of energy and savvy, both physical and mental. I know that I am smarter than a fish, but my success over the bass family is limited to one isolated victory. I relish with psychotic pleasure that only triumph over the wily species. It was crisp day in November, not your usual fishing time, in fact, it was deer season. For almost three hours I maintained silent watchfulness over the trail below my stand. A crystalline brook, four feet wide, meandered around the trees, scrubs and brush below. One tree, larger then its neighbors, fanned roots over and into the water. A rather large bass had grinned evilly at me all afternoon, as it lazed mockingly in and out from under those sheltering roots. Somehow he knew that I never saw a bass when fishing for bass. He seemed complacently aware that deer, not he, were in season at the moment. As the sun crept below the horizon and twilight invaded the lengthening shadows, that fish leered at me one last time. I was about to leave without even seeing a deer. For reasons known only to God that fish spit water at me in derision. That did it. In a moment of insanity (my plea, if the statute of limitations has not expired), I stared back at him through the scope of my rifle, then in a murderous rage, sent 180 grains of lethal lead right between his eyes. No fish ever tasted as good as that one. In less than thirty minutes, he went from smart-aleck to appetizer.

"Look, the pole is twitching." The sound of Grandpa's voice brought me back. Barely, had the second line hit the water, when the first pole twitched nervously. Grandpa had gotten a most unappetizing chunk of chicken liver to cling tentatively to the second hook. He sailed it carefully out and into the lake. He set the pole on a second forked stick after once again tightening the line.

Unhurriedly, he lifted the now bending first pole from the ground and watched, as the line began to slowly walk away from him. He gave the fish a bit more slack, then locked the reel. He extended the rod and reel in front of him and when the line tensed, he pulled sharply

Catfishin'

upward to set the hook. The rod bent almost double, as he lifted it over his head, but the line would not move. It was a very large fish, or a king sized snag.

Certain that the hook was indeed imbedded, Grandpa eased the pressure. He kept the line tight and his pole high, but didn't let the pole bend as severely. For several minutes a stalemate ensued.

"I guess it's snagged on a submerged log." Grandpa pulled every which way trying to move that line. Something was hooked real good. He held the pole pointed straight at the spot on the water into which the line disappeared and tugged until the drag clattered in its distinctive grinding chatter. Then almost imperceptibly, the line crept slowly forward. Either the log had pulled loose from the bottom muck, or something alive was about to make its move. It was the latter. Lazy and slow, but extremely powerful, the almost ten pound catfish began his adagio of annoyance. The mettle of the six pound line was about to receive the ultimate test. Grandpa knew this fish was special. He began the dance of the fisherman. Walking first one way, then another. Arms akimbo, feet slipping and sinking, he dueled that critter better than any dirt farmer in the county could have. Through it all he never let that line get slack, or tight enough to break. Luckily the water by the dam was open, that is free from cattails and lily pads that snag and break lines. In what seemed like an eternity, a huge bewhiskered head emerged, as the gigantic fish glided slowly up to the bank. With utmost care, the fish was transferred almost tranquilly to the stringer and settled back into the water.

My eyes were dry from staring. Compared to a large three-quarter pound blue gill, this ten pound monster was the biggest living fish I had ever seen. Visions of fresh, fried catfish were already causing my mouth to water.

The other pole was almost bent double!

Summer Fun

Dark, damp, constant cool
Candles flicker, then expire
Claustrophobia

The sun flared in a relentless effort to convert humidity to steam. The creek was an arid collection of stones interrupted by occasional damp nosegays of reindeer moss. The sweltering, summer day clung like a second skin. The humidity was so high that it was easier to get a drink breathing than from the arid creek. Herbie and I were bored, but too hot and uncomfortable for any strenuous activity. Grandma and Grandpa were napping, as were all other sensible members of the farm family. Spot lolled in a dust bowl under the snowball bush. The chickens hid in the shade of the barn. Kate and Pete were soundless in the stable. Only the raucous buzz of insects disturbed heavy, quiet air.

Herbie was spending another week on the farm with me. Our explorations kept us out of mischief the first four days. Herb had visited, but never lived on a farm. Taking a break from the daily chores, we splashed in the cool water from the cistern and drank deeply. One chore remained. Then youthful spirits would be on the loose until we brought the cows home that afternoon. The handful of light duties that we were assigned, served only to stir our blood for action. You could say it awakened our muscles like a pre-race exercise. Yeah, we were ripe for roguery.

Summer Fun

Eggs had been gathered from the hen house and placed in the pantry. Herb quickly learned how to bluff the terrible, setting red hen. The stock were watered. That was always the hardest job I had. Carrying a brim full bucket of water was tricky. I wasn't strong enough, yet, to handle two at a time and achieve a modicum of balance. Consequently, I learned to walk curved sideways, resigned to losing a third of the water on the way to the stable. Eventually, I attained a level of competence adequate for keeping my shoes dry. Of course, by the next day I was strong enough to carry two buckets at the same time and forced to learn a new technique once again.

Firewood spilled from the overflowing wood bin behind the kitchen stove. Alone it took me two trips, even extending my load limits, to fill the always hungry box, but with Herbie, we topped it off in one load.

The drip pan from the icebox had been splashed onto the blooming rainbow of zinnias that framed the back porch. Grandma's tea kettle was full and slowly simmering on the side burner of the stove. The drinking bucket was brim full on the sink. After we drove the cows to the back pasture, we were free till milking time.

Spot explored the familiar trails leading to the pasture. She exhibited excitement and curiosity no matter how any times she had sniffed the same bush, tree, or pile of leaves. She could read volumes with her nose. Spoor that completely escaped the "sniffers" of her two legged companions, could whip her into an excited frenzy, instantly. Not today, even Spot's enthusiasm wilted in the heat. The only sounds came from the dull plodding of the cows hooves and the incessant, vibrating cry of the cicadas.

We anticipated a cooling dip in the creek, but our spirits sagged when we saw the desiccated stream bed. Spot searched for crawdads to chase in a muck covered murky pool. She lapped gingerly at water too dirty to touch, then resumed her meandering. The cows ambled lazily toward the back pasture. We closed the gate behind the last fly swishing tail. They would be softly mooing at the same gate, ready to head home by late afternoon.

Didja' Ever Make Butter?

Herb saw the tree tops swaying almost imperceptibly on the hill. "Maybe there is a cool breeze up there."

Certainly nothing was stirring in the hollow by the creek. We decided without discussion, to climb the hill. The slope was gentle, but it now resembled a mountain, as it stared menacingly down at us. Suddenly, it was a challenge. It was there. We laughed and ran upward through the lush pasture grass. Within seconds our burst of energy waned and deserted us. Our youthful gallop became a trot, then a labored shuffle. The flaxen grasses became interspersed with unseen bushes, dewberry vines and thistles. Sumac and blackberries reinforced the obstructions in our path. We paused to reconnoiter at the edge of the dense woods. The same sounds of silence greeted us. Entering the seldom traveled virgin area, we crunched ever upward in search of the breeze. If the breeze was still there, it remained hushed and invisible above the thick hardwood canopy of oaks, hickorys, wild cherries and walnuts. Maples occasioned more open areas and a few carefully secreted persimmon trees grew on hilltop clearings.

We paused near the crest. Our breathing was as loud as Spot's panting. Usually, early morning coolness and the rising sun awakened and refreshed the almost dormant life. A rain shower, or a cool northerly breeze would do the same. On this hot day, nature was breathless. It was so quiet, that you could hear the bees hum.

"Do you hear that?" I asked.

"Yeah, what is it? Is it dangerous?" Herbie asked.

Well, I thought, maybe Herbie hasn't learned everything in four days. Then out loud, once again, "Naw, it's just a beehive in a hollow tree."

"Must be pretty close, if we can hear it. Let's look for it," Herbie suggested, looking sharply upward. Being an extremely thin boy, he really looked comical with his adam's apple protruding like a second nose. My plump and his bones were quite a contrast.

We spotted a snag that leaned precariously against the branches of some neighborly hickory trees. The partially fallen dead tree seemed like a good spot to begin our quest. One of us could shinny up the

Summer Fun

snag and be able to scan other nearby trees for the hive. I carefully weighed my manners and the dangers of climbing that precarious piece of dry wood. I concluded that being how he was my guest, it only made sense to allow Herbie the honors. The problem was how to make him demand the privilege and not question my rare act of generosity.

"You're my guest. I guess you get to climb up and see if you can spot the hive." Now Herbie wasn't completely stupid. Over the years we had "pranked" each other enough to be wary of pro-offered invitations to anything. He responded appropriately.

"Last time I climbed a tree, you yanked the ladder and left me up there for hours." His memory was infallible.

"Herbie, there's no ladder here. Besides your Mom cured me of ever doing that again." I recalled that when he finally got down, Herbie punched me without warning, right on the nose. Consequently, I chased him him home with the blood of revenge in my eyes. That blood of revenge disappeared exactly one half of an instant after a frying pan clanged off the top of my head. I can still see his mom standing there, hands on hips staring witheringly at me. Her look clearly said, "Another step and it happens again."

Between her demeanor and the horrible hollow sound, I left in great haste. I tore down the street toward home, suddenly needing to visit a bathroom. The three of us laughed for years about that incident. Today, someone would have turn her in for child abuse. She didn't hit me hard and it did put the blood of revenge in proper perspective.

Not convinced that it was totally safe for me to scale that dead tree, I made one last effort to defer to Herbie's prerogative.

"Can't climb it, can ya?" I deviously taunted him. Everyone knows a dare can't be refused, at least, I fervently hoped so. To my relief, Herbie disappeared up that trunk without another word. The snag was leaning heavily on some not so brawny green limbs of the surrounding trees. Having lost its balance in a recent summer storm, the dead tree had fallen and lodged on its neighbor's green foliage, too light to complete its journey to the ground. When the leaves shed in the Fall it would likely complete its descent. Naturally, that wasn't to be.

Didja' Ever Make Butter?

We should have heeded nature's warning. Spot was nowhere to be seen. Ever notice when your dog disappears, trouble is usually lurking. Sensible creatures want no part of Mother Nature's accidents and some inner sense seems to tell them when to skedaddle. Yeah, Spot was long gone.

As physics and luck would have it, Herbie was unconsciously cast in the role of the straw that broke the camel's back. He was ten feet or more overhead, when I heard the first groans from the complaining branches. Amidst assorted unpleasant sounds, he and the snag began the premature journey through the pliant limbs toward the forest floor.

Fortunately, I moved in the correct direction and had a marvelous view of the dead tree's majestic descent, as well as the ignominious plunge of my friend Herbie. One green branch snapped and others, relieved of their heavy burden, whipped violently upward. Dead twigs popped like a string of firecrackers, sending a shower of debris raining down, harmonizing with Herbie's panicked yowl. Some basal instinct made him leap sideways at the last instant onto something softer than the run away log. Before I could yell timber, it was over. Herbie emerged shaken, but medically stable.

The newest dead fall in the woods had splintered and broken as it crashed against the unyielding earth. Echoes of the frightening incident had hardly quieted, when an angry hum focussed our fragmented psyches. Thousands, no millions of angry insects were emerging from the shattered upper trunk. We had found the hive and the bees had found us!

"Run! Run!" I shouted, not really certain if Herbie could. He could. He did. Momentarily forgetting my manners, I led our panicked flight toward a small nearby cave on the other side of the promontory. We made it, but not unscathed. Purple hearts were the medal of the day. One attacker nailed Herbie on the back of his neck. Another accomplished his kamikaze mission on my right forearm. I frantically prevented several more from making impromptu landings on other parts of my anatomy. Herbie, never the bellwether of good fortune, had two infuriated bees attack him, simultaneously. Both died, but one by suicide as it left its stinger deep in his skin. The other was crushed beyond recognition by a panicked palm. Of course, in consolation, he once again garnered bragging rights for the frightening foray by acquiring more stings than me. At the time it seemed a dubious honor, but it grew in distinction in retelling with each passing year.

With three wounds, pounding hearts and dry mouths, we dived into the dark entrance of the cave. We headed deeply into the dark opening and stopped only after we realized that our pursuers had broken off the chase.

"Are you, okay?"

"It hurts."

"Here, put some mud on it." A small spring kept the opening of the cave moist and a daub of wet earth was always available when you needed it. The primitive cure soon lessened the pain, hearts slowed to normal and the coolness inspired a genesis of giggles. Fear is close to hysteria which is close to giggles and so went the metamorphosis of young emotions. The giggles too, faded, as rest and the appetite for adventure was once again whetted.

"Herbie. There used to be some candles in here." In short order, two candles and some dry matches were found where they had been secreted on a small ledge. The matches were preserved in a small dry container. We quickly lit two candles.

"Where are you going?" Herbie wasn't seeking fresh adventure. He was real content absorbing the cool and watching the flickering flame. Being one sting from the glory of bragging rights, I decided to work my way deeper into the cave.

Even small boys had to crouch, as the roof quickly descended, as if to meet the floor. Out of sight of the entrance, the floor curved quickly downward and twisted to the right. A narrow opening stared like a black eye as you approached. A man could squeeze through, but a boy had no problem at all.

Choosing between loneliness in the proximity of hostile insects, Herbie hesitantly followed the flickering glow of my wax taper. It was a cave devoid of stalactites and stalagmites. I had been in it only

Didja' Ever Make Butter?

twice before and each time only a few yards into it. Of course, it was forbidden territory. No one was ever to enter it without an adult.

Fortunately, it was a simple cave. It had one entrance, one tunnel and no branches. It did have a rather large room that opened just past the narrow neck, through which we were crawling. I had been there once before with a carbide lamp and was somewhat familiar with it.

The room was about twenty feet across and almost tall enough for a man to stand erect in the middle. Roughly round, it had several indentations, like fake tunnel entrances dispersed around its perimeter. My devious mind went into overdrive, "If I can really scare Herbie..."

I entered the room well ahead of my friend and hurried counter clockwise around the wall and planted my candle on a rock in one of the indentations. The dull light from my candle could barely be seen from the tunnel entrance. I went the rest of the way around the cave near the entrance of the eight foot long tunnel. There in the darkness, I hid from the unsuspecting Herbie.

The glow of his candle preceded him. Hesitantly, he penetrated the narrow opening. The candle entered the room before he did. A "poof" of breath and he was without a light.

"My candle went out. Is that your candle over there?" He called in the direction of the glow of my candle. In a heart beat, I returned silently to my wax light and hid in the same crevice. What nefarious plan swirled through my mind remains a mystery, but in my haste, I knocked my candle to the floor of the cave and plunged both of us into utter, stygian blackness. Fortunately, I felt around the damp floor and located the still warm candle, suppressing a laugh.

"Stop fooling around. Light my candle." Herb bravely ordered, but his voice's rising pitch betrayed his rising trepidation.

"I knocked my candle on the floor and it went out, Herbie, but I found it. I'll get a match and light it," I told him reassuringly. I reached in my shirt pocket for the vial of matches. It wasn't there. I figured that it must be in another pocket. Each empty pocket brought about increasing anxiety. Then there were no more pockets. No sweat, I thought. All I have to do is find the tunnel and crawl out.

Summer Fun

"Come on, stop fooling, light the candle." Herbie pleaded.

"I can't find the matches." His next sounds were unintelligible. He kind of gurgled and I heard a sharp intake of his breath. His movements were easily heard and reheard in the natural echo chamber. The scratch of his jeans and shoes against the pebbly floor located him somewhere over there, in the darkness. I heard a terrible clunk, as if his head had hit the wall, or as if a rock had hit his head. His scream froze my blood. Then silence. I was frozen with fright.

"You're next." Low and guttural, the threat reverberated in the deathly silence.

"Herbie, where are you?" Fright transformed to abject terror at the absence of his voice. Soft, almost imperceptible sounds of movement penetrated my circle of fear. I stopped breathing. I withdrew to the innermost reaches of the cave trying to force my eyes to see in the darkness. Except for my shallow, rasping breathing, there was only tomb like silence.

I waited in frozen panic for what seemed like hours. It was more likely a minute or two. I breathed, but only when my body demanded it.

"Herbie" I whispered. Overwhelming, consuming silence continued to close in on me. My trepidation ballooned toward panic. I knew whatever had gotten Herbie was stalking me as well. I held out my hand to intercept the invisible threat. I could feel nothing but the cave wall and a cold knot of fear. I moved first one way then another, trying to avoid the certainty of encounter. Cowardice had over ridden any rational thought. At last, a dull spot of light caught my eye. I had found the tunnel to safety. The bee sting paled in comparison to the knots the cave raised on my head. Moving with a speed born from fear, I bounced through the tunnel like a rock falling down the face of a cliff.

Finally, the brighter glow of daylight was before me. I could see. I saw safety. I could hear. I heard laughter. Herbie's laughter. The peccadillos of my past had immunized my friend against falling into my latest trap. When I sprung the trap, I had caught myself. Herbie

Didja' Ever Make Butter?

had cleverly reversed the results letting me feel the sting of my own embarrassment. His faked basso profundo voice in the echoing cave had stimulated my imagination into a knee quaking, spine chilling embarrassment, for which I never forgave him. For almost an hour.

Floating

Surprise everyone!
Unexpected visitor
How about a swim?

Hot sunshine whetted a burning desire for relief in the icy water. My hand languished invitingly in the cold spring fed stream. Its contrast with rest of my irradiated arm sent waves of goose bumps ebbing and flowing over pleasantly tormented skin. I splashed cupped hands of the clear cool liquid over my face, writhing deliciously in the brief deliverance from the heat. The cold droplets stimulated fledgling muscle flexes from my dirty neck to my pink belly. It was a pleasurably, self inflicted mixture of sensations, made possible by the lazy float trip, down the Jack Forks, on that hot August day.

Huge trees held hands across the narrow span of the whispering river. At most, forty feet wide, the gravel bottomed, spring fed, water way meandered slowly during this dry season as contrasted with the swift dangerous race that manifested its swelling during the spring rains. From time to time, the Queen Mary would scrape annoyingly across a too shallow gravel bar, over which, mere inches of water trickled. Usually, we pushed with the paddles and floated on. At other times we were stopped cold, forced to dismount in order to push our homemade boat free. The slow passage lent itself to appreciating the

Didja' Ever Make Butter?

lovely panorama of water carved banks, recessed limestone bluffs and the plethora of vegetation rife upon both sides of the Ozark stream.

Floating in WWII Missouri was an experience somewhat different from today. During my first great war, you could float for days, and with luck, never encounter another person. There was no staccato firing, unmuffled roar of an outboard. There were no shouts from beer swilling, pot smoking environmental rapists. Tranquillity generated appreciation then. One heard birds, the sounds of fish jumping and the occasional bass voice of a lonesome bullfrog. It presented the opportunity for the mind to work creatively. Instead of boisterous people boiling over with self-importance and boomboxes, we listened to the songs of the water interacting with the rocks, snags and shore. The chatter of squirrels in raucous conversation with jabbering birds of all description created a background symphony. In retrospect, I remember it as nature's valium. It could relax one into a Rip Van Winkle's nap. In early summer, the harmony of the birds chatting and bragging about their flightless fledglings, filled the dark shadows in the lush branches. Distant cattle could be heard mooing sporadically to each other, as the afternoon milking time neared. Other unidentified mysterious sounds from the dark shadows held the sleepy urgings of the water at bay. The mind was free to ponder life's mysteries, or conjure whatever images a young mind desired. Visions of bear, bob cats, owls or other totally impossible animals of prey lurked in my fantasies. Branches, reaching out from both shores created deeper shadows that stirred feelings of unease. Nature's carefully selected sound track produced a certain level of terror in those dark areas.

Herb and I were almost teenagers then. We had talked for days to convince Grandpa that we could safely float the small stream in the Queen. The wood box was always full and water was always available to the chickens, cows, mules and Grandma. The dish towel was fought over after dinner. It had been an eye brow raising performance. With these examples of impeccable behavior and a devotion to chores, previously unheard of, Grandpa had been convinced of our newly developed sense of responsibility and finally said, "I'll talk to the boss."

Floating

No way Grandma would agree to let us make that float by ourselves. With downcast demeanors, we followed him to the house, carrying the milk buckets. To think we had wasted all that good behavior and expended so much energy doing all of those the chores. Women never let kids do anything. Was there no justice? Maybe she wouldn't remember the bees, or the egg fight, or the clothes line.

"...and without being told. The stream is quite low this time of year and both of them swim real good. I can drop them before I go to town and pick them up at three mile point later in the day," Grandpa's speech could have talked Hitler out of Poland that day.

Grandma frowned silently and looked from one to the other of each of us. With a final stern glance at Grandpa she finally spoke, "Well, just this once." What had been but a dream then was now a reality. We were enjoying it to the max. It was hot and we were constantly thirsty. Our long-sleeved work shirts lay crumpled over our shoes in the bottom of the boat. Our overalls hung loosely from the shoulder straps, rumpling over our bare feet. The water ran clear beneath us. You could drink the water back then and we did, slurping a handful every so often just because it was there. Of course, each mini drink provided an excuse to flick water on each other. "Don't get caught doing it" was the name of the game. If you weren't seen, you weren't guilty, regardless of the fact that no one else was within a mile of us, that could have propelled the water. It was silliness that always ended in giggles.

We rounded a bend into a deep narrow channel where the trees formed a totally enclosed canopy. The sun was blotted like an eclipse. Vines hung menacingly, almost touching the deep pool. It was a perfect place for a quick swim. I grabbed a vine and hung on to stop our drift. The water seemed to be at least six feet deep, or so.

"Herb, it's perfect here, let's take a dip."

"They told us not to get out of the boat unless it was really shallow." Herb reminded me of one of the many rules Grandma had listed for us.

"It's a great spot. Let's just take a quick dip to cool off. *Grandma will never know.*" Little did we recognize the irony in those words, then.

Didja' Ever Make Butter?

Wet clothes wouldn't dry by the end of the float. Soaked clothes would be a dead give away of the disobedience of two guys restricted to the boat. Our only choice was to swim au natural. It became a giggle filled race to see who could strip the fastest. Straps were peeled from sun tinged shoulders and dropped along with underwear to the bottom of the boat. The last vestiges of civilization were still settling onto the bottom of the boat when it hit.

The only larger snake I have seen was the thirty foot python they force fed once a week at the St. Louis Zoo. Our snake wasn't thirty feet long, but it was at least eight feet from head to tail. It was easily as thick as man's arm. The elevated head, sinuously moving from side to side, was surely searching for its next meal. Herb knew that the next meal was him. I argue, certain in my truth exposing terror, that the huge reptile's next repast was me. Instincts prevented either of us from gathering the evidence necessary to winning the argument, or even starting it.

Our simultaneous howls of fright perfectly demonstrated a multi-watt stereophonic system, years before its invention. As you can undoubtedly visualize, screams of utter terror ended in gurgles, as we sank beneath the icy water. The wailing immediately resumed when we broke the surface scrambling, swimming and clawing our way to the nearest gravel bar. Walking on water seemed a realistic expectation for an instant. After those panic filled moments passed, we reclaimed a modicum of sanity, as the warm sun and solid land, helped calm our fears. After all, the snake and his accompanying impetus for panic, was rapidly disappearing a down the creek. Momentarily, we felt secure in each other's presence. The nasty invader was welcome to the Queen Mary, now floating high in the water and rapidly away from us .... He was quite welcome ....

"Herbie, he stole our clothes! What are we going to do?" A new emotion replaced the terror. The new feeling resembled panic. Suddenly, each clump of foliage had eyes. A worst nightmare had become real. Suddenly, I was totally self conscious of my nudity. I scrambled back into the cold water and sat down, wishing I was young enough to cry. Herbie was. I pretended not to notice.

Floating

Actually, it turned out better than we deserved. Grandpa, of course, had the fright of his life. He was waiting for us at the pick up point when the empty, or more accurately, apparently empty Queen Mary drifted toward him. He solemnly considered how he would tell Grandma that we had drowned. He found the snake and re-introduced it to its native environment while taking inventory of our clothes. Putting two and two together, he proceeded to pull the Queen back upstream with the definite thought of drowning us himself. His joy at finding us nude and chilled, but safe prompted him to choose an alternate plan of action that included a pledge of secrecy among the "men" of the family. Not one to lie, Grandpa rationalized that if told the truth, Grandma would never again have a restful moment when we were out of her sight. I would not care to debate his decision with Gloria Steinem, or Jane Fonda, thank you.

Fencing is Fun

Strands of wire, posts of cedar
Horseshoe shaped staples
Be careful it bites

The pale first light of dawn penetrated the crack between my pillow and the huge featherbed. You knew your time had come. Instinctively, you knew when it had come for you. Insidiously, it would creep up the stairs and surrounded my bed. When the aroma of fresh perked coffee blended with that of frying slab bacon, you knew your time had come. Your time to get up. Visions of hot biscuits slathered with yesterday's butter began to penetrate your slowly awakening senses. I heard the big spoon clanking the sides of the skillet. My mind easily pictured the thickening cream gravy.

Peeking and planning, I located every last piece of clothing before making the frigid dash from bed clothes to farm clothes. In time, I learned the trick of pulling the clothes into the bed when I heard Grandma clanking at the wood stove. That extra five minutes of stalling was usually enough to remove the chilled rigor mortis from lying overnight on the ice-like floor. Still, one didn't dawdle in covering freshly exposed skin to the icy air in the unheated upstairs bedroom. Ice, real half inch thick ice, sealed the corners of the window. In kindness, Grandma had left the door open at the foot of the staircase

Fencing is Fun

allowing warm, fragrant air from the cook stove to drive back some of the morning chill.

Grandpa was clumping his high tops on the porch to shake off the morning frost and any barnyard debris. Morning chores had passed me by once again. "Just as well," I thought, shivering into my jeans and heading for the steps, as I buttoned them, "I hate water sloshing from the bucket into my shoes on a cold day."

"I was just getting ready to call you. You would sleep forever, but never through a meal." She set a huge plate of eggs, bacon, biscuits and sausage gravy in front of Grandpa. Mine was next with hardly a smidgens difference in portions. Something about growing boys needing to eat. His steaming cup of black coffee contrasted with my cup of milk that Gram had splashed with a flavoring dash of the aromatic percolation.

"Fence needs working on today," he mumbled, pushing his words past a fork full of breakfast, "There's a gate sagging and several posts rotted off." It was Thanksgiving break and I had four wonderful days to spend with Grandpa. There wouldn't be a turkey, but no one would miss it with the huge platter of chicken and dumplings that would take its place. Most of the field work was done. There was corn to shell, but most of the crops were cribbed, baled, bagged or shipped. It was time to cut wood, repair equipment, mend fence and hunt.

Grandpa hitched Kate to the box wagon and checked to see that he had the "necessaries" loaded. The fence posts were six foot long cedar tree trunks that had aged for a year. As a rule you put one foot in the ground for every two feet in the air. Four foot fences were sufficient for cows and mules. Eight foot couldn't stop deer and nobody tried. Pigs had their own kind made from hog wire. It looked like a bunch of rectangles and came in various sizes depending on whether it was to be used for a farrowing, or a hog pen.

In the wagon, were hammers, fence nails, barbed wire, fence puller, shovel, posthole digger and heavy, leather gloves. An old bucket had several small tools inside, including metal files and a wire cutter. A double bit axe was wrapped in a gunny sack and tossed in last. Grandpa let me hold the reins while driving to get the posts.

Didja' Ever Make Butter?

After tossing in six posts, we headed for the hill by the persimmon tree about halfway to the back line of the slightly more than 100 acre spread. The farm was roughly shaped like a long rectangle running south to north. Most of the farm lay north from the house and the barn. Topographically, the land was higher in the middle and seemed to slope gently upward toward the north. A rutted wagon track roughly climbed gradually up the middle of this long slope, referred to as a hog back ridge.

Several gullies sliced the edges of the hillside, as run-off water inexorably changed the landscape. In time, even the durable cedar posts succumbed to the ravages of nature. The results could be seen. The sagging wire was now being dragged down by one post that was using the wires for support. The heavy rains had washed it completely out of the ground. Grandpa urged Kate as close to the disintegrating fence, as possible, unhitched her, put on her halter and let her graze. Kate would stay close. Pete would be long gone.

Grandpa checked the wire to see if it could be restrung, or would have to be replaced. A tug of his leather gloves and the wire parted. Out came the wire cutters and he soon freed the broken posts from their barbed wired supports. The broken posts were pitched into the wagon to be used as firewood. He pointed to a spot and suggested I try the posthole digger there. Had I been more alert, I would have noticed a certain glint in his eye that might have warned me of the set up. One downward thrust of the digger revealed what I had missed. The digger resonated in my hands, as if it had exploded. The ground was dry, hard clay. Hardpan. It would be a long day. Laughing, Grandpa took the digger and made it cut dirt like you wouldn't believe. Grandpa had the six holes ready in about forty-five minutes. Not bad for a man close to his seventieth birthday.

He set a post in each hole and tamped dirt in the bottom to let them stand unsupported. He pulled off his straw hat to take a blow and dragged his blue sleeved shirt across his forehead. He asked me to take the bucket and fill it from the creek. The creek was about 150 yards down the hill. It was boring watching him work so hard. The hike would be fun.

Fencing is Fun

Off I ran, heading straight for the persimmon tree, which was roughly in line with the small stream. The bright orange, plump, round fruit had a hint of white frosting on the outside. The dark brown stem accented it in perfect fall colors. The sweet succulent meat was a fall treat and Jack Frost's recent visit insured quality taste.

"Boy! I need that bucket of water."

"I'll bring you some persimmons, too," I hollered back. Gunga Din stuck a handful of fruit into his pocket and headed down the hill. Off to the right the flat rocks were in view. A deep pool in the midst of the unusual formation would be perfect for dipping the bucket full without getting soaked feet on this crisp November day. A wide outcropping of limestone formed the creek bed for a hundred feet at this spot. It was pitted with various size pools, but much of the white rock formation was above water and made perfect sunning spots when swimming in the summer. The creek threaded its way through the alabaster slabs, as water will do, patient and unstoppable.

I slipped and slid down the loose dirt and rocks to the creek bed. Spot pranced ahead and quickly lapped at the water assuring herself that it was still wet. I spotted several flat pebbles, the kind for skipping on water. Smoothed by the water until they were flat, at least on one side, preferably two, I selected some for throwing. The channel was narrow this time of year, but a few accurate tosses would still get three or four skips. The first one skipped all the way over the creek and landed high on the other bank. It took three more tries to get a third skip. Satisfied that it was good rock skipping day, I looked for more rocks.

A straight branch about two feet long caught my eye. I don't know why it looked like a baseball bat, but suddenly I was thinking summer. I picked up a small round rock. I threw it up in front of me and swung that stick. Thwack! It popped off the stick, a sizzling line drive that landed about fifty feet away and ricocheted across the hard flat white surface into the water. The next swing missed and then a third swing sent a pebble soaring in a high graceful arch. I could hear the applause. A big number nine was on my back. I watched the ball sail higher and higher, clearing both the rocks and the water.

Didja' Ever Make Butter?

"It might be, I could be, it is a home run!" I shouted, imitating Harry Caray, my favorite Cardinal baseball announcer. Enos Slaughter, number nine, the old, country war horse had blasted it. He was my favorite Cardinal back then.

"What home run? Home run, hell! Where is my bucket of water." Grandpa, too was shouting excitedly, as he charged down the hill toward me. I quickly dipped the bucket and scrambled toward him.

Grandpa glared, took the bucket without another word and walked off faster than I could travel. When I caught up to him, he was already pouring water into each post hole. He explained that the water settled and packed the dry dirt. More dry dirt went on top of the damp dirt and a sawed off broken axe handle was used to jam the dirt in around the post. Each post was carefully planted, as he mounded the remaining dirt around each post. They were as solid, as if they were in concrete. Now came the tricky part. Grandpa gave the lower strand of barbwire a turn around the first post next to the new one and drove two staples across the wire. Then he strung the wire from post to post, tacking each wire loosely with one staple into each post. He attached the wire stretcher beyond the last new post.

The stretcher was quite a contraption. Secured to a solid post it had a block and tackle that attached to the wire and then a lever that cranked the wire tight. When the wire was as taut, as a guitar string, Grandpa pounded the staples all the way in, securing the wire. He wrapped the end of the wire around the last post and stapled it double. The whole process was twice repeated. In no time at all, the fence was like new. We gathered the tools and reloaded the wagon.

I wondered what the rest of the day held. Before I could wonder out loud, Grandpa reached under some gunny sacks and pulled out his ancient double barrelled shotgun. "Let's get us a couple rabbits for dinner."

We walked across the hill to the west. The sun was bearing down on the southwestern exposure. A string of scrub brush and a blackberry patch delineated two fields. One field had lain fallow for two years and was only used for picking the plump, purple dewberries in

Fencing is Fun

the early summer. Grandpa suspected the rabbits might be sunning themselves nearby.

He made me walk right behind him. Spot was nearby and Grandpa "shooed" her away. She just chased the rabbits and really didn't know how to hunt like a beagle. Grandpa slowed to a stop and I saw the shotgun come up to his shoulder. The click of the hammers being pulled back by his thumb sounded loud in the silence of the field ... but that's another story.

Stove Wood and Pseudo-Bunny

Carrot in a box - Beware!
Best to dig 'em up
Oops! You're in a stew

Hasenpfeffer simmering in the oven broadcast its spicy aroma into the chilly late November air. The regular whack of the double bladed axe sent piece after piece of oak and hickory flying onto the growing pile of stove wood. The shiver of snow was in the air. Grey skies closed rapidly from the west, racing to pull the gray feather bed over the sinking sun. The wind was gusty, sending sporadic sharp slivers of wind knifing through the farm yard. The dearth of still clinging leaves, one by one, surrendered to the fickle gusts. Golden grass lay in rounded mounds, flattened by repeated frosts, hibernating, awaiting the warm southern sun of spring to reawaken.

Grandpa blew warmly into his thick powerful hands. Calluses, the rewards of years of arduous labor, accented his leathery, heavily veined skin. Again he curled his fingers around his jaw and nose to blow the warm tobacco breath onto his numb digits. I suspect it was directed toward his reddened cheeks and chilled nose, as well. His wool shirt was buttoned to the top. His bib overalls were tautly rounded over his long johns. His three quarter length denim jacket was closed tightly with each brass button carefully fastened. A nondescript, brown, felt

Stove Wood and Pseudo-Bunny

hat sheltered his mostly bald head. Thus fortified, he wielded the axe once more with surgical precision. I marveled at the uniform cuts. Each piece of wood was a perfect thickness for Grandma's wood stove. It would consume a lot of wood today between cooking and heating the old farm house.

He seldom had time for gloves. If made of leather, the dogs stole them at the first opportunity. If cloth, they got wet too quickly. If dry, they tended to be too slick. If the fool things weren't wandering off, they got misplaced and required an inordinate amount of precious time to retrieve them. Besides, Grandpa was good at warming his hands on the farm animals. The cows complained, but only at milking time. Grandpa did wear wool ones when hunting, but that's another story.

It had been a particularly fortunate weekend on the farm. Saturday we had hiked to the woods. Grandpa selected a shag barked hickory snag ready to split and haul for stove wood. The beautiful tree had died when struck by lightning, but after a year of seasoning, was perfect for firewood. A live tree had to dry for a year to burn well. Besides a live tree was a last resort and ideally, was cut to thin out a too thick stand of trees.

The path we took to the woods was circuitous by design. It led past a weathered long box in the garden, about 20 inches long and six inches square. It was concealed between two rows of turnips and baited with a stunted carrot, pulled from the ground a few rows away. Checked daily, the humane traps often produced a plump bunny for the stew pot. A sliding door was suspended by a long stick resting on a fulcrum. Two eyelets were joined to connect the door to the lever. The far end was attached similarly to another shorter stick that went loosely into the box through a hole about an inch around. The shorter piece of wood was notched and carefully hooked onto the roof of the box. A carrot, or some other tidbit was placed at the back of the box away from the door. It was really quite a simple device. Rabbit seeks carrot. Rabbit nudges stick. Gravity does the rest. The inquisitive rabbit was promoted up the food chain. It had been a good week for

Didja' Ever Make Butter?

the humans. The unfortunate bunnies caught earlier in the week were causing the delicious aroma that was conjuring delightful thoughts about dinner. But first a tall, dead hickory tree with bare scraggly limbs and fingers was beckoning for our company.

The waist thick trunk was first peeled of its loose outer bark, which was carefully set to one side. City folks would pay well for real hickory to use on their backyard barbeque pits. (Do you remember those stone and concrete edifices that fired up on summer holidays?) With swift accurate cuts, Grandpa notched the trunk with his keenly sharpened double bit. Ten minutes of sweat rendering swings spread a layer of fresh chips around the tree, now bearing a deep, wedge shaped cut in its side.

It was time for the two man cross cut saw. It was big deal to have the responsibility of manning the cross cut with Grandpa. The long sharp blade was attached to two broom handle like projections. Unlike broom handles, these foot high pieces of hickory were brown from sweat and oil from the hard working hands that powered them. They were silken smooth from years of rubbing and caressing by the calloused hands. They were used to grip and convey the metal monster back and forth across the fibrous wood. With each stroke, the snaggle-toothed, six foot, serrated saw blade sprayed sawdust in an incessant shower at my sturdy ancestor. Occasional spurts came my way, as if an after thought.

"Grandpa, can we check the other traps on the way back?" I talked, because I really wanted him to stop sawing for a minute. My arms felt like lead weights and I needed a blow.

Without missing a stroke, he said, "Check them later. You can do it while I split the trunk into lengths."

Lengths are what he usually called the eight foot pieces of split tree trunk that he hauled on his shoulders to the wood shed. Sometimes he called them splits, which he assured me meant the same thing. I watched him carry four six inch thick lengths at a time, while I struggled with one sledge hammer. I bet those pieces of wood must have weighed twenty or thirty pounds each. The sledge only weighed twelve pounds.

Stove Wood and Pseudo-Bunny

As my strength increased with my years, I realized the lack of saw dust flying in my direction was an unspoken concession to my youth and an accurate measure of my contribution to the felling process. In the truest traditions, Grandpa never uttered a discouraging word on my non-productive performance. He did suggest that I pull the saw and not push it. About the third time this reminder had to be uttered by him, it was accompanied by growls and some words of German intermixed with his steamy breath. I was certain that he would never have uttered those words in Grandma's presence. A keen disappointment was never giving Grandpa the pleasure of watching me match his pile of sawdust. There came a day when I easily could have, but he and the farm were gone by then. I never matched his patience. Never taught my kids how to use a cross cut saw either. The chain saw ended that tradition.

Age and repeated reminders, at last provided the insight, that pushing the blade caused buckling, making Grandpa's pull stroke twice as difficult. When you laid on a saw the way he did, a buckled blade binding in the wood could just about wrench his arms from his shoulders. In a proper rhythm, he needed me to pull the saw straight back preparing the saw for his next power stroke. I thought all along, that I was doing all the work for my "old" relative.

Grandpa could make a tree fall uphill. That may seem like a funny statement, but when the wood had to be carried out of the woods on your shoulders, it was important which way the tree fell. Notches on each side of the tree governed to a major degree the direction of the falling wood. Trees leaning slightly in a wrong direction could be corrected by driving an ash wedge into the upper notch. This forced the tree to disobey gravity, usually. The most obtuse cases were conquered by a block and tackle.

A long rope was tossed over a high limb. This in itself is an art. It is important to get it high enough on the tree to provide adequate leverage. More importantly, a heavy enough weight must be used to pull the free end of the hemp rope far enough down to where you could reach it. Once the loose end was retrieved it was attached to a

Didja' Ever Make Butter?

block and tackle secured to the base of another tree. The trunk could be carefully enticed in the proper direction by the overpowering block and tackle.

There were very few trees that Grandpa couldn't drop on a dime. Many farmers were injured felling trees. Grandpa respected nature in every way and tolerated no horseplay, or inattention. To my knowledge he never got hurt cutting wood. Later I used those lessons many times, impressing, as well as scaring friends and relatives. My skills at felling trees between wires, roofs and other endangered structures seemed awesome to the uninitiated. Lacking Grandpa's conservative bend, I admittedly "showed off" from time to time. Luckily, I never had a serious mistake. One of my favorite students wasn't as fortunate. Jerry Lakin almost got killed when a big tree kicked back and landed on him. He lost a leg and died a few years later from complications. A scholarship at Northwest High School was established in his memory by his loving family.

There is an indescribable thrill caused by the sound of a falling tree. I appreciate and respect nature, trees and animals, as much as anyone. I would never fell a tree for the hell of it, but when needed, there is no hesitation on my part to harvest nature's bounty. Felling a carefully selected tree has almost become a ritual. First come those soft cracks that whisper a warning to the sawyer. A few more strokes of the saw produce loud popping cracks that announce the loss of support, as the last severed fibers part. A crescendo of noise begins as the swishing and "whapping" limbs duel neighboring limbs, as the tree begins its unpracticed, never to be repeated, angry descent. The majestic bass thump of the weighty trunk, "thunking" onto the hard earth, lends a note of finality. An anti-climactic crush and snapping of limbs under the heavy stem continues, then finally subsides, leaving the forest once again silent. Even the birds halt their song in respect. It is a sad, yet glorious moment, that brings a strange thrill. Is it the small assertion of man against a formidable opponent, kind of like tweaking a giant.

"You can check the traps now." Grandpa had already picked up the double bit and was trimming the limbs from the trunk, after which,

Stove Wood and Pseudo-Bunny

we would use the cross cut to measure and cut the eight foot long sections. The splitting would follow. Splitting wood is a science. It is necessary to learn to read a trunk, locate knots, burls and other hindrances to the clean split. Many times a single stroke of the axe can lay open the mightiest piece of wood. Other times every wedge in your arsenal is needed to separate a cohesive log. Some trees like the elm were never split. The grain of an elm is like the blueprint for the Gordian Knot. If an elm had to be felled, it was used to fill a gully.

I hurried for the orchard, knowing Grandpa would need me to help carry tools and wood back to the house. There were three more traps amongst the apple trees. Like the garden trap the first was still open and hoping for company. The second trap invaded my senses long before I actually saw it. I knew at once that a rabbit, unfit for consumption, was inside. The air was no longer filled with the aroma of hasenpfeffer. It had been replaced by the panic sprayed perfume from an extremely frightened skunk. In one of the smarter moves of my young life, I left the trap exactly where it was and ran to report the circumstance to Grandpa.

"It'll be there later. Hand me that wedge." I couldn't believe his apparent lack of interest. He had cut the first eight foot piece by himself and was almost finished splitting it into smaller sections. Light sprinkles of snow laced the gray air. The subject seemed closed, as he continued his efforts. A carefully peeled long pole took shape from an unusually straight branch.

"We'll finish cutting tomorrow, bring this pole," he directed.

The perpetually moving old man shouldered a gunny sack full of tools, balanced the saw on the same shoulder and somehow put two sections of split hickory across the other as he strode quickly up the hill toward the orchard. His nose led him in the right direction toward the now irritated, trapped skunk. It slowly dawned on me the purpose of the almost ten foot pole. Years later when the story was retold, the pole had grown to eleven feet. That way it could be used for friends you wouldn't touch with a ten foot pole. That day we certainly had a "friend" that qualified. Our only advantage was that "Brer" skunk

Didja' Ever Make Butter?

had to back out giving us a running start. And run we did, just as soon as Grandpa laid that pole on the lever to open the trap. No we didn't stand any where near the door. That door popped up and we sprinted away, laughing at the almost predicament. Minutes later the pole was inserted into the trap and both spoiled pieces of wood were carried quickly to a downwind gully. Both pole and trap were flung deep into the erosion sculptured wash out.

As we returned and neared the house, the aroma of hasenpfeffer once again aroused our appetites. The hasenpfeffer and potato dumplings were delicious.

Iron Crazy Horse

Kids in disfavor
Aromatic Incident
Iron Crazy Horse

Warmed by the bright autumn sun, the tractor sat like a sentinel over looking the battle weary fields. A lone tree held fast to a few, now brown leaves. The last doves had flown south soon after the corn harvest. Spot searched the edges of the fields for errant bunnies. One of her most recent litter imitated her every move, save for tripping clumsily over random dewberry vines.

Herbie went to the farm with me for the weekend. It was a rare cloudless day. The fates smiled and we were surrounded by opportunity. Grandma, reticently embarked on one of her rare shopping expeditions to Manchester. She needed thread, lace and such things that men are totally inept at finding. After many attempts to describe the needed purchases, she reluctantly admitted that she would have to once again undergo the rigors of an automobile ride to town. Grandpa was forced to oblige. Thus the opportunity for two inquisitive twelve year olds to seek out forbidden pleasures. We didn't even consider messing with Grandpa's shotgun or anything like that. We considered riding the mules, but Pete was too scary for us and we had reached an age where riding double wasn't appealing any more, unless it was Betsy.

Didja' Ever Make Butter?

We each munched on a crisp red apple picked up from under the tree. Both were still damp with remnants of the morning's light frost. Wiped on our jeans, they quickly polished to a high gloss. Taking small bites so as to inspect carefully for foreigners, we ate the choice parts surrounding the worm holes. I carefully inspected Herbie's apple as he looked for his next bite.

"Is that a worm hole?" I asked innocently.

"Where?!" Herbie was instantly attentive.

"Can't be," I continued, "the hole is moving."

Red and white flecks of apple spewed the landscape. Disgusting sounds burst from his mouth. Herbie flung the apple as far as he could as if to sanitize himself by its absence. In a coordinated attack, my laughter assaulted his ears and ego simultaneously. He drew a deep, knowing breath and the chase was on.

"Gotcha!" I hollered derisively, as only nasty disposed, adolescent boys can. Once again memories of my humiliation in the cave (Herbie's finest victory in our never ending one-ups-man-ship struggle) had been revenged. That's how we got to where the tractor stood warming in the sun. Invitingly alone. Unsupervised. With a half a tank of gasoline. We swarmed over it, imaginations feeding on contact with the warm, red metal.

"Didja' ever drive it?" Herbie asked.

"Sure, Grandpa let's me drive it all the time," I lied. Hanging onto the reins of a mule that could walk a furrow out of habit, yes, but driving the dangerous and unpredictable gasoline powered creature was totally forbidden. But to admit that to Herbie was not possible to an image conscious kid.

"Wow, I wish I had a Grandpa with a tractor." Herbie had neither.

"Yeah, it's really neat feeling all that power under ya'. I pretend that I'm Patton in his tank when I drive it."

"Can you give me a ride?"

"Grandpa won't let me drive it unless he is around." My feet dug into the plowed ground. My eyes darted from toe to toe. I probably looked as shifty as I felt.

Iron Crazy Horse

"Aw, he'll never know." Herbie pretended not to notice.

"I can't." The far tree line held my interest momentarily.

"I bet your fibbin'. You don't know how to drive it." The challenge stung like glove in the face. It was an irresistible dare. It was drive that tractor or lose a major battle in our ups-man-ship war. I stalled while trying to remember the starting procedure. Silently I listed the steps, "Put gear shift in neutral. Open the petcock. Set the throttle. Pull the choke out. Turn the..."

I was saved! "I don't have the key, Herbie."

"It's right there in the ignition," Herbie smugly announced, a sly grin crawled across his face. My heart sunk once more into the depths of my fear churned stomach.

"Yeah, it sure is." My bravado was far short of convincing.

"Well, let's do it." Herbie urged me onward. Like a professional racer, a Barney Ross of the plowed ground, I strode imperiously around the gigantic beast. Stalling for time, I hefted the grease gun from tool box and carefully squirted grease into and around several of the more visible fittings on the front axle. I wiped the excess on the accompanying rag, soon filling it with stiff amber globs. Unable to find room for additional grease, I turned our attention to the dip stick. I professionally wiped the dip stick on my pants. Hopefully the oil would not be up to level. It was.

"Grandpa will be back any minute..." I was running out of diversions.

"They just left," Herbie's tone indicated that he was sensing victory. "You really don't know how. Do you?"

"You just watch. Stand back." I set the levers, opened the valves and climbed onto the seat, barely making the steel spring quiver. I stretched my left leg and just managed to depress the clutch and wiggle the gear shift into neutral. Turning the key I pressed the starter with my right foot. The harsh sound scared me. I jerked my foot from the starter. Herbie saw my trepidation and his body talk was derisive

"I knew it..." he muttered slowly walking away. I hit the starter once again with fearless determination born from humiliation. There

Didja' Ever Make Butter?

is nothing as dangerous to young people as peer humiliation. The poorly muffled creature, fired loudly. It grumbled in response to the grinding starter before settling into a rhythmic rumbling. The engine ran ever faster then dwindled, almost dying before I remembered to adjust the choke. Herbie stared at my proudly focused eyes. I saw his newly found wide eyed admiration. Smiling, he jumped on the axle, grabbed the edge of my seat and yelled, "Let's go!"

We pulled the pin divorcing the plow and the tractor. Growing in confidence, I pushed the clutch down as far as I could and tried to shift into gear. There was a terrible grinding sound as my too short leg didn't depress the clutch far enough.

"Grind another pound for grandma," my friend chided. I stretched as best I could, pushed the clutch even further and finally yanked the machine into a forward gear. I let out the clutch and Herbie was flung backwards as the beast reared, both front wheels clear off the ground. It was by far a more effective buck than any of our "rodeo" animals had provided. Fortunately the one lurch killed the engine, but not our enthusiasm. Within moments, I had the engine running smoothly and Herbie once more in place. I tried increasing the throttle as I eased the clutch out. It worked. We were moving. Right out of the plowed field we went. We were going pretty fast. Too fast my instincts said. A wash out was rapidly approaching so I yanked the steering wheel all the way to the right. Just then I recalled Grandpa talking about how Mr. Price got hurt real bad when he turned his tractor over.

I adjusted the wheels just as the rear wheel began clawing the edge of the washout. The tractor tilted precariously and Herbie shrieked but fortunately or even miraculously, the iron beast sought firm purchase on higher ground. With the passing of the initial panic, the danger was soon forgotten. I throttled back to a more leisurely speed and began our tour of the acreage.

We were in heaven. All around the farm we drove. Through the orchard, around the barns, past the stable. We even caught Rommel napping and gave him a feather flapping chase until he got smart enough to swerve at a right angle and lose us. I even increased the throttle for him. We were clipping along pretty good when he "skeedaddled" out of the way. We laughed so hard at his antics that I almost missed the woodshed. Luckily I swerved with a quick jerk of the wheel and only tore off a section of corner molding. I looked back at Herbie who was now white with fright at the near miss. His eyes were like saucers. His knuckles were white from gripping the metal seat so determinedly. His mouth was working like a fish gasping for air. I couldn't rip my eyes away from his comical look. He kept trying to tell me something, but I couldn't hear the words, just garbled sounds. At least I thought those were his intentions. I yelled, "Talk louder!"

That was either simultaneous with or an instant before we flattened the outhouse. As if to compound our dilemma, a huge rear wheel dropped into the waste pit and quickly ground its way axle deep into the muck. Indescribable is the most gentile way to describe the aroma that circled slowly around the tire. I increased the throttle, hoping to get back on firm ground and merely succeeded in flinging odoriferous materials in a long narrow band in the alfalfa field. That band displayed a rich dark green for the next several growing seasons. In final desperation, I turned off the ignition. We sat in stunned silence, a silence broken only by the sound of a Model A Ford chugging up the driveway. Spot was obviously and noisily telling Grandma and Grandpa what awaited them.

Herbie and I visited the farm again. It was on our bicycles. No adult member of the family would drive us any longer. They had previous engagements whenever we asked for a ride. There was some compensating good from the incident. The new outhouse was needed. The pit had needed cleaning.

On the other hand, Grandpa had a dickens of a time getting Kate and Pete near enough to pull the tractor to dry ground. I remember their eyes getting wide and spooky as Grandpa led them toward the tractor. I swear till the day he died, Pete had a look of hatred in his eyes every time he saw me. Kate seemed all right, but I was never too sure of Grandpa.

Growing Pains

From cocoon, the butterfly
Long limbs, rounded flesh
Emerge young woman

The wheat harvest was a memory. Glistening, yellow stacks of straw bore witness to the passing of the workers. It had been several years since Grandpa had first permitted me to work the wagon on thrashing day. Now, at thirteen, I was almost a man.

We were experiencing those oppressively hot, lazy days of the corn growing season. The morning chores were completed. Grandpa was older and slower now. He depended upon me a lot more. Much of the crop land was now rented to younger farmers for shares. It was planted in corn and beans this time of year. A small patch of corn was grown by the creek, to feed the two cows and the mules. (Minotaur had long since been a veal meal.) It was the only field crop that Grandpa planted this year. Of course, there was the garden, but everyone, even Grandma, helped with that.

The garden still provided a busy canning season. Betsy was here helping Grandma today. Betsy came to help Grandma a lot. I ended up helping her dad pretty often, too. There weren't a lot of other kids our age around, so I suspect we did a lot of this helping just to be around someone our own age.

Growing Pains

Grandma and Betsy had snippled beans all morning and packed them tightly in cobalt blue mason jars. Layers of beans were snippled, then separated by a thin sprinkling of coarse salt. It was the same as making sauerkraut. In about three months a unique tasting soup base developed. It was called *"Schnitte bohne suppe"* or literally, snipple bean soup. Snipple beans, a ham bone, navy beans and diced potatoes, simmered for hours, produced a culinary delight enjoyed by many generations in our family.

Betsy gently touched my arm. "Time for lunch."

Since moving to the country three years ago, she had grown rapidly. The first buds of womanhood were calling attention to her beauty. That beauty was not apparent to me, not from my lack of interest, but by the complete unimportance of anything relating to sex, or gender in our relationship. Like any friends, we spent considerable time helping each other with chores and homework. Enjoying each other's company and conversation, our friendship was independent from the inhibitions and prohibitions of boy, girl interactions.

"I'll get Grandpa and be right there." my smile followed her, as she headed for the house. Grandpa was chopping wood. Nostalgically I thought, "It won't hurt for me to help him carry the wood. He took the heavy loads for me often enough. Guess it's my turn, now."

As it turned out, we each took a small load of wood, washed up and took our seats with Grandma and Betsy. Soon we were digging into plates full of country goodness. A fresh peach pie could be seen cooling on the shelf. As appetites dulled, conversation commenced.

"The chores are pretty well caught up..." I mumbled, seeming to make polite table conversation. We were finished eating except for the pie, but having an ulterior motive, I spoke only loudly enough to be heard talking. The object was to sound polite, respectful and end with a request that hopefully, would be answered in the affirmative, by half listening adults. Therefore, my circuitous palaver ended up with something like, "...can we ride Kate?"

Grandma usually gave Grandpa a knowing smile, almost invisible in the deep creases that 80 years of farm life had etched into her face.

Didja' Ever Make Butter?

Obviously, their logic determined that a quiet nap was more likely with two boisterous children out of the house, than if they were scuffling around and laughing every other minute. Forever practical, Grandma was compelled to add several responsibilities, in order to make permission to play seem utilitarian. "Water Kate and Pete first and remember to close the gates. Be careful of Pete and don't be gone too long."

"Not bad," I thought, a mite cynically, "She traded three chores and two conditions for one yes. If the Cardinals could trade like that, Ted Williams would be playing along side Stan Musial." Betsy and I ran for the door before another list of barnyard duties were tacked on.

Kate stood docilely by the fence. I scrambled up on the rails and swung my leg over the mule's strong back. Betsy followed. I clasped her hand as she scrambled up behind me. As always, her arms circled my waist and came to rest at my belt. She let her body relax against me, I felt her softness press lightly against my back. We were completely comfortable with each other, whether touching, or not, but lately I seemed to noticeably enjoy any excuse to be touching.

Without the heavy leather harness, Kate must have sensed it was to be an afternoon of leisure. With only love and a rope halter, she sashayed slowly up the road. Kate ambled past fields that she and Pete had walked hundreds of times in that powerful, measured, "all-day-pace" that broke the ground, crumbled it fine, injected the seeds and cultivated out the intrusive weeds. Of course, a mule had no intelligent realization of these things, but Kate seemed of happy spirits, for whatever the reason.

Looming ahead was the big barn with its inviting hay loft. Inside, we had spent many enjoyable hours playing hide-and-go-seek, cowboys and indians and other fantasy games invented on the spur of the moment. Sharing these silly childhood games with a friend, seemed to double the fun. There were times when we left the loft, both of us "grungy" from head to foot, stained a light tan from the dust. Only our cornflower blue eyes shone through the grime.

I laughed, remembering the time we jumped from the loft, slid down the straw pile and almost landed on Spot, who had been nap-

Growing Pains

ping in the straw. We must have been so besmirched, as to be unrecognizable. Poor Spot, whether severely startled, or terrified by the apparitions before her, ran off yipping in terror. Betsy and I went limp with laughter, rolling in the dust until our sides ached and tears cut dark paths down our dusty faces. We had taken one look at each other and ran for a cleansing dip in the creek, clothes and all.

Today, with the sun beating down and the humidity soaking our clothes, the creek seemed more inviting than the wonderful, dusty, old barn.

I opened the gate that Grandpa and I had built in the fence by the persimmon tree. It was a short way to the creek from there. Betsy closed the gate and I took the rope off Kate's halter and let her graze. She immediately lay down and rolled over in the dust, legs akimbo, high in the air.

"What in the world is she doing? Has she gone crazy?" Betsy had not before witnessed that sight.

"She's fine. Mules do that to get a coat of dust on their back to keep the horse flies off." Can you imagine the sight of a thousand pound animal, rolling on her rounded back? There she was, rolling around with all four legs thrashing in the air, trying to keep her balance. She twisted and turned like a snake twisting bronco, only upside down. We both watched, laughed together, then remembered the creek.

During most of the day, the white rock area of the creek was in shade. For about four hours at mid-day, the sun poured brilliantly through a hole in the green canopy formed by the tall trees clinging to each bank. The deep shadows contrasted sharply with the brilliant glare reflecting from the white limestone rocks. The formation of rocks resembled slabs of chalk, or solidified, white sand. Pools of water, from a few inches to several feet deep, had been worn into the rocks. The resulting individualized sized holes looked like sales displays for marble spas.

The water felt icy cold, as its only source in mid-summer was the ever flowing springs so common to Missouri. In the springtime, tad-

Didja' Ever Make Butter?

poles swam in the pools and grew rapidly, feeding on their tails, until they transformed into frogs, returning to the water for food and haven. Now "crawdads" puffed their backward way from one hiding spot to another. At fishing time, we caught them by the dozens. They made wonderful bait.

Betsy and I had enjoyed this swimming hole many times together. We were quite unconscious about state of dress having been scantily clad many times in each other's presence, like washing up, dressing for bed, etc. We stayed over at each other's houses quite a bit, always strictly chaperoned. We both swam in our underwear and I hadn't particularly noticed that she wore an undershirt while swimming, this year.

I had been embarrassed by her once. She came to our house unexpectedly, one day this summer. There I sat, on top of the old cistern, naked as a jay bird, in a tub of water, taking a bath.

"Grandma!," I hollered, diving under water. The mere remembering of the incident made me glow in the dark for a week. I thought Betsy and Grandma would never stop laughing. Of course, she didn't see a thing except my bare shoulders, but it was just the idea and the surprise of her walking up on me unexpectedly. I guess I was a prude back then.

Betsy was less than two years younger than me. Being on a farm, not having television and all, made for a simpler, unsophisticated lifestyle. Nature was accepted as is. There wasn't a lot of prurient advertising to titillate the imagination. Consequently, I didn't think about sex, not at thirteen years of age anyway. It wasn't something romantic, any way. It was gender and it was about what the animals did to make more animals, if you get my drift. Sometimes a lewd joke was told in the locker room at school by the older boys. But sex, it just wasn't an important part of me...yet.

There comes a time, however, when no matter how ignorant, uninterested, or holy you are, that something called hormones disrupts the tranquil innocence of young men and young women. In certain circumstances, two people look at each other and see much more

Growing Pains

than a comfortable old friend. They catch a disease called puberty, symptomized by a fever called desire.

As always, I unbuttoned my shirt on the way down the hill to the creek. As always, we chatted and bantered, just enjoying the day. As always, I bolted ahead to the flat rocks and dumped my shirt, dropped my jeans, slipped off my shoes and split the deep pool with an awkward, flat splashing dive. I let out the usual yelp when I surfaced, exploding water from my mouth and hair, teeth flashing amidst the shattered crystal surface.

Turning, I looked for Betsy. I had seen her undressing lots of times. Something seemed different. Somehow I felt I shouldn't look, but I was unable to tear my eyes away. he lifted the cotton dress over her head. Her back was discretely turned toward me. I stood quietly in awe. As if for the first time, I saw two slim legs curve gracefully from ankle to knee. She seemed to pirouette on tip toe, sending ripples up her thighs and chills up my spine. Her bottom was no longer boyishly flat and firm. It curved round and soft, scrolling a french curve upward to her well defined waistline.

"My gawd," I barely mouthed the words. My mouth hung slack-jawed, as the realization of her femininity, dawned into my consciousness. Life seemed to be happening in slow motion. Her back flexed gracefully, as each rib added a new dimension to her nascent womanhood. Her undershirt had separated from the dress and slowly glided back where it once again met the top of her underpants. One arm came free as her hand slipped through the sleeve of the dress. Her other arm continued up over her head until she resembled a statue waving a cotton flag. A tiny breast bloomed visibly under her undershirt. The dress cleared her head and a rivulet of curls tumbled downward, as if crowning a princess. As she turned, her laughing face lit up the heavens for me.

She warned in her tinkling voice, "Here I come ready or not."

A little girl in a new body ran for the water. I was thunder struck. I was dumbfounded. Obscene boys had told fantasies about things like this in the locker room. Some of the younger farmers made com-

Didja' Ever Make Butter?

ments from time to time and occasionally would brag about things I didn't quite understand. I had overheard some bits and pieces about grown up girls, and let me tell you, I wasn't ready for that. This was Betsy, my best friend. I can't think of her "that way." But I was.

Betsy dove right at me. Her dainty shriek was as light as a melody. The sparkling water shattered and splashed over me, as she surfaced, quickly. Both of her hands landed heavily on top of my head in an attempt to dunk me. I braced and stiffened, bracing for her attack, but it was too late. She shoved me under. Sucking in a quick breath on the way down, I grabbed her arms and pulled her down with me. I opened my eyes as she came down, saw the laughter on her mouth and a curious desire in her eyes. She drifted closer and let her arms circle my head. Instinctively, I urged her closer and touched my lips to hers. Her eyes widened, then closed and she pulled me tightly to her for an instant. Her tender lips covered mine, as we sealed our first fleeting kiss.

Parting only slightly, we surfaced, still clinging. Silently, we stood perusing each other and this newly found dimension of our friendship. Neither smiling, nor frowning, our gazes alternately drank in each other before sneaking furtively away. This new relationship had made us uncomfortable. We were both thrilled and confounded by the surging emotions it brought.

I felt a heat such as I have never felt before. Simultaneously, I shivered as goose flesh invaded my body. Betsy's teeth were chattering. Never had either of us gotten this cold in such a short time. Silently, as if afraid to break the spell of the moment, we waded from the pool to a bright patch of sun warmed white rock. Side by side we lay on our stomachs, barely touching.

We were naive, but not ignorant. We both realized what was happening. Of course, we didn't understand all the ramifications, but we knew we were on dangerous ground. It was both awesome and frightening. It was bliss and fulfillment. We wanted more, but something held us back. The awareness that we had been in love for a long time became suddenly clear. We hadn't been in love this way, however. What was "this way?"

Growing Pains

Long shadows walked over our backs. Tenderly, our fingers touched. Silently, our thoughts ranged, searching for the quixotic, ethereal answers that danced just beyond the reach of our young minds. We had entered a world of uncertainty, insecurity and supreme bliss. Passage through it could be tender, or torture. That day, rational minds overcame urgent bodies. Both of us wanted much more, but neither of us were quite sure what. Both of us knew that uncharted waters held many a reef and shoal. With only ignorance for a lighthouse, we steered in the safe waters.

Tenderly, we relinquished contact and dressed. When our clothes once again shielded us from the heat of our bodies, we turned toward each other once more and allowed our lips to gently touch. With the sweet taste of innocence on our lips, we walked slowly home.

Helmet Potato Salad

Rich, dark earth; forest green vines
Rounded mounded rows
Kartoffel below

"Those are potato plants, Fred," I whispered, emphatically. Many times I had watched Grandpa Rausch pull the potato hook through similar mounds and pull those luscious lumps into the light of day. Many times I had planted carefully cut seed potatoes into a similar mound in the spring.

"Make sure each piece has an eye and face it up," Grandma Rausch and every other person over thirty would caution the youngsters. One pass in each direction by the mule powered, single bottom plow made the long mounded furrows. Sprinkle straw on top and you had what the old timers called straw potatoes. Nobody ever told me why they put the straw on top. I always figured it was to keep the seedlings warm on those chilly spring nights. Found out later it holds the weeds back, keeps the soil loose and holds moisture. All important to grow the big ones. Back during WWII, no one explained, or questioned it, they just did it.

Fred was convinced. It was a cold night in Germany many years and many miles removed from the family farm. Nothing was visible from our listening post. It was joint maneuver time in West Germany.

Helmet Potato Salad

NATO was showing off for the Warsaw Pact. Our 293rd Engineer Battalion was supporting the 2nd Armored Division out of Baumholder. I was finally living my childhood fantasies in real time. Sadly, Rommel was long since gone, both of them.

It was quiet. It was routine. The officers were in their heated lowboy "motels." Old truck shells had been carefully salvaged, then outfitted by the company scavenger with the best. Beds, storage, lights, table, chairs, and a coal burning stove had been installed at taxpayer's expense. (The little briquettes of compressed coal dust were expensive and hard to find that winter of 1956, but they produced a lot of efficient heat.) You could bet that mock battles were being planned over a well worn deck of cards. Usually Jack Daniels helped with the planning, even though he was banned from the premises. Thus, did some officers, in particular Captain Jensen, adapt to adversity.

"You get 'em, I'll cook 'em, Fred." In short order, my description of the imagined results overcame Fred's fears of the sergeant of the guard or, worse yet, an angry German farmer. The crisp, thirty degree night air had aroused an appetite for hot, German potato salad in both of us.

The loamy soil was frost bitten on top but dry and loose underneath. A thrust or two with Fred's trenching tool and a tug on the vine rolled plump rounds of brown skinned potatoes into view. There were two all purpose army tools, the trenching tool and the steel helmet. Tonight my steel pot was first used as a grocery bag. The WWII steel pot was issued as a helmet but had more uses than baling wire in a barnyard. Ask any G.I. That two pounds of metal was umbrella, bag, bucket, cooking pot, bath tub, wash basin and anything else ingenuity could invent. Tonight we planned to test its mettle. Thirty minutes later our relief sent us heading for the bivouac area — raw materials intact.

A midnight raid on the mess tent, resulted in the acquisition of salt, pepper, sugar, onion, bacon, vinegar, flour and parsley. When I returned, Fred had the freshly washed spuds boiling in one pot (helmet) on a coal stove. Thirty minutes later and we had a sterilized

Didja' Ever Make Butter?

helmet (bowl) and five pounds of boiled heaven. When the spuds had cooled enough to peel and slice, I did the honors, while Fred fried the bacon and onions in another helmet. I tried hard to remember how Grandma mixed it all up. I poured most of the fat away, then made a roux with the flour and poured the water and vinegar and spices to make the gravy. I crumpled the bacon and chopped the parsley onto layers of potatoes, adding salt and pepper, as I went. Finally, I mixed in the gravy and tasted. All right it wasn't as good as Grandma's, but that night, to us it tasted like it was the world's best.

Mouths slathering out of control, it was time for the still warm mixture to be shared. Armed with appetites known only to young men, the five tent mates enjoyed real German "Helmet" potato salad. My place in army history was secured. Thus, did some G.I. farm boys adapt to adversity in 1956 with the first recorded instance of America receiving foreign aid.

Fraidy Cat

Tranquility reigns
Broached by dis-harmonic cats
Let sleeping dogs lie

Mouth watering, eye tingling vapors wafted into my face, evoking visions of the succulent feast to come. The hickory chips had done their job. The lovingly prepared lumps of ground beef were searing with mild sputtering protests on the hot grill. It was a tranquil day on the farm. I even watched Rommel walking amidst his flock without rancor. One last sip from my cooled cup of milk, laced with a shot of coffee, and I would close my eyes and allow my thoughts of the soon to be served meal drift into my fantasies. I'm sure my smile was working overtime.

The menu was special that day. Any time that the barbecue grill was fired up was special. It was a simple, homemade stack of concrete block with some salvaged grates that Grandpa had constructed by the wash house. Not much to look at, but it worked just fine. Thoughts of barbecued burgers smothered with onions, fresh sliced from the garden languished, complemented by the drifting smoke from the grill. I got to watch the burgers cook, while Grandma put the final touches on the german potato salad. Grandpa stopped by in between chores, to check the fire. Earlier, I saw Grandma pull down a new jar

Didja' Ever Make Butter?

of homemade pickles from the pantry. Visions of the sharp dill taste had my mouth watering. The pecan pie cooling on the porch didn't even enter my mind. Believe that, and we can discuss some beach front property in Florida that I can sell you real cheap. Visions of food, coupled with the peaceful, sunny day, had me lulled into a euphoric state. Suddenly, a loud caterwauling jarred my sensibilities.

"Phffft...rrrowwarrrgh!" and other assorted feline expressions, ripped through the silence. My eyes flew open and I inhaled sharply, managing to ingest a particularly bilious puff of smoke. Undoubtedly, even the charcoal suffered adversely from the same shrieks that jarred me from my cat nap. Through tearing eyes, I saw a lump of pulsating white, black and brown fur meandering erratically on the gravel. What an apparition! Six or more legs, two or more tails and at least two discernible heads. As my eyes focused more accurately, it became apparent that two members of the cat family were having a territorial disagreement and decided against taking it to the People's Court. Unlike their human counterparts, they parted quickly without bloodshed and went in divergent directions. Almost the end of the story.

Secretly, I was disgruntled at the intrusion upon my peacefulness, but being in a most mellow mood and showing the decorum of my upbringing, I made not a modicum of effort to extract revenge. It was all but forgotten. Then, out of the corner of my eye I spied a tan shape slinking cautiously along the fence, partially hidden by the tall grass. Nose low to the ground and tail slowly languishing to and fro, the cat approached the corner of the fence with extreme care.

I watched as his nose broke the invisible plane of sight at the corner. Obviously, he wished to see around that corner without being observed.

The idea for revenge flashed into thought at that precise moment, not a second sooner. All my years spent on the farm, watching and imitating the antics and sounds of animals came rushing out from the recesses of my temporarily twisted mind. You should hear me imitate a contented cow, or better yet a chicken, swelling with pride over a freshly lain egg. Then, from the recesses of my cat file, I recalled my

Fraidy Cat

best impersonation of an attacking cat. Loudly! Suddenly! Phffft ... rrrowwarrrgh!

The tan bully reacted in a manner that fully exceeded my expectations. He, being the cat, of course, from a position described as flattened to the ground, ascended perpendicularly to a height exceeding two feet, landed stiff legged on all fours, flared every hair on his body to a wire brush attentiveness and headed for a hole under the fence about three fourths of his normal body size. In diving through the hole he miscalculated on the high side and hit a board with his head. His shriek, or the blow set off a reverberation like that of a yardstick tweaked while hanging over the edge of a desk. The board's staccato like rattle added impetus to his hastily unexpected departure.

If my laughter, at the sight, added insult to his injured pride, so be it. My revenge for broken tranquility had been extracted. The barbecue was a gourmet's delight.

Watchin' and Walkin'

Panorama of color
Yellow, red, green, brown
Joseph's autumn coat

If this be death and dying, this annual Fall display, I need no further proof of the beauty of the hereafter. It seems to say, "Rest easy weary child, this is but a hint of what awaits you."

The yellow cast hickories compete with the purple, red and brown oaks. Framed in the deep greens of the wild cedars, it's as if the artists of the world have smeared huge palettes with reds, yellows, umbers, and burnt siennas. Each delightful color vies for attention, while blending into a harmonious masterpiece. Then, breathtakingly, like a crown jewel, like a beauty pageant winner, like a blue ribbon lemon meringue pie, one tree captures your attention. It glows as if spotlighted. The others exist to accentuate its glory. The phosphorescent hues of a sugar maple tree invades your sight. Resplendent in an unbelievable blend of reds and yellows that mixed to golden orange, highlighted till it glowed like a living flame. The ostentatious maple modestly whispers, "Look at me."

The visual perceptions and memories of a recent late September drive from Tampa to St. Louis and return demanded remembering. I was reminded how Grandma's only positive desire to ride in the Model A was during the Fall display of color.

Watchin' and Walkin'

An overture of the ornate display revealed itself south of Macon, Georgia. White puffs of scattered cotton left on scraggly bushes, composed a portrait in basic black and white. The unharvested fields unfurled, as row upon row of unpicked white fiber, became a sea of white. The distant brown and yellow hillsides gave hints of the glory to come.

The rising hills pressed ever closer to the highway. Glowing reds near Chattanooga matured into brilliant splendor from Nashville throughout the entirety of Illinois. It must have been a good year. Sufficient rainfall fires the colors. The hues were outstandingly rich.

Missouri's display had peaked. The shades of browns were many and beautiful and would challenge a master artist to capture the many subtle tones. I had missed the prime performance, yet I knew what it had looked like after more than 50 years in residence. I visualized the grooved trail winding through our farm's miniature forest. Once again the dry leaves crunched beneath surreptitous bare feet. Roots reached up through the dust sporadically catching unsuspecting pedal digits. How quickly the tender tootsies had become bloodied, crusted, then calloused by the harsh realities of farm life in the raw. Pain was worn like a badge. Complaining distanced young boys from manhood. Funny thing, the boys made a macho production of their hardships, while uncomplaining women did their thing every waking moment, from the age of ambulation, till time for their sombre wake. Never complaining, always nurturing; they were the foundation upon which men received the credit for constructing a nation.

Missouri weather could swing from frost in the morning, soaring to the searing eighties by noon. On such a fall morning, Grandpa led me along a wooded trail. He traversed quietly and efficiently, like native Americans and settlers before him had done, causing only the merest whisper while negotiating the dry leaves. Imitating him was beyond my ken. My bare feet crunched leaves, snapped sticks and in general alerted every smart squirrel in the woods to our presence. Still, in spite of the handicaps of age, grandson and arthritis, Grandpa was able to move silently onward, spotting the little rodents, as they

Didja' Ever Make Butter?

rustled furtively through the high boughs of the hickories and the oaks. A squirrel, cutting nuts, can be heard, according to Grandpa farther than a stampeding buffalo herd. A nut dropped from forty feet to a dry bed of leaves he continued, reverberated as obviously, as my careless feet. The incessant chatter of the gregarious rodents echoed resoundingly, in the otherwise quiet woods.

There were many unanswered questioned from my farm days. One such query was the almost coincidental placement of stumps. It seemed that near every good squirrel tree was a "rump high to a man" stump cut perfectly flat. The sharp splinters that characterized the tops of other stumps always seemed to be missing. Some almost seemed shiny, as if polished over time by some craftsman. Grandpa, sighting these convenient friends, would settle comfortably, squiggle his overalls a bit to remove the wrinkles from under his tender parts and rest the butt of his huge, double barrelled twelve gauge shotgun on the ground between his feet. Silently, he would point a little behind him on the uphill side to a spot where I was to sit. The listening and watching would begin.

Without conversation, or motion to stave off the pressing boredom, my fantasies would be stimulated by nearby critters. Ants scurrying to and fro became armies rushing to battle. A doodle bug rolling his gross ball of manure toward his castle, became a huge earth mover. At some point the inevitable glance upward would scope the trees for scurrying reds or grays, hustling the nut crop for a living. The gray squirrels were the hardest to spot. Smaller and generally more shy than the reds, it took a keen eye to see them in the more distant trees. They tended to flatten against limbs and trunks in the upper shadows and disappear from sight. The wisp of a tail might be the only clue to their existence. The reds, what a contrast they provided. Loud and raucous, bright in color, plump in size. Peek-a-boo was their sport. Just as keen as the grays, they spotted you instantly and darted to the far side of the tree. Within minutes they would peek around, or over their cover to spy on the strange animal below. It was at that precise moment that curiosity, in the loud form of Grandpa's twelve gauge, harvested the rodent.

Watchin' and Walkin'

Curiosity and experimentation, at age nine, led me to notice that the colors in my crayon box could duplicate the fall foliage. I liked to color as a boy. I have seldom admitted that, fully considering the act of coloring to be much too feminine a pursuit. Isn't it a shame that my generation was pigeon holed by so many gender prejudices? Any way, that is when my appreciation for the beautiful leaves took root. Squirrel hunting began in late summer. The many toned greens of the thick lush forest roof slowly thinned, as leaves fell casualty to fierce summer storms and the inevitable aging process. First came hints of yellow that would tinge the edges of the dying leaves in late September, or early October. The first of the maples would turn yellow, later the sugar maples, fiery red. The oaks held out longest, doing their thing until well past Thanksgiving, with some varieties steadfastly grasping their leaves until the new growth forced them to give up in the spring.

If the first heavy frost had spread its white crystals, the hunt would invariably lead to persimmon hill. The persimmon tree's dull yellow leaves were among the first to fall leaving bare limbs resplendent with bright orange fruit. I do remember that biting the orange Halloween colored fruit before that first frost was a mistake, an extremely bitter one. But picked in a timely fashion and appropriately wiped, those small round fruits had a delectably sweet flavor, highly prized by human and wildlife. Did Grandma really know why Grandpa and I seldom returned from the field hungry at that time of the year? Probably. Did she secretly laugh in amusement at our frequent visits to the "two-holer" in the garden? Probably.

Most of the time we returned with two, never more than three squirrels. I always wanted the tails, after they had been salted and dried, but was disinclined to touch them after having discovered the colonies of fleas that infested the critters. Total farm boy I never became. I did take a squirrel tail home from time to time. I wanted it for my bicycle, but they always looked scraggly compared to the ones from the store. Another problem was that they always seem to get lost within a few days. Every single one of them. I could never seem to remember where I put them. After so many tails, coincidence has

Didja' Ever Make Butter?

to be ruled out. Mom, did you throw them all in the trash?

There were two schools on skinning squirrels. Some swore to the method of encircling the body and pulling the skin inside out toward both tail and head. The other method said to start at the tail, carefully peeling the hind legs and then pulling the entire skin toward the head. It was then cut from the body in one piece with the head covered by the inside out skin. Seemed less gross that way. Grandpa tended toward the latter. The fine hair from the animal seemed hardest to removed from the bare skin. Cleaning a squirrel was harder then a rabbit, or a quail. Depending on the size, it only took two or three to make a bountiful meal. First breaded and fried like chicken, then simmered until tender in natural gravy, served with mashed potatoes, it was a completely enjoyable treat. Was it the wood stove, the recipe, or the fresh air appetites? Maybe it was just real, fine eating.

I know this, Grandpa always left a lot of squirrels in the woods. He could have shot a lot of them in very little time, but I think his visits to the woods, with gun in hand, were like a vacation. They always took several hours whether I was with him, or not. He didn't talk a lot at any time and even less in the woods. But short phrases spoke volumes when he would point and utter, "Pretty tree. Some red. They're playing tag."

Call them lectures remembered. I was fascinated then and now by the three toned oaks. They had distinct colors of brown, green and purple, all on the same tree. In fact, all on the same leaf. The leaves, when in clusters, appeared to be the Black Watch of the forest. Plaid-like in appearance, I easily imagined bagpipes yowling melodiously in the breezes. Interspersed were bright yellow hickories standing attentively, like scouts. Dark evergreens and richly shaded pines formed a constancy of background. Crimson sumac defined the lower border of the portrait. Regardless of the stunning variety, my thoughts always returned to the fiery maples. I constantly scanned the forest to find the one with the reddest red, the one with orange that resembled a ripe tangerine and the one that possessed the golden Midas touch blend, that made it seem like a burning bush of non-consuming fire.

Watchin' and Walkin'

Could the celebrated bush, from which Moses was handed the tablets, have been such a maple?

Once again I was hurtling along Interstate 24. Time on the return trip passed almost too quickly, as nature's "exquisitence" permeated my senses. I felt vibrant stirrings, provoked by the beauty of the moment, as well as the memories of the farm. Thoughts rolled by, as quickly as the passing miles. In peaceful meditation, I wondered whether Julia Ward Howe had once gazed upon a similar aesthetic Fall scene that caused her to write, "Mine eyes have seen the glory of the coming of the Lord."

Solitude

Quiet solitude
Tree filtered sunlight
Nature's Holy Communion

"Comes a time when the old folks wait for the rooster," Grandpa reminisced, as the years began to advance somewhat faster than he did. When I was younger, I came to believe that Grandpa awakened old Rommel each day when he rattled the stove grate, while building the fire. The barnyard bully, my arch enemy, upon hearing the metallic clatter would sheepishly squawk a hoarse cock-a-doodle-doo at the peeping sun. Over the next few minutes he would add volume and quality, until he signed off with a hen raising, milk curdling blast that translated, "Hey, ya'll! The sun's up. Why aren't you?"

This summer Grandma and Grandpa seemed less concerned about awakening Rommel. Younger neighbors now worked the farm on shares. Only the garden and one cow remained from the glory days. Pete, the gray, had passed on to the land of alfalfa reserved for hard working mules. Kate, sweet gentle mare, was now gray in the muzzle. She lazed her remaining days in fresh straw, munching contentedly on her daily ear of corn and flake of hay. She and Hilda kept each other company on their leisurely daily trek to the pasture. Once upon a time they would have been escorted each way. Now they were unaccom-

Solitude

panied in either direction, unless I had an urge to head their way. If it weren't for Hilda's still productive udder, they probably would have come home even more infrequently.

With the hens dwindling down to a precious few and having long since entered menopause, Rommel merely took up space and feed. Fertilizing eggs for those thin feathered old hens must have been as pleasurable, as a daily dose of cod liver oil. It was with mixed emotions that I tasted the Sunday dumplings he finally flavored. Turned out to be his final revenge. He was as dry and tough after four hours in the stew pot, as he had been in the barnyard. At least, he wasn't there to enjoy that last laugh. Actually, the dumplings were delicious, affected more by Grandma's recipe than by his attitude.

Hours before, Grandpa had offered me the axe, but I yielded the honor to him and at the propitious moment, conveniently remembered that Kate needed a bucket of water. As much as I hated that old rascallion rooster, he had been an honorable opponent.

Now that morning chores were at a minimum, the old folks slept in. My early rising habits remained. Upon awakening, I liked to head for the porch swing and wait for the sunlight to sneak through the leaves. It only took Spot a minute to find me. Her warm tongue on my bare toes seemed to send a special message. Nothing I know expresses such unconditional love and loyalty, as the unsolicited tenderness offered by a family dog. I looked down and scratched her ears to acknowledge her presence. Her tail slowly thumped the wooden porch floor, as if to cement a renewed vow of fealty. Her big brown eyes rolled upward in adoration. Her soft muzzle melted onto the porch floor like a scoop of ice cream.

Nearby, the huge snowball bush came alive with sound. Off to our left, mated with the fence, it hosted a veritable mixed choir that sang praises to faithful old sol. Worker bees by the hundreds buzzed their way to the blooms then back to the hive. Thumb sized bumble bee bombers accompanied by yellow jacket fighter support, bombed the intruding red wasps.

Humming birds flitted from flower to flower on the pale blue morning glory blossoms, tapping the deepest part of the blooms for

Didja' Ever Make Butter?

nectar and dew. Occasionally, the male would dive bomb its mate, as if in play. I feared for real damage once, as he exploded into the smaller female with a recklessness of a run away linebacker. But, outside of a loose feather floating away, it seemed just another game in nature's scheme of things.

I don't remember thinking about much in those early morning moments of solitude. Instead, I observed. I listened. What would Mom Nature be saying today? I watched the morning glories unfold into magnificent blue fullness, only to close before the sun reached mid-morning. I saw squirrels chase each other in games of follow the leader, that only another squirrel could follow. How quickly they ran, leaped and twisted in every conceivable direction. They found purchase on branches unbelievably small, but seemed to sail over them so fast, as to hardly disturb them. It was like skating on thin ice, go like blazes and for darn sure don't stop. A hilarious moment was provided, from time to time, when one of them mistakenly stopped on a too thin branch. The branch would dip sharply, as the panicked rodent tried to scramble for a better hold. Often as not, he would drop to a lower branch and hope for a lucky grab. I have seen them drop from dizzy heights to the floor of the woods and suffer only wounded pride before scampering off to the nearest trunk.

The birds were cheery. On any given dawn you could see blue birds, jays, robins, mockingbirds, finches and of course my favorite, Mr. Bob White, the quail. Is there any creature prettier then the quail. The soft browns, black, white and yellow blend into a perfect camouflage for the plump ground huggers. The male wears a daring slash of white on both side of his face. The female prefers her distinctive band to be yellow. Even their eggs are a beautiful beige, accented with mottled brown splotches.

Their conversations would echo throughout the woods, "Bob White, Bob Bob White." Sweet and clear, with surprising loudness. I tried to answer them and got pretty good at my imitation. Many times I called them toward me, as close as the fence. There, the one on display would strut and whistle, as Spot and I remained perfectly still,

Solitude

watching the jaunty bird search for his true love. Over the years many birds answered my call. None stayed long enough to be considered a serious date, but always the conversations ended with a hand on my shoulder letting me know that my conversation with Mr. Quail had once again awakened Grandpa. On the best mornings, unlike the quail, Grandpa joined me on the swing and together, we would try to call in one more Bob White.

Eternal Rest

Mourn the crying sky
Tears flow from man and nature
Embrace them warm earth

Her dull, glassy eyes had no target. I watched them slowly roll, unfocused, hopefully unaware of her suffering, or our abject misery. The heat of her fever warmed my hand, as I cradled her listless head. The once shiny, cool nose breathed warm and dry. Once perky ears lay limp, like curls on a humid summer day. Her white plume tail showed the merest of motion, as if movement was painful. Shallow breathes became intermittent. A contraction caused her body to shudder, as if she were making an heroic effort to escape the haunting spectre of death. In heart rending finality, Spot exhaled softly, then relaxed in eternal sleep.

As I write this almost fifty years later, my eyes tear again, remembering the long ago parting of a most precious childhood friend. Shared days of proximity and the joyful moment of her glorious greeting following an absence are among my cherished memories. The verve of the chase, her excited bark as she closed on the pursued the hare, still has freshness in my mind. The laughter in her bark belied her spurious attacks. Spot never caught a rabbit, or any other creature to my knowledge. She trailed them for the sheer joy of it.

Eternal Rest

Spot and I never argued. We never fought, except in mock war over a stick, or piece of rope. Can we say this about any other friends? Pure, unselfish, undemanding love was the sum total of her relationship. Both childlike minds found only perfection in the other. Yes, she gave more to me than I to her.

Tears leaked hotly from my tightly closed eyes, as self-imposed pity engulfed me. The surging emotions ebbed and flowed in synchronous rhythm. Flashes of experience exploded through my pain ridden mind. Just as in life, her presence in my memory was real and overpowering.

Spot exhaled her last loving breath months before. Now Grandma lay inside Bopp's Funeral Home, surrounded and honored by mourning friends and relatives. In a short while she would be consecrated to mother earth, to be seen no more, but remembered forever. At eighty three years of age, she was as seraphic in death, as she had been in life. I stared expectantly, desperately wanting her to shake off the ghostly sleep, awaken from her nap and ask Grandpa to help her out of the ornate metal box. I was comforted by the silken, quilted padding that surrounded her. The heavy aroma from the flowers promoted an air of oppression in concert with the sombre dirges, barely discernible from an unseen organ.

Repressed whispers were punctuated by occasional bursts of normal spirited speech. Grandma was old. Sympathy was offered with hope. Fond memories were shared with intermittently smiling progeny. Adults comforted other adults. I was left to my own mental gyrations. Ever notice how kids are generally overlooked at times like this? Does anyone really know what to say to young people? I was thirteen years old, kind of an awkward in between age. Too young to mingle and too old to leave at home.

Grandma died three days before on April 5, 1945. I was taken to visit her on the Sunday before she died. She lay serenely in her bed, covered by the hand made quilt she had lovingly stitched. The family had brought her bed downstairs and reassembled it in the dining room, there was no heat upstairs. A huge feather bed lay fluffed at her feet.

Didja' Ever Make Butter?

Her pale countenance showed no emotion, or recognition. She lay so silent and breathed almost imperceptibly. A cerebral hemorrhage had staked its claim on her ancient body. The stroke would prove fatal. The doctor left her at home, medically certain of her proximate passing. The damage had been massive and irreversible. She had neither awakened, nor had she moved since collapsing in her beloved kitchen.

Grandpa had been torn between leaving her to get help, or staying at her side. He had entered the house weary from the day's labors, anticipating supper, but encountering tragedy. After tenderly placing her in bed, he walked and ran to the nearest neighbor imploring their assistance. She survived five comatose days before peacefully expiring, surrounded by our family and her pastor, Reverend Hoeh. I was spared that final day. Consequently, my memories recall the serenity of viewing her, as if asleep, both in her bed and the casket. Unlike with Spot, who's final shudder brought a flood of tears and the relief of body racking sobs, my mourning for Grandma lasted longer. My mind would not accept her death.

Another impression from those days of sadness invades my memory. Admittedly, I recently checked the dates, because my recollections of the two events become juxtaposed. Grandma's death and the demise a week later on April 12, 1945, of Franklin Delano Roosevelt, merged into an inseparable crescendo of grief. Not the raw searing pain of personal tragedy, but the oppressive heaviness, like that period before a violent thunder storm. Arthur Godfrey's trembling voice describing the funeral procession of FDR remains so vivid, that it imposed itself yet again when I watched the procession for John F. Kennedy 18 years later. For years, the sound of Godfrey's voice would trigger memories of Grandma's last days. Blessedly, the public mourning for the president in 1945, allowed me to release my grief in floods of tears.

Grandma's death determined the pattern for my personal behavior at funerals. She was my first experience with mortality. I did not understand the transience of life in 1945. Its meaning becomes clearer with each passing year. Sometime after age fifty, death seems to lose

Eternal Rest

a little of its sting. Grief achieves the mellowness of acceptance with subsequent loss of friends and relatives.

I sorely miss Grandma and Grandpa. They were the perfect relationship. They were free from the total responsibility of parenthood, yet lovingly accepted it. They gently imposed discipline, tempered by wisdom, developed from experience. Parents often panic in their desire to nurture and thus, be overly dramatic, premature and sometimes too harsh in their disciplinary lessons. Imparting these same lessons seems to come more comfortably to the older set, especially those who learned from practice rounds with their own children. It's difficult for children to forgive the mistakes of imperfect parents. It is difficult to be a perfect parent, as well. Oh, to have even been close.

I visited Grandma's grave, frequently. My children have been there. We have stopped at random times. Hunting trips, family outings and other occasions find us stopping at the hillside plot of grass. Grandpa rests beside her now and has for many years. I miss, but do not mourn him. Chauvinism will not permit me to extend the sensitivity to him that I feel automatically for Grandma, even though our relationship may have been closer. Comforting is the belief that both are securely in the care of their Maker.

Grandpa and I buried Spot at her favorite resting spot, deep in the shadows of a sprawling snowball bush. The location gave her clear view of house, drive, barn and hen house. The shaded rich earth cooled her in summer's heat and sheltered her from windy winter's blasting breath. A nearby lilac bush honored her with its sweet scent. I insisted, that she be cosseted in a ragged shroud. We reverently interred her in the warm earth. The tears stopped, eventually.

Epilogue

> *Sad separation behind*
> *Put to rest the past*
> *New dawns, new friends, begin again*

Life continues. Loss is sad. Seen from a distance, closure is a natural part of life's cycle. Certainly more harsh is an interruption of the natural cycle by the loss of someone not yet fulfilled. The tragedy of a young life encountering accident, disease, random violence, for example. These are certainly more tragic than the passing of aged grand-parents, a pet dog or a formidable rooster. Neither loss attempts to measure to shocking initial sadness or the quality of the love. Passing and sadness go inevitably hand in hand. I remember the perspective in what Grandpa used to say, "Ain't no one ever got out of this world alive."

The poignancy found in the memories of the deaths of a loved one was explored and experienced in the last chapter, *Eternal Rest*. Rather than leave the reader despondent, bearing a sense of loss, look on it as closure on a piece of history, now well over fifty years past. It describes, in full, a portion of some lives, endings for some and the end of beginnings for others. It was a happy period that like all things human, ends, making way for new happy times. In the ending it gains definition, as it marks the beginning of a new phase and in some cases

Epilogue

a parallel phase, the urban adventures of Doug, Herbie and a whole new set of friends and relatives.

If you have enjoyed *Didja' Ever Make Butter?* then look for the soon-to-be-published *Didja' Ever Kiss A Girl?* Gary Corbett's next novel will be brought to you by Polo Springs Publishing Co. in the spring of 1996.